The
Baker's
Daughter

Also by D. E. Stevenson

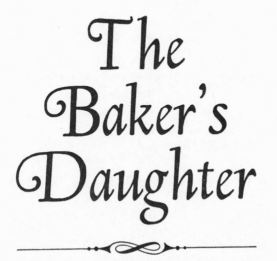

The Baker's Daughter

D.E. STEVENSON

Holt, Rinehart and Winston | New York

Library of Congress Cataloging in Publication Data

Stevenson, Dorothy Emily, (date).
The baker's daughter.

I. Title.
PZ3.S8472Bak12   [PR6037.T458]   823'.9'12   76-6109
ISBN 0-03-016856-2

First edition published in the United States
in 1938.
Second edition published in Great Britain in
1973 under the title of *Miss Bun, The Baker's
Daughter*; first published in the United States
in 1976.

Printed in the United States of America

10   9   8   7   6   5   4   3   2   1

*The people and places in this book are
imaginary and bear no relation whatsoever
to any people or places bearing the same
name.*

The
Baker's
Daughter

FOREWORD

This book was written in 1938 and published soon after, but although many of the facts have proved untrue it is still artistically true of any little town in the Scottish Border Country and the people are as real today as they were thirty-four years ago.

In writing the history of Miss Bun I have avoided the use of dialect (which is ugly and troublesome to read) and have relied upon the turn of a phrase and an occasional Scottish word to gain my ends. The people of Beilford and others of their ilk are bilingual, and can speak good modern English when they please, but slip into the comfortable vernacular when they are conversing amongst themselves or are moved by any strong emotion. The Scottish nobility and gentry such as Sir James Faulds of Beil and his friend, the Admiral, speak cultured modern English in everyday life but often use the vernacular in conversation with their tenants. It would be difficult to say whether they use it unconsciously or for the sake of friendliness and Auld Lang Syne. In their early days, when they ran about their fathers' estates and mixed freely with gamekeepers and the village boys they would naturally pick up the contagious lilt and expressive phrasing of their tongue.

"And remember this," said Darnay. "The old Scots language is a grand language, hoary with tradition. They spoke it at King James's Court and at the Scottish Bar; poets used it and made it live for ever."

CHAPTER ONE

A CURLEW, winging its way across Southern Scotland, would see the little town of Beilford as a handful of grey pebbles cast down on the banks of the river Beil. It is all grey—grey stone houses, grey roofs, and grey stone setts paving the streets—for the stone of which it was built came from the quarry at the base of the Castle Rock.

The Castle is the seat of Sir James Faulds and is one of the oldest inhabited buildings in the land ; it is set upon the cliff overlooking the town, and here the river makes a double bend before flowing away south-eastward to the sea.

Beilford is an old town with an East Gate and a West Gate—narrow arches set in thick walls—and the street which runs from one to the other through the middle of the town is narrow and winding. On market days this street is congested with traffic, for Beilford is the shopping centre of a prosperous farming community—ironmongers, saddlers, butchers and drapers all thrive well—at one end of the High Street, near the West Gate, a fine frontage displays the sign of " THOMAS BULLOCH, WINE MERCHANT AND ITALIAN WAREHOUSE-MAN."

Thomas Bulloch was a well respected man in Beilford. He had inherited his business from his father, and had extended it by hard work and capable management.

His shop was patronised not only by the townspeople but also by the surrounding landowners, for he had a large and varied assortment of goods and his prices were moderate. The shop was served by a good staff of assistants, but Mr. Bulloch could quite often be seen there himself, for he believed it to be good policy to show a personal interest in his customers, and he enjoyed the work. When Mr. Bulloch was not in the shop he was probably in his office at the back of the premises—a queer stone chamber, three-cornered in shape, wedged in between his ample store-houses—here he sat, day after day, writing letters, interviewing travellers and agents, ordering wines and spirits, butter and bacon, oranges and spices and a hundred and one necessities and luxuries which it was his business to retail.

There was a very fine smell in this wedge-shaped office, for Mr. Bulloch liked to keep samples of his wares on the shelves which lined its walls: tins of fruit, jars of ginger, glasses of preserves, spices and cereals and dried fruits of all kinds; and, in a very special cupboard which was always locked, a few bottles of very special wines, liqueurs, and brandies. When any of Mr. Bulloch's old customers had reason to visit the shop —customers such as Sir James Faulds of Beil or Admiral Sir Rupert Lang of Bonnywall—they made a beeline for Mr. Bulloch's sanctum, knowing full well that they would be welcomed there, and regaled with a glass of old brown sherry and a thin biscuit or perhaps asked to sample some especially delectable brand of ginger or fine cigar. The gentlemen liked that, but perhaps the chief attraction which brought them to "Bulloch's den" was the man himself.

Bulloch was tall and big boned, with shaggy white eyebrows and strong white hair. The eyes beneath the shaggy brows were grey and keen. There was something bird-like about the straight glance, the slightly hooky nose, and the big spare frame, and when Admiral Lang remarked to the Earl that Bulloch reminded him of "a benevolent eagle," the Earl was startled at the aptness of the comparison. There was dignity in Bulloch, and wisdom, and a quiet humour.

One cold November day Mr. Bulloch was sitting at his desk in his wedge-shaped office. Ostensibly he was engaged in writing a letter to his agent in Calcutta to point out that the last consignment of Orange Pekoe had been distinctly below standard, but the pen had fallen from his hand and he was staring with unseeing eyes at the small coal fire which winked and blinked cheerfully in the polished grate. To-day was Mr. Bulloch's birthday, and birthdays are the milestones of life, inviting reflection upon the road that has been travelled, or the road that lies ahead. At seventy there is more road behind than in front, and Mr. Bulloch was looking backward down the years. He was looking back a long way, forty-five years or more, to his courtship of Susan Smart, to their marriage, and the happy days that followed. He thought of the birth of his only child, Mary, and of the joy that the baby daughter had brought to the comfortable house above the shop. Those were happy times, thought Mr. Bulloch, Mary's childhood, Mary's schooldays—how quickly they passed !

When Mary was barely nineteen she had married Will Pringle—the baker whose premises were at the other end of the street—it was a good enough match as far as money went for the bakery was a large and prosperous concern, but Will was dour and taciturn, with no humour and less kindliness in him, and the Bullochs had never been able to like him however hard they tried. They could not understand what Mary saw in Will, but they had always given her all she wanted, and a habit of this kind is hard to break. To do Will justice he had been very fond of Mary and good to her in his own way, and as far as his limitations would permit. Mary had borne him two children: a girl who was called Sue after her grandmother, and a boy called Alexander. The years sped on—they were calm contented years in retrospect—and then the blow had fallen.

Mr. Bulloch sighed, for Mary's death did not bear thinking of—it was so unnecessary. If only they had realised *in time* that her cold was serious! If they had put her to bed and had proper advice she might be alive now! They did all they could when once they knew, but it was too late then, for pneumonia is swift and cruel and tarries for no man.

One evening when Mr. Bulloch was sitting with Mary she had opened her eyes for a moment, and seeing him there she had caught at his hand and whispered, "Dad, take care of Sue, she's too serious." She had drifted away into unconsciousness again before he could answer, but he had known then that there was no hope, Mary was dying.

Sue was fourteen when her mother died, and Will took her away from school to keep house for him. The neighbours talked about it—as neighbours do— some saying that Will Pringle had no right to take the child from school, and others that it was the best training she could have, and she would make a better wife when the right man came along.

Nobody predicted that Will would remarry, for Will was no "ladies' man," and he seemed quite comfortably off with Sue as housekeeper. He waited a long time —until his daughter was twenty-two—and then electrified Beilford with the news that he was going to take a second wife. It is possible, of course, that he may have envisaged Sue's marriage (for there were several young men who would have been glad to have her) and looked about him for a wife-housekeeper before it was too late, or he may have fallen in love with plump Grace Simpson. Nobody knew what was in Will Pringle's head and nobody was ever likely to know, for he was a man who kept his own counsel.

Will's remarriage was a shock to the Bullochs, for *they* had not forgotten Mary, and her place in *their* hearts could never be filled, but they kept their bitter feelings to themselves and were friendly and pleasant to Will's new wife. It was necessary that they should keep on good terms with the Pringles on account of the grandchildren.

All this passed through Mr. Bulloch's mind as he sat and stared at the fire, and then—because he was weary of unhappiness—he switched his mind back to the happy times and thought again of the young Mary—of Mary the child. What a gay pretty creature she was, a fairy princess who had danced her way through life ! They had all sorts of foolish little jokes together—he and Mary—and childish secrets and games. And they read fairy tales—for these were her chief delight—Mr. Bulloch sitting in the big arm-chair and Mary on the floor by his knee. The tale of Goldi-

locks and the Three Bears was their favourite (Mary's
own hair was spun gold) and he had read it to her so
often that, even now, he knew it off by heart, ". . . and
when Goldilocks reached the little cottage in the
woods she crept up to the door and knocked softly—
three little taps, and then three little taps again, and
then another three little taps for luck . . ." and always
Mary had knocked upon Mr. Bulloch's office door in
the same way, with three times three little taps, so that
he would know it was Goldilocks calling on the Big
Bear. Then, before he had time to answer, she would
rush in, laughing merrily, her gold hair blown about
by the wind, and swinging her schoolbooks at the end
of a little strap; "Big Bear!" she would cry, "it's
tea-time now—school's over for the day!" Mr. Bulloch
had that little strap still—it was in his table drawer—
a queer keepsake for a hard-headed business man.

It was this gay irresponsible creature who had said
to him, ". . . take care of Sue, she's too serious," and
Mr. Bulloch often pondered on the words. Did Mary
realise that life is hard on serious people, and that her
own lightheartedness had saved her from hurt?

CHAPTER TWO

MR. BULLOCH was so lost in dreams of long ago that he was not surprised when he heard Mary's own private signal—three times three taps on his old oak door. He cried, "Come in," and raised his eyes from the fire expecting to see Mary's fair merry face, but it was not Mary who came round the edge of the door, and for a moment Mr. Bulloch gazed at his visitor with a blank unrecognising stare.

"Sue!" he said at last, like a man awakening from sleep.

"Yes, it's me," declared his granddaughter, somewhat bewildered by her reception, "can I come in? You're not too busy?"

"Come in, child, come in," said Mr. Bulloch. "I was dreaming, I think—very reprehensible in business hours. Have ye been up to see Granny?"

"No, it's you I've come to see," Sue replied. She had a small parcel for him—a woollen scarf which she had knitted for his birthday—and Mr. Bulloch drew her head down and kissed her soft cheek with rare tenderness.

"You're a good lass," he declared; "sit down and talk to the old man for a wee while, Sue."

The mists of the past still lingered so that he had almost called her Mary—yet she was unlike her mother in every way. Different in appearance, with her small pale face and grey-green eyes and the heavy mass of chestnut hair which waved back from her wide serious brow, and different in nature with her thoughtful quiet ways. She was not like Mary's daughter at all, she was more like Susan his wife. He looked at her, searching her face, wondering if she was happy (how could she be happy with that woman in her mother's place), wondering what sort of thoughts were hidden behind that quiet mask-like look, and it seemed to him that she was too old for her years, her mouth too firm, her expression too reserved. He remembered that even as a child she had worn a quaint air of maturity, of responsibility—perhaps that was what Mary had meant.

"You're not old, Grandfather," Sue said, leaning against the edge of his desk and surveying him critically.

"I'm seventy to-day."

"I know that, but you don't seem old. You're interested in things."

"Things are interesting," he replied.

There was a little silence and then Mr. Bulloch asked, "Why did ye knock like that?"

"Knock?" she repeated questioningly. "Oh yes, I see. It was just that mother always knocked on your door with three times three. I used to see her do it and wonder what it meant."

Mr. Bulloch did not tell her about Goldilocks for Sue would not understand—not for her the foolish tender make-believes which had so entranced her mother, "It was a bairn's trick," he said, "that's all, Sue, a bairn's trick. But never mind that now, tell me all the news."

Her face clouded over. "There's no news," she said, "or at least nothing important. Have you fixed on the music for the Hogmanay Party, Grandfather?"

Mr. Bulloch was fully aware that this was a red herring, but it was such an attractive red herring that he could not resist it. "We have then," he declared, brightening perceptibly. "Andy Waugh was in last night. It's to be Haydn this year—wait till I tell ye about it, Sue."

It was a time-honoured custom for the Bullochs to give a party on New Year's Eve; a fine dinner first and then a small concert of chamber music. Mr. Bulloch played the 'cello exceedingly well, and his great friend Mr. Waugh, who kept the music shop in Beilford, was no mean performer on the violin. This year (as Mr. Bulloch proceeded to explain) the party was to be on an even more ambitious scale than usual.

"Hadyn's not easy," declared Mr. Bulloch seriously, "and the piece Andy's chosen has an awful hard solo for me. It'll need a good bit of practice, I'm tellin' ye, but it's beautiful music, Sue."

They were still discussing the subject when they were disturbed by a knock on the door—no three times three this time, but a perfectly sane and sensible "rat-tat, rat-tat."

"That'll be Hickie!" said Mr. Bulloch. "What'll Hickie be wanting? *Come in.*"

Hickie came in. He was Mr. Bulloch's chief assistant, a sturdy well set up fellow of about twenty-eight with thick brown hair and bright brown eyes. His eyes fell upon Sue and kindled with pleasure, for he had loved her, and waited patiently for her ever since she was a small girl. Sue did not love him, of course, and Bob Hickie knew that, but he was willing to wait for her another nine years if necessary. He knew that she was old Bulloch's favourite grandchild and most probably his heir, and, although he would still have loved her if she had been a pauper, her position was certainly an enhancement of her charms.

"Mr. Bulloch," said Hickie, when he had greeted Sue and asked her how she did. "Mr. Bulloch, it's that Mrs. Darnay—she's asking for you. Will I tell her you're engaged?"

"No, no, I'll see her," declared Mr. Bulloch, "I'll come this very minute. You'll stay and have dinner, Sue. Away upstairs to your grandmother till I see what Mrs. Darnay's wanting."

Sue accepted the invitation, but instead of going upstairs she followed the two men into the front shop. The fact was she wanted to see Mrs. Darnay; she had heard of her, of course (for the whole of Beilford was interested in the Darnays, and talked about them unceasingly), but Beilford folk were not good at describing people, and Sue wanted to see Mrs. Darnay with her own eyes. Sue knew—as everybody knew—that the Darnays lived at Tog's Mill, an old disused flour-mill which stood on the river bank about two miles above the town. They had taken the place on a long lease and had done it up and made it habitable. Everybody thought that this was a very strange thing to do, for the Darnays could have got a villa on the out-skirts of Beilford for less money than they had expended on the mill—a comfortable modern villa with electric light and other conveniences—but Mr. Darnay was an artist, and artists were well known to be "queer" so perhaps that was why they preferred a tumbledown mill to a decent modern house.

Sue stood a little apart, and examined the artist's wife with thoughtful care; she had never seen an artist's wife before, and had expected something picturesque, something artistic, with graceful flowing draperies and untidy hair. Sue had seen an amateur production of *Patience* which the Beilford Dramatic Club had presented to its admiring neighbours and fellow townsmen the previous year, and she had imagined Mrs. Darnay would be "like that." Mrs. Darnay was not the least "like that," but she was sufficiently peculiar and striking to obviate disappointment. She was tall and slim, with very fair hair set in sculptured waves, and her face was "made up" with paint and powder—red lips, pink cheeks and dark blue shadows round her eyes. Her clothes were peculiar too, for she was hatless, and her leopard-skin coat, sleek and shiny, reached only as far as her knees, while her slim legs were clad in stockings so fine that they looked as if they were bare. Sue gazed at Mrs. Darnay, fascinated by the strangeness of her.

Mrs. Darnay turned from the assistant who was attending to her order and smiled at Mr. Bulloch engagingly. "So good of you to spare me a few minutes," she told him in a high light voice.

"What can I do for ye, Mrs. Darnay?" he asked. "No complaints, I'm hoping."

"No complaints at all," declared Mrs. Darnay, "the fact is I want you to help me. I don't know many people about here, you see, and I wondered if you could tell me where I could find a cook."

"A cook?" echoed Mr. Bulloch in surprise.

"I brought my cook with me," Mrs. Darnay explained, "but she had to go home—it is dreadfully inconvenient. I haven't got anybody now except my French maid and she can't do everything; besides she isn't a good cook and my husband is *so* particular."

"Well, it's not quite in my line," said Mr. Bulloch smiling. "I've enlarged the scope of my business a good deal but this is the first time I've been asked for a cook."

"Oh, I know!" Mrs. Darnay cried, "of course I know it isn't really in your *line*, but I hoped perhaps you might be able to suggest somebody—I'm really almost desperate."

"What about me?" enquired Sue in her quiet voice.

Neither Mr. Bulloch nor Mrs. Darnay had noticed Sue, for she was a person who could fade into the landscape when she pleased, but now they both turned and looked at her: Mrs. Darnay critically, Mr. Bulloch with incredulous dismay.

"I can cook quite well," Sue continued, "and I'm a good washer, too. I don't mind getting up early——"

Mrs. Darnay looked at her searchingly and liked what she saw. She was so desperate for a cook that she would have taken almost anybody and had an absurd impulse to seize upon Sue then and there and abduct her forcibly; but it was better not to seem too eager, so she curbed her feelings and asked the conventional question, "Have you got good references?"

Sue was about to reply that she had no references at all, but she was forestalled by Mr. Bulloch.

"This is my granddaughter, Mrs. Darnay," he declared in his most kingly manner, "my granddaughter, Miss Pringle."

"Then of course I shan't require references," said Mrs. Darnay smiling sweetly.

"But it's a mistake!" Mr. Bulloch cried. "I mean there's no need for Sue—I don't want her to——"

Mrs. Darnay summoned all her tact and charm (for she *had* to have a cook and she had set her heart on this nice superior-looking girl). "If Miss Pringle would come temporarily," she suggested, "just to help us out —just until I can find somebody else."

Miss Pringle agreed. She agreed to everything that Mrs. Darnay said, quite regardless of her grandfather's objections; she agreed to go to-morrow, and to stay for a week to see how she got on, "and then we'll see," Mrs. Darnay said, with her charming smile. "We'll see how we get on—but you'll stay until I can get somebody else, won't you ?"

Sue assented to these somewhat ambiguous terms.

CHAPTER THREE

MR. BULLOCH had not been able to interfere, nor to prevent Sue from making the arrangements with Mrs. Darnay, but when Mrs. Darnay left he took Sue upstairs to her grandmother.

"Susan!" he cried, bursting into the dining-room where the dinner was being laid, "Susan, look at this girl—she's daft."

"My," said Mrs. Bulloch, smiling calmly, "so Sue's daft, is she? That's a pity, Thomas."

"Wait till ye hear what she's wanting to do," Thomas told her. "She's engaged herself to go and cook for the Darnays—did ye hear what I was saying? Susan, she's to go to-morrow and cook for these people."

"I heard," said old Susan softly, and young Sue, watching intently, saw her old thin hand hesitate for a moment as she laid down a spoon.

"Ye heard!" Mr. Bulloch cried. "Well then, tell her the thing's all nonsense. She's to come here if she's wanting away from home."

"Sue knows we'd like that," Mrs. Bulloch declared, looking up and smiling tenderly at her granddaughter. "Sue knows, so there's no need to say it. I'm thinking we would be more sensible if we listened to Sue and heard her reasons, instead of argle-bargling over her as if she was a dummy." There was a glint of humour in her eyes—though her voice was perfectly quiet and grave—and Mr. Bulloch's clouded face broke into a reluctant smile.

"My gracious, woman, you're smart!" he exclaimed. "Come away, Sue, and let's hear what possible reasons ye can have—are ye wanting away from us all?"

"No, no, Thomas," interrupted his wife, "that's no way to get hearing about it."

"I want something to do," Sue said. "I want to be useful. It's difficult to give up everything you've been doing and just stand out of the way. I'm not complaining about anything," she added with a quiver in her voice. "It's not that, Grandfather, it's because there isn't enough for me to do—two women—in one wee house——"

"But ye can come here," Mr. Bulloch cried. "Leave Grace to get on with it and come here—ye can help me in the shop. Susan, for maircy's sake tell her we're wanting her!"

"Sue knows that," declared Mrs. Bulloch again.

It was true that Sue had known she could go to the Bullochs, for they had suggested it in a tentative manner when her father married again, but Sue had not known that Mr. Bulloch wanted her to help in the shop or she would have accepted the invitation forthwith. She had visualised herself helping her grandmother with the household duties, and, after considering the matter carefully, had decided that there would not be enough for her to do (Mrs. Bulloch had one small maid who came in daily but she did all the cooking herself and obviously enjoyed the work) and Sue was too proud and independent to go and live with her grandparents unless she could be useful to them. All this rushed through the girl's mind like an express train, and she began to regret her sudden impulse and to wish that she had spoken to her grandfather and found out what was in his mind.

"I've promised Mrs. Darnay," she said at last.

"If ye've promised, ye've promised," Mrs. Bulloch replied. "It was a kind thought to help them out, and when they've got some other body to do for them ye'll just come home to us." She looked at her husband as she spoke and the words of protest died upon his lips, for they were so near in spirit that she could speak to him with a glance. *It will be easier this way*, her glance said, and Mr. Bulloch saw that this was true. It would be easier for Sue to come to them from the Darnays' than straight from Will's house to theirs.

"They'll have to find some other body soon, then," he declared, "for we're wanting Sue ourselves."

. . . . . .

It was six o'clock when Sue got home, for she had some necessary shopping to do in the town. She found her father and her stepmother and her young brother sitting down to tea. There was a large piece of boiled bacon on the table, and a fine smell of kippers filled the air.

"I've got a job," she announced as she drew up a chair to the table. "I'm going to cook for Mrs. Darnay at Tog's Mill."

"A job!" exclaimed Grace. "Where's the sense of that?"

"What do ye want to take a job for?" enquired Will. "There's no need for ye to go out to service when ye've a good home."

"I want something to do," she explained. "There's nothing for me to do here."

"What'll folks say," grumbled Will, and scowled at

her gloomily. He knew quite well what folks would say; they would say he had remarried and turned his daughter out of the house—a nice thing to be said, and too near the truth to be comfortable.

"It doesn't matter what folks say," replied his daughter tartly.

Will thought it mattered a good deal, for the truth was he liked to stand well with his neighbours. He would have liked folks to say—as they said of old Bulloch—that he was a fine fellow. He would have liked them to seek him out and talk to him—but nobody did. Will knew that he was unpopular in Beilford, but he could not change his nature and the knowledge that he was disliked made him more gloomy and taciturn than ever.

He thought of all this, and consumed a large slice of ham before he answered. "That kind of talk is bad for business. They'll say the business is going down if I can't afford to keep ye at home."

"I'm going anyway," said Sue.

He banged on the table with his hand. "Then ye'll not come back," he declared in a voice that trembled with passion. "Ye can go, and stay—I'll have no defiance in my house."

The threat did not move Sue at all, for she did not intend to return home. When her time at the Darnays was over she would go to the Bullochs and help in the shop. She said as much to Will, and said it without tact, for she was too straightforward and independent to beat about the bush.

"The Bullochs!" cried Will. "I'm sick of hearing about them. It's the Bullochs this and the Bullochs that from morning to night. It's the Bullochs

have put ye up to this nonsense—I know that
fine."

"You know wrong then," she replied calmly. "The
Bullochs aren't wanting me to go, but I said I'd go,
and I'll go."

"Go, then," raged Will. "Go for any sake. We'll
maybe get a little peace in this house when ye've
gone."

Grace had been silent during the discussion, but
afterwards when they were washing up the dishes she
had a good deal to say.

"It's a daft thing to do," she told Sue, as she rinsed
the plates and put them on the rack to drip. "Ye'd
be much better off married, with a house of yer own
than cooking for other folks. Ben Grierson would
have ye to-morrow——"

"I don't want him," declared Sue. "I'm sick of
hearing about Ben."

"Ye're daft," Grace said, "clean daft, that's what ye
are. Ben's a good steady man and he's mad about ye,
forbye. Ye've kept him dangling too long already—
maybe ye'll lose him altogether if ye wait much
longer."

"It's you that's kept him dangling," retorted Sue
with some heat. "It's you that's encouraged him, not
me."

Grace sighed. She had a long and draughty sort of
sigh which Sue found most annoying.

Sue was surprised at the opposition she had encoun-
tered from Will and Grace, for she was aware that her
presence in the house was a trial to them both. Sue
was impatient and impulsive and it was impossible
for her to stand aside and watch Grace doing things

differently without making any remark. In fact Grace had not been in the house twenty-four hours before they had fallen out over the arrangement of the cleaning materials. The things had always been kept in the boot cupboard, on a particular shelf, and Grace moved them into the kitchen without consulting her step-daughter. "But they've always been there," Sue had cried, "Mother always kept that shelf for them."

Grace had never forgiven those injudicious words. She had made sweeping alterations after that just to show Sue who was the rightful mistress, and she had taken an even stronger line because she felt uncomfortable and insecure. Grace did not feel that the house really belonged to her—she felt like an interloper, and this annoyed her. She fixed the blame for her discomfort on her step-daughter—how could she settle down contentedly in her new home when Sue was there, disapproving of all she did and comparing her methods with Mary's? Grace wanted Sue to marry —that was the sure way to get rid of her—it was no use playing about with temporary jobs. Sue would soon get tired of cooking for the Darnays, she would miss her chance of a comfortable marriage, and they would have her back in the house for good.

"Could ye not give Ben a chance?" she enquired, stifling her annoyance and trying to speak in a friendly manner. "He's a real good sort, Sue."

"I wouldn't marry Ben Grierson if he was the only man in the world," declared Sue flatly, "and you may as well know the truth."

Sandy had taken no part in the argument at the tea table. He was a peace-lover, and he kept aloof from unpleasantness whenever it was possible to do so. He and Sue were very fond of each other, and were allied together against Grace, but Sue was aware that Sandy was a very poor ally when there was trouble brewing.

The evening passed without any opportunity for a private talk with Sandy and, this being so, his sister was not surprised when she heard a gentle tap on her bedroom door. She had not yet started to undress, so she opened the door and motioned Sandy to come in.

"I had to speak to you," he said in a whisper.

"What do you think of it?" she asked, in the same conspiratorial tone.

"It's a good thing for you to get away from here."

"And for you too," returned Sue dryly. "You'll have peace now—and that's what you like."

Sandy did not attempt to contradict this, he sat down on Sue's bed and looked at her thoughtfully. "My, I wish it was me," he said, "I'd give anything to get away."

"You haven't got much longer," Sue pointed out. "You're sixteen now, and you're going to the University——"

"But I'm not!" he cried. "It's all off now. Father spoke to me to-day. I'm to leave school at Easter and help in the bakery."

"Oh Sandy!" exclaimed Sue in dismay. "Oh Sandy —but he promised you."

"That was before he married Grace," Sandy reminded her. "I've known for some time that Grace was working against me. She thinks it's all nonsense me going to the University, and she's made him think the same . . . a waste of money, that's what he said."

"What did you say?"

"Nothing," replied Sandy wretchedly. "What could

I say? If he won't spend the money, I can't do it, can I? Oh Sue, I can't bear it. Think of me living on here with father—and Grace—all the rest of my life. Just think of it—all my work wasted."

Sandy was very near tears in spite of his sixteen years of manhood.

"Why don't you stand up to them?" Sue said, but she said it without conviction, for she knew Sandy too well to have much hope that he would ever be able to stand up for himself.

"I hate rows," he said, kicking at the bedpost with his toe. "You know I hate rows. It would be hell if I didn't do what he said."

"We won't sit down under it," she declared in a brisk tone. "I'll think of a way, Sandy."

"But you won't be here——"

"You can come out to Tog's Mill and see me. Don't worry, Sandy, we'll find some way—perhaps grand-father would speak to him."

They talked for a little while longer, and at last Sandy went away. Sue had cheered and braced him— as she always did—and he began to think there might still be hope.

When Sue woke it was grey dark. She sat up and rubbed the mists of sleep from her eyes, and looked round the little bedroom which she had slept in as long as she could remember, and which she might never sleep in again. The furniture was barely visible in the gloom, but the small round mirror near the window shone like a silver penny, gathering light from the sky.

Sue had been unhappy here, but all the same she

could not contemplate leaving her home without a pang and her heart gave an unpleasant lurch when she thought of the immediate future. "I must have been mad to say I would go and cook for those people," said Sue to herself.

She lay down again, and considered the whole thing carefully, and the more she thought of it the more worried she became. It was the venture into the unknown that troubled her: the prospect of arriving at a strange house, of taking up her abode amongst strange people, of sleeping in a strange room. And then there was the cooking—supposing they were not satisfied with the food—supposing they asked her to make a cake, and it was a failure, stodgy, heavy, the currants congregated at the bottom in a solid mass!

"Oh *dear*!" cried Sue, rolling over in bed and burying her head in the clothes, "oh goodness gracious me, whatever was I thinking of!—but I'll just have to go through with it now—there's no way out."

CHAPTER FOUR

THE morning passed quite quickly, for Sue had much to do. She looked over all her clothes and decided what to take with her and what to leave behind; she washed and ironed and mended industriously and was considerably cheered and strengthened by the doleful prognostications of Grace. Sue was an obstinate creature and she disliked her stepmother a good deal, so the more Grace predicted disasters and discomforts the better Sue felt, and it was not until she had said good-bye to her family and was sitting in the bus with her suitcase beside her on the floor that her spirits began to fall again like a barometer in a typhoon.

The bus stopped at the top of the hill about two hundred yards from her destination, and Sue got out and stood for a few moments while the bus rattled out of sight. It was growing dark now, for dusk falls early in November. The sky was still luminous—pale primrose and orange near the horizon, and lilac overhead—but the land was all dark with the coming of night, and the trees and hedges stood out against the brightness, black as charcoal.

Sue lifted her suitcase and walked down the rough track which led to Tog's Mill. She saw it as a dark huddle of buildings jaggedly outlined against the bright sky and she heard the rushing sound of the river as it leapt over the rocks. An owl hooted dismally as she approached, and, although she was by no means

31

easily frightened, Sue shivered involuntarily at the sound. What an eerie place it was! What a strange place to choose to live in! Surely the people who chose to live here must be queer themselves! It was so lonely, so deserted-looking that it was hard to believe that the brightly lit streets of Beilford were no more than two miles away.

The door was opened to Sue by a sallow-faced woman with dark hair and black beady eyes. She was dressed in black satin with a filmy lace apron. Sue noted that she wore silk stockings—almost as fine as Mrs. Darnay's own—and wondered how she could do any work in them.

"Mon Dieu, so you 'ave come at last!" cried the woman. "Come in queeck—do you sink I want to keep ze door open all night in zis dreadful cold?"

It was not a very pleasant welcome, but Sue comforted herself by reflecting that at least the woman seemed glad she had come. "I didn't know I was expected sooner," she said humbly, as she followed the woman into the kitchen.

"Sooner! Why not come at once, yesterday, or two days ago? 'Ere, zere is all to do an' only me to do it— one pair of 'ands—ze fires, ze meals, ze washing up ze dishes. Mon Dieu, quel horreur! Me, Ovette, washing ze dishes an' making ze fires! Nevaire 'ave I 'ad to do such work. Oh, it is not you to blame," she added with a sudden somewhat wolfish grin, "I am not reasonable, but 'oo could be reasonable wis all zat work to do."

It had never occurred to Sue that there could be any excuse for unreason, but she was much too bewildered to reply, and indeed it would have been difficult for her to get a word in edgeways if she had wanted to do so.

The Frenchwoman gabbled on, her broken English liberally sprinkled with French words, and Sue thought it was the strangest language she had ever heard for she was used to the slow quiet speech of her own people. She had not been an hour in the house before she knew all about her employers. It was against her principles to pry into their affairs but, unless she had stuffed her ears with cotton-wool, she could not have avoided hearing about them.

"We do not like zis Scotland," Ovette told her, pursuing her into the scullery where she was peeling the potatoes for the Darnays' dinner. "Bah, wot a 'ole! No vairs to go—no lights—no fun. Paree is wot we likes, Missis Darnay an' me. Paree is so gay. Mistaire Darnay 'e drag us 'ere to live in zis awful 'ole."

Sue pursed her lips. She was indignant at the insult to her country but she decided not to reply to the Frenchwoman's taunts. It was no good quarrelling with the woman before she had been two hours in the house.

"You not zink zis is a 'ole," Ovette declared, "but you not know any bettaire—see? You not know Paree, you 'ave nevaire been at Londres—ze streets, an' se lights, an' ze preety shops—ze preety 'ats in ze windows an' ze gowns—all so lovely—but 'ere all is cold an' meeserable."

"Why do you stay, then?" enquired Sue, losing all patience with the woman's complaints.

"Per'aps we not stay so vairy long as you sink," replied Ovette with that wolfish smile of hers. "Missis Darnay she not like it 'ere any more zan me, an it is Missis Darnay zat 'as all ze money—see? Ze one zat pays ze piper calls ze tune, an' she choose ze gay tune like me. It was zis morning she say to me——"

Sue looked up from her task surprised at the sudden silence and she saw a strange look sweep over the sallow face.

". . . nevaire mind," Ovette continued, "zat is none of your beesness, Sue. Your beesness is to cook ze nice dinner, n'est ce pas?"

Sue did not answer, she carried her pot of potatoes into the kitchen and put it on the fire (there was no gas at Tog's Mill nor any other modern convenience) but, if she thought that she had escaped from Ovette, she was mistaken.

"We were so 'appy at Londres," said the French-woman's voice at her elbow. "Missis Darnay she was 'appy wis all ze parties, an' Mistaire Darnay 'e paint ze preety peektures, an' all ze people say 'e is great artist. 'E make a lot of money too, but 'e is selfish as ze devil, zat man! Eet is not enough zat people say 'e is great artist an' buy 'is peektures—no—'e must leave ze town an' stop painting ze preety peektures zat everybody likes, an 'e must come to Scotland—Mon Dieu, qu'il est bête!"

"Are there any children?" Sue enquired, hoping to divert the woman's flow of talk into a more comfortable channel.

"No, 'an zere will not be," Ovette told her with a sly leer, "Missis Darnay she know too much."

Sue disliked Ovette thoroughly by this time, she was a horrible creature, disloyal and sly. Sue felt almost physically unclean after contact with her, and had begun to wonder how she could possibly remain a whole week in the same house. And yet the woman

was quite kind to Sue in her own way, she declared
that the cheese soufflé was "a râvir," and that Mr.
Darnay had asked for a second helping, and when
dinner was over and the dishes washed up she urged Sue
to go up to bed.

"You are tired—yes—it is natural," she said. "Me,
I will put ze 'ot bottles in," and she came upstairs to
see that Sue had everything she wanted.

The top floor of the house consisted of a tiny passage
with three doors opening off it. "Zis is my room,"
Ovette said, pointing to a half-open door, "an' zat is
yours. If you desire any sing—but no, you will not."

"No, of course not," Sue declared.

She had no wish to see Ovette's room, but it seemed
rude to show no interest at all, so she looked in and was
somewhat surprised to find that it was in a state of the
utmost confusion. Clothes lay about on the bed and on
the floor, and a bulging dress-basket was pushed under
the washing-stand. Sue was all the more surprised
because the untidy room did not seem to fit in with
Ovette's personality—she was meticulously neat.

"I 'ave been tidying up," explained Ovette, shutting
the door hastily, "an' when I tidy up all ze sings gets
untidy first. 'Ow you say ' It must be worse before it is
better,'" and she laughed.

Sue did not know what to say.

"Come zen," Ovette continued, "zis is your room.
You will be comfortable 'ere, yes?"

"Oh yes, it's a nice wee room," Sue declared. It was a
small but very pleasant room with a low camceiled
ceiling and a wide window seat let into the thick
wall. The window looked on to the river, she could
see the gleam of it in the darkness, and could hear the

rushing sound it made as it swept past the wall of the house.

"I will wake you in ze morning," Ovette said. "Do not rise till I come—it will be early enough, I promise —an' if zere is noise in ze 'ouse do not trouble. Sometimes zey are vairy late. Missis Darnay will speak to you in ze morning. You will sleep sound, eh?"

"Very sound," Sue replied. She was so exhausted by Ovette's yatter that she felt as if she could sleep for a week.

CHAPTER FIVE

It was daylight when Sue woke, and for a moment she could not think where she was. The window was in the wrong place, and the ceiling had come closer down—then suddenly she remembered all that had happened. The sun had risen and was shining in at the window and Sue realised that it must be late—why had not Ovette wakened her? It was most annoying for there was a great deal to be done before breakfast. She rose and flung on her clothes, but in spite of her desperate haste she could not help glancing out of the window for it had been dark the night before and she had not seen the view.

Her window was at the end of the house and looked eastwards, down-stream, and, in the glow of the rising sun, she saw the water leaping and glinting and hurrying away from the mill. At the other side of the river was a steep slope, well wooded with mixed trees. There were still a few brown withered leaves clinging to their branches, waiting for an easterly breeze to blow them away. The river had fallen considerably in the night and passed with a lapping rippling sound, and the black rocks in its bed were surrounded by tiny frills of foam.

Sue hurried downstairs. The house was very quiet—too quiet somehow—it gave her a vague feeling of uneasiness and dread. In the kitchen, which faced the gate into the road, she could not even hear the sound

37

of the river—there was no sound at all save the sounds which she was making herself. She stopped once or twice in her preparations for breakfast and listened for movement overhead but there was nothing to be heard.

It was difficult to know what to do, for the bacon would get spoilt if she cooked it before they were ready—she had done everything else. I'll have to waken Ovette, she decided, I'll just have to.

There was no answer to her timid knock on Ovette's door, and, when she opened the door and peeped in, the room was empty—it was not only empty of its human occupant, but it was swept bare of all her belongings. There was no brush or comb on the table, no washing materials on the wash-stand, and the door of the cupboard stood open showing empty shelves. A breeze swept in at the window and fluttered a torn piece of tissue paper which was lying on the floor.

Ovette had gone! Sue was absolutely dumfounded at the discovery, she stood in the middle of the room and looked round her in dismay. Ovette had gone in the night and obviously did not mean to return—so that was why her room had been in such a state of confusion!

Sue was still standing there (trying to make up her mind whether to wake the Darnays and tell them the news, or to wait until they wakened themselves) when she heard the front door slam so violently that it shook the house. She ran downstairs to see who it was, arriving so early in the day, and saw a man in the hall taking off his coat—a big fur-lined coat of heather-mixture tweed—his soft hat was lying on the hall table where he had thrown it.

"Hallo!" he said, looking up at Sue as she hesitated on the stairs, "hallo, *where on earth* have you come from?"

Somehow or other Sue was aware that this was Mr. Darnay himself. She did not know how she knew it, and it was all the more odd because, until a moment ago, she had imagined Mr. Darnay lying asleep behind that closed door upon which she had been afraid to knock and he was not at all like her conception of what an artist should be, for he was tall and straight with a lean brown face and piercing grey eyes—he was more like a soldier than an artist Sue thought—but all the same she was sure that this man was Mr. Darnay and no other. She stopped on the stair and gazed at him and he gazed back.

"Well," he said at last, "well, who are you, may I ask, and what in Heaven's name are you doing here?"

"I'm the cook," said Sue.

"The devil you are!" Mr. Darnay exclaimed. He was silent for a moment and then he continued, "I'd forgotten all about you—and Elise must have forgotten too—of course that fiend, Ovette, took care not to say anything about it."

"I only came yesterday," Sue pointed out. "That's why you haven't seen me before."

Mr. Darnay looked at her in a strange way. "What are you going to do?" he enquired.

"I was just going to fry the bacon."

He threw back his head and laughed—it was a curious mirthless laugh.

"—unless you want me to do something else," Sue added in a bewildered voice.

"Dear me, no," Mr. Darnay replied, "what else should I want you to do? Fry the bacon, by all means. Though dynasties fall we must eat—eat or die—and I have no intention of dying yet," he added.

Sue thought he was very strange. She came down a few steps and hesitated. "Will I wake Mrs. Darnay, or will you?" she enquired.

He had turned away, but now he stopped and looked back. "My good girl they've gone," he said quietly. "D'you mean to say you didn't know? Yes, they've both gone—I took them to the station. There's nobody left in the house but me—and you. Of course I don't expect you to stay, I had forgotten all about you."

Sue went into the kitchen and fried the bacon; she worked mechanically, her brain busy with the extra-ordinary behaviour of her employers. It's as if they were daft, she thought, as she laid the rashers of bacon tenderly in the pan, yes, it's just as if they were daft, engaging me to come and cook for them and then hareing off in the middle of the night, but it's none of my business, of course.

It was none of her business how her employers chose to behave, but her own future was her business and she viewed it with dismay. She saw herself returning to Beilford with her tail between her legs and producing this absolutely incredible tale to account for her dismissal.

Sue set the table and rang the gong, and almost immediately Mr. Darnay came strolling up from the river over the close turf. She left him, and went to have her own meal, and she had barely finished when he came into the kitchen to find her. He was frowning, she noticed, and biting the stem of an unlit pipe.

"Look here—er—of course I must pay you," he said, stammering a little with obvious embarrassment. "I don't know much about—but you've come here, and I suppose you were led to believe that—that you would be kept on—so—so——"

"It doesn't matter," she put in hastily.

"Mrs. Darnay was called away suddenly—er—on business."

"Yes," said Sue. She looked up and met his eyes and he flushed under his tan; Mr. Darnay was an extremely bad liar.

"You don't believe a word of it," he exclaimed somewhat bitterly. "Why should you believe it? But all the same I should be much obliged if you will give that explanation to your friends. I'm not particularly keen for the whole of Beilford to know that I've quarrelled with my wife. They think I'm mad already."

Sue was embarrassed by the way he spoke. She realised that he scarcely knew what he was saying. He was all on edge, wounded and bitter at heart. He would regret his frankness later when he had time to consider it.

"I suppose you heard the row," he continued, "and all the fuss of packing—it lasted most of the night."

"I didn't hear anything," Sue assured him. "I was tired, so I went to bed at nine. Ovette never told me they were going away. I saw her box packed when I went up to bed but I never thought——"

"What!" he cried, turning upon her so suddenly that she started back in alarm. "You saw her box packed at nine o'clock! But it wasn't until after that they decided to go. Wait a moment, we must get to the bottom of this."

"Maybe it would be best if we didn't. Maybe it would be best if I just went home—I'll not say a word to anybody."

He looked at her for the first time as if he really saw her and the hard lines of his face softened. "That's damned good of you," he declared. "I appreciate that, but I must *know* you see. There's something odd here and I must understand it.

"The fact is this place does not suit my wife. She always hated it. But I had to get away from everything —the parties, the late nights and all the other stupid waste of time and energy—I had to get away from all that," said Mr. Darnay, starting to walk up and down, speaking more to himself than to Sue. "Last night things flared up and we both said things—things we had been thinking for some time—and the end of it was Elise decided to go back to her people. She got Ovette out of bed and they packed——"

"But Ovette knew they were going," Sue cried in a breathless voice, "her clothes were half packed, I saw her box."

"You're sure?" he asked her, "you're quite sure you saw that woman's box half packed when you went to bed? It's important to me, you know."

"Yes," said Sue. "Oh dear, I wish I could say no, Mr. Darnay. I see how it was—they had settled to go— before——"

"And the whole row was engineered," he added bitterly. "Oh well, I suppose it doesn't make much difference."

She waited for a little and then she said timidly, "You'll be shutting up the house, of course."

"No, why should I?" he answered. "I'm just beginning to—there's something about this place that suits me. I'm getting the feel of it. No, I shall stay on here by myself. I shall manage all right—I'm used to camping—and it will be good to be alone with nothing to distract me from my work."

Sue wanted to offer to stay and "do" for him, for it seemed to her impossible that he should "manage." He might be used to camping but it was quite different living in a big old-fashioned house. She trembled to think what the place would be like after he had lived in it alone for a week—but that was none of her business of course, he had said she was to go, so she must just go. Before she went she would cook his dinner and put the place to rights.

Sue glanced at him again and saw that he was far away, lost in dreams, and had forgotten her existence. She was quite sure that he was not even thinking about his wife, or the mean trick she had played on him. Sue did not know what artists thought about when their faces wore that strange rapt expression, and, because she was interested to know, she followed his eyes and saw that he was gazing out of the window. A cloud, white and billowy as eiderdown, was sailing across the sky, trailing its grey shadow across the sunlit hill.

"Gorgeous!" he said softly. "Could you ever get

the feeling of that softness—even Constable—but you might try——"

I don't believe he would notice whether I was here or not, said Sue to herself with a little secret smile.

CHAPTER SIX

IT WAS, of course, a ridiculous idea that Mr. Darnay would not notice whether she was there or not—Sue chuckled over it herself at the time—but she found, as the day wore on, that her idea was not very far from the sober truth. She stayed and cooked Mr. Darnay's midday meal and, because she was sorry for the horrible way his wife had treated him, she took a lot of trouble over the meal. She gave him soup and curry (made from some cold meat which she found in the larder) with snow white rice and crisp little curls of potato. She also made a coffee soufflé with a crystallised cherry on the top. She had to go and look for him when the meal was ready and, after some trouble, she found him on the river bank painting a willow tree. He was so engrossed in his work that she had some trouble in making him come, but at last she managed to drag him back to the house.

It's dreadful, Sue thought, as she trotted off to the kitchen for her own dinner, it's simply dreadful. He'll never remember to cook anything for himself—he'll just starve—he's thin enough already. She decided to stay and cook his supper and then go. He would have to stop painting when dusk fell and then she could talk to him and show him where everything was. Sue was rather pleased with her cleverness in perceiving that an artist's working hours must necessarily be limited by the fall of dusk, but she

45

found that although she had been right in her presage she was wrong in her deduction.

Mr. Darnay certainly gave up painting when it grew dark, but he shut himself up in his studio and was no more get-at-able than before. She peeped in to tell him that the butcher had called and to ask him what she should order, and saw him standing before a large table covered with bottles and bowls and knives; he was measuring powder and mixing liquids and pounding up something in a pestle and mortar for all the world like a chemist. She shut the door softly and came away, for it was obvious that no good could be got out of him until he had finished what he was doing.

The butcher's vanman was surprised to see Sue at Tog's Mill.

"Are ye here for long, Miss Pringle?" he asked with interest.

"I'm here to oblige," Sue told him. "Have you got a nice wee bit of pope's-eye, Mr. Farquharson?"

"I'll cut ye a piece," he declared, diving into his van until nothing of him but his legs were visible. There was a short silence while he cut the meat, and then he enquired amicably, "How would ye like a sheep's heid, Miss Pringle? I've a good one left."

"No," replied Sue shortly.

"Och, ye'd better take it," he told her, handing it out of the van as he spoke, "it's a real nice heid—I never saw a meatier one—and ye can have it for saxpence."

It was certainly a fine head, and Sue would have taken it like a shot if she had been staying on, for it would make nourishing soup, and nourishing soup was exactly what Mr. Darnay needed, but Sue was not staying on, so it was no good.

"No," she replied regretfully, "I'm not needing a head to-day. I'll just take the meat, thank you. Is there any news, Mr. Farquharson," she added enquiringly, for, although she had only been at Tog's Mill for twenty-four hours, she felt as if she had been cut off from the outer world for weeks.

"News?" he enquired, "what kind o' news? The Spanish Government has taken yon place wi' the queer name—is that the kind o' news ye're meaning?"

"Franco'll get it back from them," said Sue confidently, "Franco'll win."

"Franco!" exclaimed the van man scornfully. "*He'll* no win. He's nought but a rebel—ye're surely not on his side, Miss Pringle?"

"I am, then," Sue declared, "I like Franco, he's got a nice face. I saw a photo of him in the papers."

"You an' your Franco!" exclaimed Farquharson in disgust. He got into the van and drove off.

It was not until he had vanished up the road that Sue found she still had the sheep's head in her hands. She turned it over and looked at it. The man had been right, it was a fine head with plenty of meat on it and very cheap at sixpence.

"Well, if that isn't provoking!" she said aloud, and then she smiled to herself and added, "it was Franco's fault." She carried it into the larder and put it in a bowl to soak.

When Sue went to call Mr. Darnay for supper she

saw that he was "awake" (it was the word she used in her own mind to describe his awareness of everyday matters).

"Hallo, I thought you'd gone!" he exclaimed in surprise.

"No," said Sue gravely.

He considered her—"Your home is in Beilford, I suppose?"

"Yes. Mr. Pringle the baker is my father."

"I'll take you home in the car," Mr. Darnay said. "Yes, that will be best."

"And how will you manage?" enquired Sue, speaking somewhat truculently in her nervousness. "How can you cook the food and wash the dishes when you're working at your painting all day long? The thing's ridiculous, you'll just starve, that's what'll happen."

"You mean you want to stay?" he asked her in amazement.

"I mean I'm going to stay," declared Sue boldly. "I've taken in a sheep's head, and you'd never boil it long enough. Where's the sense in wasting a good head?"

Mr. Darnay roared with laughing.

Sue waited patiently until he had finished. "Well?" she said at last.

"Well," he repeated, "well, it's really awfully good of you. We must have it on business terms, of course. What—er—salary do you get? I don't know much about these things you see."

"I was to get a pound a week," Sue admitted, somewhat diffidently, "it seems a lot, but grandfather said it was the thing."

"It isn't a lot at all," replied Mr. Darnay hastily, "you're a very good cook. I should have told you how much I enjoyed my lunch, but the fact is I was thinking. Sometimes I lose myself and don't realise what's happening. Painting is so exciting, you see."

Sue nodded gravely. "You ate it, that's the main thing," she said.

"I've had a splendid day," he continued. "It was so nice and quiet, and I was in the mood for work. You're sure you want to stay?"

"Quite sure," replied Sue, nodding again.

He sighed—perhaps with relief. "That's good," he said, "I see now that it will be much the best thing. What's your name? I can't go on calling you 'look here' or 'I say.'"

"It's Miss Pringle," she told him seriously.

His eyes twinkled. "Of course, how stupid of me! You told me that before, didn't you, Miss Bun the Baker's Daughter."

Sue knew the game of "Happy Families"—it had been a great favourite when she and Sandy were small, so she appreciated the jest and retorted immediately, "and you're Mr. Pots the Painter, I suppose!" She blushed rose red as the words left her lips for they sounded a wee bit cheeky, but Mr. Darnay didn't seem to mind.

"Of course I am!" he cried, laughing heartily, "Mr. Pots the Painter! We shall get on like a house on fire, I can see that."

"I'm sure I hope so," said Sue gravely.

Sue settled down into a steady routine, and soon felt as if she had been at Tog's Mill all her life. The mornings were occupied by the work of the house, but the afternoons were free, and she made a habit of walking by the river or on the moors. She was back at four for a cup of tea and then the butcher called. Tog's Mill was so far from the beaten track that the van could not call there in the morning and indeed Farquharson made it obvious that he was calling there as a favour, and that the small orders she gave him scarcely paid for the petrol he used. Sue had known the butcher, Mr. Anderson, since she was a child, and his son was her contemporary at Beilford Academy so she was able to take a strong line with Farquharson. She made him bring her groceries, and a copy of the daily paper. She had discovered somewhat to her surprise that no paper at all came to Tog's Mill and had determined that this state of affairs must not continue. (Sue liked what she called "a keek at the papers" herself, and she was of the opinion that a gentleman like Mr. Darnay ought to read the news.)

"It's like heathens," she told Farquharson. "Just like heathens. Anything might happen and us not know a thing about it."

The vanman agreed to lighten the heathen darkness of Tog's Mill and brought Sue *The Scotsman* regularly every day, and for this indulgence Sue gave him a cup of tea and argued with him over the conduct of the Spanish War.

Her father's van, with its load of new baked scones and cookies, only called twice a week and the ancient vanman could not be threatened nor cajoled into calling more often. "Yer father would no' stand for it," he declared. "He's awfy near wi' the petrol. If yer wantin' me oot three times it's himsel' will hae tae gie the orrder."

Mr. Darnay was out painting all day long—or as long as the light lasted—he had explained to Sue that he was "experimenting with a new medium." Sue translated this into her own practical language and enquired, "Are you trying to paint in a different way, or is it with different kinds of paints?"

"It's both, really," he told her. "I feel I've got hold of something which can't be expressed in the old way —it was getting too easy—I was making too much money——"

"Will you make more money with the new kind of pictures?"

"No, I shan't. In fact I don't suppose anybody will buy them, but that isn't the point."

Sue understood that this "new medium" was the underlying cause of the quarrel which had resulted in the break-up of the Darnay menage. She considered the ethics of the case as she roamed down the path by the river's edge. Darnay felt that this new way of painting was more important than fame and money and the companionship of his wife—that was strange. Could it be right? As she came to know him better, however, Sue began to feel certain that whatever he did, or had done, was right, for she could no more imagine him doing a mean thing than she could spread out her arms and fly. His nature was a pledge of conduct, for he was keen and shining like a sword, contemptuous of hypocrisy and all half-hearted things. Sue had never met anybody the least like him before, never anybody so natural and free and indifferent to what other people thought.

Sometimes when Darnay was "asleep" as Sue called it (though indeed the word was a poor description of the sort of trance in which he worked) she came and went all day without getting a human glance from his eye. It made her uncomfortable sometimes to have him look at her as though she were not there—he looked at her, Sue thought, as you would look at a sofa, or a familiar chest of drawers—but at other times when he "woke up" he seemed to feel the need for companionship and would call her into the studio and talk to her, or drift into the kitchen and sit on the table and interfere with her work. His visits interfered very seriously with Sue's work for his conversation was so difficult to understand, and so interesting—perhaps on that account—that she would stand and listen to him while the pudding boiled over and would forget whether or not she had salted the potatoes. She was fully aware that he talked to her for want of some one better, and that he scarcely knew or cared whether she understood, and at first Sue resented this. It's all daft nonsense, she told herself comfortingly. But the odd thing was that it wasn't daft nonsense at all, and Sue, remembering afterwards what he had said and pondering the words, would suddenly be enlightened. The things he said kept knocking against her mind until she was forced to wrestle with them and tear out the meaning.

Sometimes she was annoyed with him, for he did not trouble to be tactful—his mind was too full of his work for him to consider the feelings of his housekeeper—and Sue, like all proud people who find themselves in an inferior position, was easily insulted.

"You can hear the river plain, to-night," she said one evening, as she brought in his supper and arranged it on the table. Darnay was reading *The Scotsman*—he read it daily now, accepting it as manna from the skies without bothering himself about how or why it came.

"I can hear it plainly, Miss Bun," he declared, without looking up.

Sue understood the rebuke and resented it—her hackles rose—"I speak like my neighbours," she said in a stiff little voice.

Darnay looked at her and smiled—what a queer bundle of complexities she was! Ignorant as a savage, proud as the devil, independent as be damned and yet humble and intelligent, and kind.

"You needn't, Miss Bun," he told her.

"I needn't?"

"No, because you know better. It's a kind of inverted pride——"

"I don't want to be better than my neighbours—why should I—they're good enough for me."

His eyes travelled down to her feet. "And yet you don't wear down-at-the-heel shoes," he said quite casually.

Sue retired to the kitchen without another word. He was daft, she decided. Down-at-the-heel shoes indeed! No, she wouldn't be seen dead in such things. She was proud of her feet (and justifiably so, for Sue's feet were very small and well-shaped). *She* wouldn't go slopping about in down-at-heel shoes like Mrs. Watt, and old Mrs. Bain, down-at-heel shoes!

And then quite suddenly she *saw*—down-at-heel language, what a horrible thought! She pondered it as she held the omelet pan over the fire and eased the crisp edges of the omelet carefully with her knife. Then she slid the omelet on to a hot plate and carried it into the dining-room.

"I see what you mean," she said, as she placed the dish before him on the table.

Darnay had been reading the weather forecast. He lifted a puzzled face and stared at her.

"Down-at-heel language," she explained. "I don't want to talk like that."

"Good heavens, you don't!" he cried.

"Could I learn to talk like you?"

"You mustn't try," he declared. "Honestly, Miss Bun, I couldn't bear it. Your talk is just right for your country. It's as right as the heather on the hills. You have just enough of the 'Scots' to add salt to your conversation—I love to hear you talk—and remember this," added Darnay seriously, "the old Scots language is a grand language, hoary with tradition. They spoke it at King James's Court and at the Scottish Bar; poets used it and made it live for ever. It was just the one word I was carping at—ungrateful prig that I am."

"Plain for plainly," said Sue, nodding, for every word of the conversation was indelibly printed on her mind.

"Plain for plainly," he agreed, "and slow for slowly. That isn't Scots, Miss Bun, it's just slovenly down-at-heel English and somehow or other it always makes me angry. It's a sort of complex, I suppose," he added smiling, "but that's a poor excuse for my rudeness, I'm afraid."

Sue flushed, for an apology always made her feel uncomfortable. "Your omelet's spoiling," she said and fled for her life.

CHAPTER SEVEN

UP TILL now Sue had always lived in a town (not a very big town, of course, for Beilford is a small compact place, scarcely straggling outside its sixteenth-century walls), her life had been in the town, and all her interests, and she knew little more of the country than a city-born urchin. Now, however, on her afternoon walks she began to enjoy the country. She saw it all the better because her walks were solitary, and because her mind was jolted out of the groove in which it had run for so long. This life—busy, useful, independent— was so different from her old life that she felt like a different person. In fact her old life seemed like a dream, and all her own problems were shelved to make room for her new interests.

It was beautiful country, even in its winter bareness. The silver river wound between great rocks, or slipped along silently between green banks, or gurgled over shallow beds of gravel. She saw trout leaping in the pools below the rocks and the silver glint of a salmon as it passed up the river to spawn, and she saw all kinds of birds (some standing by the river's edge, and others flying low over the moving water) and wondered about them, and wished she knew their names and how they lived. Down here in the valley by the stream there were little rounded hills, green and friendly, and tall stately trees, graceful in their tracery of bare boughs, but when she climbed on to the moors she found bigger hills covered with brown withered heather and coarse yellow grass. Jagged rocks stuck out through the thin skin of earth, and dry-stone dykes flung themselves in sweeping curves over the shoulders of the hills. There were sheep here, small mountain sheep with black faces and black legs, seeking their food amongst the coarse herbage and scattering in all directions when Sue approached, and there were different kinds of birds—larks and grouse and others that she had never seen before. Here the wind blew cold and clear, and big clouds, white and billowy or dark and threatening, sped before its chill blast trailing their skirts over the far-off tops. In these high places the whole feel of the day could change in a moment from warm friendliness to cold hostility. A cloud moved up and hid the sun, and the very same hills, which had seemed so kind, were suddenly grey and lonely and formidable, and the wind was suddenly chill.

Sue found little paths over the hills, and wondered about them not knowing that they were sheep-tracks, age-old. Here and there she came across the ruins of a bothy—a mere rubble of stones—and wondered who could have built it, and why it had been built with such labour in that deserted spot. Small burns ran down from the tops towards the river below, small cheerful burns prattling busily in their stony beds, and in the creases which they had carved out of the hills there were clusters of hazels and rowans, and an occasional oak, stunted and twisted by the wind's force.

On the slopes of the hills were small farms, nestling in hollows and screened by trees, surrounded by patches of fields like coloured handkerchiefs spread upon the ground to dry—brown fields of plough, green fields of pasture for the cows. The farther hills, higher than those of Beil, were clad with pine and fir, but bald at the summit where the naked rock cropped out, and farther still was a distant line of mountains which changed from blue to grey or violet as the clouds moved past.

One afternoon Sue found herself near a little farm —a small whitewashed cottage surrounded by chicken coops and bee-hives. It was so well kept and tidy that she paused at the gate and at that moment the door opened and a girl came out, a girl about Sue's own age with a merry face and crisp brown hair. They stared at each other for a moment with interest, for the place was so deserted that human beings were at a premium there.

"It's a fine day," said Sue at last.

"It's grand," agreed the girl. "Are you going far?"

"I'm just taking a walk," Sue told her.

They fell into conversation and Sue learnt that the girl's name was May Grainger and that she and her brother had started the poultry farm and were running bees as a side-line. "They pay well here," the girl told her, "for it's heather honey of course, but Alec looks after the bees, I'm rather scared of them."

Sue was scared of bees too, for she had been stung when she was a child and had never forgotten the incident, but fowls were harmless as well as useful, and these white leghorns were attractive too. She had time to spare so she went round the coops with May Grainger and helped her to feed her charges, and she asked all sorts of pertinent questions and marvelled at the cleanliness of it all.

"They lay better if you keep them clean," May declared, "at least Alec says so—and anyway it's nicer to have eggs from clean hens, don't you think so?"

Sue agreed with that. "Could I buy eggs here?" she enquired, somewhat diffidently, "or are you sending them into town?"

"You could have three or four dozen a week, but you'd have to fetch them," replied the girl.

It was the beginning of a very pleasant friendship for they had much in common. They had both been bred in town and were now discovering the delights of the country, and discovering its sorrows also. The Graingers' cottage was every bit as antiquated and inconvenient as Tog's Mill, and it was even farther from the shops so the two housekeepers could commiserate with each other on the difficulties of laying in supplies. They discussed ways and means of alleviating their lot and Sue picked up some useful hints from her new friend; an electric torch for instance, was an invaluable adjunct to an early riser, and a small dab of luminous paint on a box of matches saved a good deal of time and trouble when you wanted to find them in the dark.

"Good-bye," said May. "I wish you could stay to tea and see my brother. Come back soon, and come as often as you can."

"I'll come every Wednesday afternoon for the eggs," Sue promised, "and maybe oftener if I can manage it."

Sue stopped to wave at the turn in the track, and May waved back to her in a friendly manner. It had been a pleasant adventure, Sue decided, the kind of adventure you could never have in a town.

The way home to the mill lay along the path by the edge of the river and past the willow tree where Darnay was painting. He had been painting that same old tree for a whole week now—a stunted, misshapen tree it was—and Sue wondered why he did not paint something else for a change. He looked up as she passed and waved to her to come, and taking her by the shoulders he stood her in front of his canvas and held her there.

Sue had never really looked at any of his pictures before; she was shy of looking, for it was no business of hers. She was aware that if she had been painting she would not have wanted anybody to look at what she was doing, it would be "sort of sacred." To-day Darnay was in what Sue called his "wild mood" (she had noticed that the "wild mood" always followed periods of intense concentration) and when he was like this you never knew what he would do or say.

It was quite impossible not to look at the picture now, so Sue looked at it, and her heart sank. She had been so sure that what he was doing was wonderful, for he himself was wonderful and he worked at it with all his might.

"Oh!" said Sue, so dismayed by the strange sight before her eyes that she could not hide her consternation.

"Well, Miss Bun, you've said it!" he declared, and there was a quiver of laughter in his voice. "A whole column of criticism in one word—eh?"

"Of course it's not finished," she said, trying to find excuses for what she saw. "Maybe it will be quite different when you've finished it."

"But it is finished," he told her. He took up a brush

and signed it with a few quick strokes and flung himself down on the grass. "You don't like it, Miss Bun," he said, smiling at her happily, "I didn't think you would, somehow. Perhaps nobody will like it——"

"I don't know much about pictures."

"But you know what you like," he suggested with twinkling eyes. "Dear Miss Bun, you run so true to type, and yet there's a flavour about you that never palls, so you don't like my Willow Tree in November."

She looked at it again, hoping that she would like it better this time. In the foreground was the willow tree, and looking up through the bare brown whips you saw the sky, grey with flying clouds. The whole thing was done in a cold tone of grey and thickly plastered with whorls and streaks of paint.

"You're too near," he said, watching her face with amusement. He had lighted his pipe, and now he pointed with the stem of it in a gesture she had learnt to know. "Go and sit down on that rock," he added.

"There's tea to get," Sue objected, "and the butcher——"

"Never mind tea and the butcher."

She went and sat down on the rock and looked at the picture again; it was certainly much nicer from here, but even now Sue did not think it was pretty.

"Well, what's the verdict?" he enquired.

"I don't know anything about pictures, so what's the good."

"It's interesting—the impact of my experiment upon an uneducated eye."

Sue bristled—uneducated indeed! She had had a perfectly good education.

"Well, you are from my point of view," said Darnay,

laughing at her disgusted expression. "From my point of view you are a savage, Miss Bun, an intelligent savage of course, a sort of woman Friday, cast up upon my desert island. Yes, that's exactly what you are. Come along now, forget about the advent of the butcher and tell me what you see."

Thus adjured Sue tried to forget about the butcher (it was somewhat difficult, for there was nothing in the house for to-morrow's dinner) and fixing her eyes upon the picture she gave it her full attention.

"Yes," she said, "I see it a lot better from here. Yes, it's very real looking—the branches of the tree look so near, and the sky seems very far away. How did you make it look like that?"

"Go on," said Darnay, sitting up and looking very alert. "Go on, Miss Bun."

"The clouds look awful soft and sort of puffy," Sue declared, "and you could almost think they were moving along with the wind, and that wee hole in the clouds with the blue sky showing through looks terribly far away."

"Thank you," he said softly.

She looked at him in surprise.

"Go on," he adjured her, "and please be absolutely honest. This is interesting."

"It's queer," Sue continued, "but somehow the picture makes me rather—frightened. There's something sort of fierce about it—sort of cruel. It's like a tiger, Mr. Darnay."

There was a little silence when Sue had finished speaking and she felt more frightened than before (it was a dreadful thing to say about his picture, and foolish too—how could a willow tree be fierce like a tiger?) but he had asked for the truth and something stronger than herself had prompted her to give it to him.

"Out of the mouths of babes and sucklings," said Mr. Darnay at last.

"You're not angry?"

"No, only humbled to the dust. You're dead right, Miss Bun, I was in a tearing rage when I painted that picture. I thought I had sublimated my rage—but I hadn't."

Sue understood now. "Why, of course," she cried, "you painted your feelings into it."

"But I shouldn't have," he told her. "You seem to think that makes it right, but it's all wrong. What are my feelings worth? I must be no more than a seeing eye, a crafty hand. I must allow the tree or the flower I paint to exhibit it's own nature—that is art. I thought I was painting the soul of the willow, but it was my own black soul I was painting—that's no good. An artist must paint as though he were God. Supposing a man sat down at the piano in a tearing rage and played one of Beethoven's Sonatas, putting his own feelings straight into the music, would that be right ? No, but if he were able to sublimate his rage it would sharpen his perception and enable him to understand and express the emotion of the composer. We must use emotion to strengthen our souls, not allow emotion to use us."

These were difficult words, and Sue was wise enough not to reply. She understood vaguely what he meant, but she could not see the importance of it. Of course he was angry and hurt—who would not have been—and it seemed to her that if he were able to paint his rage into the bare whips of a willow tree and a clouded sky it was a good thing and a clever thing to do. She had been surprised at the quiet way in which he had taken his wife's departure—many a man would have shouted and raged over it, or moped about the place like a sick jackdaw (thought Sue), but Mr. Darnay had gone on with his work as if he didn't care—she saw now that he had got it all off his chest by making a picture of it—an excellent plan. It was good for himself to get rid of it and good for other people that he should get rid of it in such a nice quiet way. When Mr. Waugh's wife had run away with a commercial traveller he had played his fiddle night and day for a week until the people in the next house had been obliged to send in a message asking him to stop. And when Jamie Duguid ran away to sea his father had threatened to go after him with a gun, and, when forcibly restrained by his friends, he had drunk himself silly and run round Beilford in his nightshirt. It was a little different in Mr. Darnay's case (Sue was forced to admit) because Mrs. Darnay had not gone off with another man, but all the same she had treated him badly and Mr. Darnay had just cause for wrath. Now that he had relieved his feelings he would paint something prettier and more comfortable to look at—Sue was sure of it.

They were walking back to the house by this time, Mr. Darnay striding ahead of her along the narrow path, burdened by his easel and all the other equipment which was necessary to his art. She had wanted to carry some of it for him, but had not been allowed—whether for politeness sake, or because he was afraid she would drop it into the river, she could not tell.

The river was very winding here, and all at once he stopped and looked back at her.

"D'you know that poem by Burns about the Doon?" he asked.

"Yes, I know it," Sue replied.

"Say it then, Miss Bun. Let me hear the real thing."

"Is this the bit you mean?

> ' Amang the bonnie windin' banks
> The Doon rins wimpling clear.'"

"That's the bit," he declared. "It's lovely. The Beil rins wimplin' clear too, doesn't it? Say it all to me, Miss Bun."

For a moment Sue hesitated—it was a daft sort of thing to stand on the river bank and say poetry—but Mr. Darnay was waiting, and she wanted to please him, and comfort him for her hard words about his picture, so she threw back her head and said the poem all through rather slowly. Her soft deep voice mingled with the prattle of the river and the song of the birds.

Darnay listened intently, and when she had finished he said, "Thank you. That was perfect, I shan't forget it as long as I live."

She saw that he was happy again, his vexation past and forgotten, and she was glad. As they rounded the last bend the old mill came into sight; the sun was setting behind them and the whole building was illuminated with a pinkish glow. It had grown old well and the queer rough hewn stones of which it was built had weathered with the landscape so that it was now actually part of the trees and rocks. The old wooden wheel still remained, and a gentle stream of water trickled over it and fell into the pool below. There were long strands of green weed hanging from the wheel and a few small ferns had taken root in the crevices. The whole building was now mirrored on the smooth dark surface of the intake pool so that the house belonged to the water as much as to the earth and sky. Sue looked at it and liked it. She liked it in the same way as you like a person, and she realised that you could never be fond of a modern house in quite the same way. She would probably be annoyed with it again, when she rose in grey dark and groped for the matches to light those smelly lamps, and to struggle with the evil spirit that dwelt in the old-fashioned kitchen range, but at the moment Sue felt a very real affection for the place and a sensation of homecoming such as she had never experienced before.

CHAPTER EIGHT

IN SPITE of Sue's preoccupation with her new life she
had not forgotten Sandy's problem, but had thought
about it quite often as she went about her work, or
lay in bed at night, and at last she decided to speak
to Mr. Darnay about it. She chose a time when he was
"awake"—it happened to be breakfast time and a thin
drizzle had started to fall which made painting out
of doors impracticable.

"How long will this last, Miss Bun?" enquired
Darnay as she brought in his bacon.

"It might go on all day," replied his housekeeper
pessimistically and then, as she saw his face fall,
she added, "or it might clear up quite soon."

Darnay laughed.

"Well, you never know," Sue told him, "if the wind
got up it would blow the clouds away."

"We must whistle for a wind," he replied.

He was looking through his letters as he spoke, and
now he pushed them aside distastefully.

"Don't you like getting letters?" Sue enquired.

"I hate it," he replied. "Put them into my desk,
Miss Bun, they just upset me. Why on earth can't
people leave me alone to get on with my work!"

"But you haven't opened them——"

"Take them away," Darnay said, "I know what's
in them. They want me to go back to London and
paint pictures that will sell."

67

Sue took the letters in her hand—they wanted him to go back to London, did they?

"Put them in my desk," he said, "put them all there. I'm fed up with letters. I want to get on with my work, I'm fed up with the weather too," he added ruefully.

Darnay sat down to his breakfast, but his housekeeper still lingered.

"Would it bother you to hear about my brother?" she enquired somewhat diffidently.

"No, it wouldn't," he replied at once, "what's the matter with your brother, Miss Bun?"

Sue launched out into her story and, seeing that Mr. Darnay was interested, she told him the whole thing. He listened patiently, and asked several questions, and at last he said, "Has your brother got a definite career in view, or does he just want to go to the University and escape from Beilford?"

"It's animals," Sue declared, "Sandy's mad for animals. He wants to be a vet, and of course he would have to take his degree—he wants to escape from Beilford too, of course. But you see, Mr. Darnay, the real difficulty is Sandy himself. He'd do anything for peace."

"Tell him to come out here and speak to me," Darnay said.

Sue accomplished this quite easily. She sent a note to Sandy by way of Mr. Farquharson, who was now her faithful slave, and the next evening Sandy arrived at Tog's Mill looking very smart and clean in his best Sunday suit.

"Grace asked me where I was going," he declared, as he came into the kitchen and looked round him with interest, "so I just said I was going to supper at the Andersons'."

"There was no need to lie, surely," said Sue a trifle sternly, "Grace couldn't have prevented you coming here."

"She'd have wanted to know why I was coming, and all about it," Sandy explained.

Sue sighed. "It'll maybe mean more trouble for you before you've done," she pointed out. "Grace may find out you weren't at the Andersons', and then where will you be? But never mind that now, Mr. Darnay's waiting for you."

She led him into the studio and left him there, for she thought that the interview might bear better fruit if it took place in private. What kind of fruit it would bear she could not imagine, but she had great faith in Darnay. She took up her sewing and sat down by the kitchen fire and waited patiently, wondering what was happening and what was being said. She hoped Sandy was making a good impression, but he would, she was almost sure of that, for Sandy had nice manners and took pains to make people like him. It was this desire that people should like him that was really the base of all the trouble, for Sandy would rather tell a lie and make a good impression than tell the truth and make a bad one.

The interview lasted for nearly an hour, and Sandy came out of the studio with pink cheeks and glowing eyes.

"He's great, Sue," declared Sandy.

Sue had known that before. "What have you decided?" she asked with her usual practical common sense.

"I'm to have supper with you," said Sandy, "and then I'm to go straight home and speak to father. Mr. Darnay says he'll help me to get into a Veterinary College—he knows a man who's the head of one in England—but he says I must speak to father myself."

"That's fine," exclaimed Sue.

They sat down and had supper together. Sandy was full of excitement and optimism. Already he saw himself a "vet" tending sick horses and curing them of diseases which defied the efforts of every other "vet" in the country.

"Then you'll speak to father to-night," Sue said, as she saw him off at the door.

Sandy hesitated. "Maybe I'll wait till Sunday," he said doubtfully, "there's more time on Sunday. It would be a pity to spoil everything by speaking too soon. There's plenty of time. I'm not to leave school till Easter."

"Speak to him to-night," Sue told him. "Get it all settled."

"Well, we'll see," said Sandy vaguely, and he walked off slowly up the hill.

He had to wait for some minutes before the bus hove in sight, and during this cold wait his spirits sank. He began to visualise the interview with his father and to make up his mind what he would say. He knew quite well that the interview would be a very unpleasant one, and he hated unpleasantness. I *can't*, thought Sandy miserably, I'll have to wait a bit and get him in a good mood—perhaps Sunday—or next week sometime—I'll wait.

When he got out of the bus at the Market Cross his spirits had risen again, for he had decided to put off the unpleasant interview indefinitely, and the mere fact that this unpleasantness had receded into the distance was a relief to his mind. He walked home up the High Street, and as he walked his pocket jingled in a most delightful way, for Mr. Darnay had given him five shillings to spend on something he wanted. What did he want?

He stopped dead outside the window of the saddler's shop. The shop was closed of course, but there in the window was the air-rifle which he had wanted for months. "Yours for 5/-" said the notice in large letters, and below, in smaller letters, was added "and 1/- weekly."

Sandy's eyes gleamed. He could buy the air-rifle now, or at any rate he could buy it to-morrow. It would be his very own, he had the 5/- in his pocket. The weekly payment of 1/- did not bother him much for he would manage that somehow—he could save up his pocket money, or borrow from Grace.

The next day was Saturday, and Sandy was off to the saddler's directly after breakfast. He was much relieved to see that the rifle was still in the window, for his dreams had been haunted by the fear that somebody else might walk in and buy it before he could get there. Mr. Hogg, the saddler, was in the shop himself, and received Sandy with a smile.

"Aye, it's a nice wee gun," he said, "I'll get it out of the window for you."

Sandy put down his five shillings and took the rifle in his hands; it was smooth and shiny. His heart was thumping with excitement.

"Ye'll come and pay me yer shilling every week, mind," continued Mr. Hogg, "any day that suits ye."

"I'll pay you on Saturdays," Sandy said quickly. "Can I take the gun now?"

"Surely ye can," replied the saddler, smiling.

Sandy took it and departed, walking on air. He was meeting his crony, David Brown, and they had arranged to go for a bike run together, but the new acquistion changed their plans. They rode up to the moors and spent the day shooting at rabbits instead—it was a splendid day.

"We'll do this every Saturday," Sandy declared, as they rode home in the falling dusk, "and when the days get lighter we could come up here after school."

David agreed enthusiastically.

CHAPTER NINE

MR. AND MRS. BULLOCH were sitting by the fire. Mrs. Bulloch was knitting a grey sock, and Mr. Bulloch was reading out tit-bits from the evening paper. They were very happy and completely in harmony. The fire burnt merrily in the grate, and was reflected in dancing points of light in the lenses of Mrs. Bulloch's spectacles and on the highly polished surface of her knitting needles. Outside the wind howled, and now and then the windows rattled, but this only served to accentuate the comfort of the cosy room.

Sue, who had taken an evening off, found her grandparents sitting there and felt a sudden surge of affection for them—like the affection felt by a traveller in foreign lands when he beholds the white cliffs of Dover looming out of the haze—here they were, and here they always would be, solid and reliable, and loyal. She had never realised before how much she loved them, nor how much she depended upon their love.

The Bullochs were delighted to see their granddaughter and to see her looking so well and happy, they did not rise to greet her, for it was not their nature to be demonstrative, but their two heads turned towards her, and their kind eyes smiled.

"My, you're a stranger!" Mrs. Bulloch declared.

"Granny and I were thinking you'd forgotten us," added Mr. Bulloch.

"It's my first outing," Sue told them, "and I came straight here, so you don't need to complain."

"Ye're liking it?"

Sue nodded. She had established herself on a footstool between them and the glow of the fire was on her face. Mr. Bulloch thought that there was an "alive" look about her which had been absent from her since her mother's death, and he noticed that the small bitter lines round her mouth were smoothed away.

"It's good to be useful," Sue said frankly. "It's worth while. Yes, I'm liking it."

The Bullochs waited for a few moments hoping for more information, but none was forth-coming.

"Is Mrs. Darnay kind?" asked Mrs. Bulloch at last.

Sue sighed. She had known that she would have some such question to answer. "Mrs. Darnay's not there. She was called away—it was on business," she added, hating the lie.

"And the Frenchwoman, what like is she?" enquired Mr. Bulloch with interest. "She's been in the shop once or twice and I've never cared for the look of her— a sly boots if ever there was one. Don't you trust yon Frenchwoman a yard, Sue."

"She's not there either," Sue said.

"Ye're there alone!"

"It's nicer, really. Grandfather's right, she was a funny sort of woman. She nearly had me deaved with her talk the first night—it's much better now she's gone and I can do things my own way."

They looked at each other over Sue's head and read a certain apprehension in each other's eyes.

"I'm thinking ye'd best come home, Sue," said Mr. Bulloch slowly. "It's a queer sort of thing altogether."

"It's lonely for ye," Mrs. Bulloch declared.

"I like it," she told them, "and how could I come away and leave Mr. Darnay to do for himself? He paints all day and every day—who's going to do for him if I come home?"

"It's a queer sort of thing," her grandfather repeated, frowning. "I'm not liking it at all for ye, Sue. I'm thinking ye should tell Mr. Darnay ye're leaving and let him get some other body to do for him—an older person."

Sue was surprised at the strength of her objection to this suggestion—she felt quite angry with her grandfather—and yet she had known that some such suggestion would be made. She was wise enough, however, to hide her feelings, for if they thought she was too anxious to remain at Tog's Mill they would be all the more determined on tearing her away.

"We'll see," said Sue equably. "Maybe later on."

The Bullochs were not deceived by this diplomatic reply for they knew their granddaughter pretty well, and nobody could know Sue without being aware of her stubbornness and independence, but they could do nothing more at the moment, so they held their peace.

"I'm worried about Sandy," said Sue, after a moment's silence.

"What's Sandy been up to?" enquired his grandmother.

"I wish he had been up to something," Sue declared. "He's never up to anything. He just lets things slide."

"Will tells me he's to go into the bakery," said Mr. Bulloch, "is that right, Sue?"

"He doesn't want to," she replied. She hesitated for

a moment wondering whether to say any more about it or not, and finally decided on the latter course. She had discussed the matter very fully with Mr. Darnay, and he had pointed out that nobody could help Sandy unless he would help himself. It was Sandy's own nature that was the real problem.

"He should tell his father what he wants to do," declared Mrs. Bulloch sensibly, and so saying she rose and began her preparations for supper.

"Grandfather," said Sue, "will you come down to the shop? I'm wanting some things to take back with me."

Mr. Bulloch laughed. "Ye are, are ye? Maybe ye've forgotten the time. The shop's been shut two hours, Miss Pringle, I'd have ye know."

"It'll be all the quieter for me, and I'll see what I want all the better," Sue told him with a twinkle in her eye. "If you're feeling tired you can give me the key and I'll take what I want myself."

"Save us all!" cried her grandfather in mock alarm.

He heaved himself out of his chair and led the way down the narrow corkscrew stair which descended from the house to the warehouse, turning on the lights as he went, so that when they reached the ground floor the whole place was brilliantly illuminated. Sue was quite dazzled by the glare after the soft glow of lamps to which she had become accustomed.

"It's bright," she exclaimed, looking round her and blinking a little.

"Aye, it's bright," agreed Mr. Bulloch with pride. He loved his shop and he loved to see it like this—swept and garnished, full of delectable goods from every country in the world. There was romance in this business of his (though he would never have admitted it, for he liked to pretend that he was a hard-headed business man). All those cases, packed by white men and yellow men, brown men and black men, and consigned to him from the uttermost parts of the earth, were unpacked by his own staff in his own warehouse and displayed to the good folk of Beilford on his ample shelves—was that not romance? The mere names of the goods he sold were like a song in his heart, and made little coloured pictures in his mind. Sugar, for instance, was no mere comestible, used to make puddings and cakes, or to sweeten a man's tea, for Mr. Bulloch knew the history of sugar and how, long before Christ was born, the sugar-cane was known and valued in the East—in Persia and Egypt, and Bengal. He knew how it had been introduced into Southern Europe, and later, as an experiment, to Southern America and the Indies; he knew what the plant looked like growing in the fields—the tall straight cane, with its graceful fronds, and the flowering stem bearing its feathery flowers—and how it was tended by brown men and black, the juice extracted and prepared for use. He could see in his mind's eye the packing sheds—long low buildings, shaded by tropical trees—and the gaily coloured clothing of the natives as they went about their work, packing the very cases which now stood in the store-house behind his shop.

All this passed through Mr. Bulloch's mind when Sue, in her soft low voice, remarked prosaically, "A quarter stone of granulated, and a pound of the best cube."

But sugar was not the only commodity which had history and tradition; tea and coffee, ginger and spices, in fact everything in the place possessed a history and was interesting in its own way. Even the comparatively recent "Canning Industry" had its own particular thrill, for how amazing and wonderful it was to think of men picking peaches in Africa or California and sealing them in tins so that folk in the bleak winter of Beilford could share the prodigality of their warmer clime!

The big tubs of golden butter, which stood in the corner by the window, brought Denmark with its tall fair people and its green meadowlands before Mr. Bulloch's eyes; and the round red cheeses evoked visions of the Netherlands, visions of canals, with slow-moving barges, of windmills and fields of tulips and sleek fat cows. Mr. Bulloch had seen most of these places with his own eyes when he was young for he had had a passion for wandering over the world and his father had encouraged him to travel. He had combined business with pleasure and had built up useful connections for the firm with all sorts of strange people in all sorts of strange lands.

Sue, though less knowledgeable than her grandfather and less romantically minded, had a great affection for the shop, and was extremely interested in its contents. She looked round the well-stocked shelves and felt a sudden surge of greed—what marvellous, what succulent dishes she could make for Mr. Darnay if she had the run of this place! The list of groceries with which she had armed herself seemed meagre and inadequate indeed, but she pulled herself together and decided that necessities came first.

"This isn't your best rice, Grandfather," she said, taking up a handful and letting the pearly grains trickle through her fingers.

"It's not," he agreed, laughing delightedly at her cleverness. "Are ye wanting the best rice, Sue? Can he afford to pay for it?"

The question pulled her up short and she hesitated a moment for she had not the smallest idea of Darnay's financial status. It was Mrs. Darnay who had the money—Ovette had told her so—and Mrs. Darnay had gone.

"I was only teasing," Mr. Bulloch declared. "The bill's always been paid—a bit late at times, but that's carelessness and not the want of money. The Darnays are the kind of folk who have always had money to spare, and it's that kind ye find being casual about their bills. Ye don't need to worry, Sue."

"No, I'm not worrying."

"Does he get big money for his pictures?" Mr. Bulloch enquired, pausing in the act of weighing out two pounds of his best rice. "Some artists do, but maybe ye'll not know what he gets."

"He used to get big money," Sue replied—she was wandering round the shelves now, selecting tins of peaches and pears, and smaller ones of asparagus tips for the little savouries which Darnay so enjoyed— "He used to get big money, but he's given that up now. He's started painting in a new way and he may not get so much."

"That's a queer set-out," declared her grandfather.

"What's queer about it?"

"Supposing I was to give up this shop that pays me well, and start trying to run a different kind of business—would ye say that was not a queer thing to do?"

"It's different altogether. You're contented with the shop—it's not only the money, is it?"

"No, it's not only the money," he agreed.

There was silence for a minute or two, and then Sue said, "Bacon, Grandfather," and added defiantly, "the best Wiltshire, please," for whether Darnay could pay for it or not he should have the very best.

"Pick it yerself, then," Mr. Bulloch invited her with a twinkle in his eye.

Sue considered the sides of bacon with the utmost gravity. "I'll take three pounds of this," she said at last, "and I'll slice it myself if you'll put it on the machine for me—he likes it thin."

"Never!" exclaimed Mr. Bulloch in mock surprise. "He likes the best Wiltshire, and he likes it cut thin! Ye'll be telling me he likes a couple of the best new-laid eggs with it next."

"I'm getting my eggs from a farm near," she told him.

"Mine'll not be fresh enough for him, I suppose!" said Mr. Bulloch humbly.

Sue had to laugh then—she couldn't help it—and her grandfather joined in with such a lusty roar that Mrs. Bulloch heard it in the sitting-room and came down to ask what the joke was.

"Mr. Darnay likes the best Wiltshire, cut thin," declared Mr. Bulloch, between his gusts of laughter.

"Well, and what of it?" said his wife, raising her eyebrows in surprise. "What's to laugh at in that, Thomas? It's the way ye like it yerself."

By this time the pile of groceries on the counter had grown to considerable proportions—bags of cereals, tins of fruit, bacon, butter, sugar and cheese

were but a few of the treasures which Sue had culled
from her grandfather's stock.

"I'm thinking it'll have to go in a crate," he said,
looking at the pile doubtfully, "or maybe Alec
Anderson would take it out to ye for an oblige-
ment."

"You'll send it out early with your own van," said
Sue firmly, "the butcher doesn't come till late. What's
the van for if you can't send out an order in it—a big
order like that."

"Did ye ever hear the like!" cried Mr. Bulloch with
feigned dismay. "I've to send the van four miles with
one order, and petrol at one and eight the gallon!!"

"It's one and sevenpence halfpenny," amended Sue,
who happened to be in possession of this useful piece
of information owing to a similar but far more heated
argument with her father's vanman.

Supper was a cheerful meal for Sue was in excellent
spirits and kept her grandparents amused with racy
accounts of her doings at the mill. She told them of her
struggles with the kitchen range, and how she was
sure that it harboured an imp of darkness in its vast and
gloomy interior, and she told them about her walks
on the moors, and how the birds sang in the early
morning. In fact the Bullochs had never heard her
talk so much, and it was only afterwards, when she
had gone, that they discovered how little she had told
them.

"It's queer her not going along to Number Three,"
Mrs. Bulloch said thoughtfully. "Will and Grace'll
not be best pleased that she came here and never went
to them."

"She hadn't time," Mr. Bulloch replied, as he took

his beloved 'cello from its case and prepared to practise a tricky passage in Haydn's Concerto.

" She could have made time," Mrs. Bulloch returned, "and ye'll remember she said that Grace was too inquisitive—who minds folks being inquisitive unless they've something to hide?"

"Ye're thinking——"

"I'm not thinking anything, Thomas," said Mrs. Bulloch somewhat inaccurately, and she took up her half-knitted sock.

CHAPTER TEN

His willow picture finished, Darnay had started on an entirely different régime. Instead of working day after day at the same subject he moved about, ranging the country-side, and brought back sketches and queer half-finished studies of clouds and bare trees and rolling hills. These he stuck up in his studio on a shelf he had made himself, and sometimes Sue, going in to call him to a meal, would find him standing in the middle of the room, staring at them, his hands in his pockets and an unlighted pipe in his mouth.

When Sue got back from Beilford, after her visit to the Bullochs, she found Darnay sitting in the kitchen reading *The Scotsman*. "It's warmer here," he told her, somewhat apologetically, for he was aware that Miss Bun was a stickler for propriety and liked him to keep to his own part of the house.

"You should have kept up the fire in the lounge," said Sue sternly. "I knew how it would be if I went out."

Darnay smiled, it amused him to be called to order by his housekeeper. She was such a quaint little creature, so practical and serious, and yet with a sense of humour all her own.

"What have you got there?" he asked, as she laid her parcels down on the table. "What's this, eh?"

He pointed to a quarterly magazine which Sue had purchased in Beilford. It was entitled *Brothers of the*

Brush, and the outside cover displayed a highly coloured reproduction of a surrealist painting.

She blushed, she had bought the magazine with the idea of educating herself in art so that the next time Darnay asked her to give her opinion on a picture she would know exactly what to say. Glancing through it in the bus, she had seen at once that it was the very thing she wanted—when she had mastered this she would no longer be an uneducated savage in his eyes.

"Miss Bun!" he said, half laughing and half serious, "Miss Bun, I won't have it. You were going to study this frightful abortion in secret—deny it if you dare—and in a few days I should have had you prattling to me about depth and grouping and impasto—and oh, how I should have hated it!"

"But I thought——"

"It does credit to the kindness of your heart that you were willing to take all this trouble, but, believe me, I prefer my gentle savage, my Woman Friday."

"I could learn," she began breathlessly.

"You could learn," he agreed quite gravely, "you could learn all the jargon of the art critic—there isn't a doubt of that—but it would take you years of study to even begin to understand what you were talking about."

She gazed at him wide-eyed. "Then it's no good," she said hopelessly, "I could never be any help."

"But you are a help!" he cried, "that's what I'm trying to tell you. You taught me more about my picture in two minutes than the best art critic in London could have taught me in half an hour."

"I only said——" began Sue, unable to believe her ears.

"I don't know *what* you said," cried Darnay excitedly, "I neither know nor care. All I know is that you made me see what I was doing and turned me from the path before it was too late. Your vision is intuitive and unspoilt—do you understand?"

It was the first time he had ever asked her if she understood what he meant, and Sue realised the importance of this. Hitherto he had talked on—not caring whether she understood or not—he had talked to please himself, because he felt like talking and there was no one else there; but now he was actually talking to *her*, communing with her as a person, anxious for her to understand his point.

"I don't think I do understand—altogether," admitted Sue.

"You know nothing, but you can see clearly with your eyes. You're not muddled up with a lot of other people's ideas about pictures," Darnay explained carefully, "that's quite clear, isn't it?"

"Yes," said Sue meekly, "I won't read it, then."

The magazine was lying on the table between them. Sue pushed it towards him and Darnay picked it up and dropped it into the fire. It went to Sue's heart to see the magazine consumed (she had paid a shilling for it) but she made no move to stop him, and the two of them watched it burn. At first the flames licked round the edges of the glazed paper, charring and blackening the leaves; and then as it grew hotter, the whole book burst into flames and subsided into a mass of black fragments.

Darnay looked at Sue speculatively. "To-morrow I shall paint *you*," he said, and lay back in the chair with a sigh.

Sue had not forgotten that she was going to be painted, but she imagined, in her ignorance of painters and their whims, that Darnay would await her convenience. She had her work to do, and work was more important than painting. Sue was busy scrubbing the kitchen floor when Darnay appeared at the door and announced that he was ready.

"But *I'm* not," said Sue, plunging her scrubbing brush into the pail, and retreating another yard on to the dry part of the floor. "I've got the potatoes to peel when I've finished this, and the pudding to make—maybe I'll be ready about noon."

"Maybe you'll come now—this very minute," declared Darnay, laughing. "The kitchen floor won't run away, and we'll have bread and cheese for lunch."

"What!" cried Sue, "but I can't leave all the work and——"

"You can and will."

She looked up at him and saw to her dismay that he was quite serious and determined. She would have to go, that was obvious, and perhaps if she gave in and went now she could escape later and get the dinner on. The kitchen floor would have to wait until the afternoon.

"I'll go and change my dress," she said, rising reluctantly from her knees.

His eyes narrowed. "I'll paint you like that," he said. "No, don't take that thing off your head. I like it."

"It's a *duster*!" Sue cried.

"I don't care what it is."

"You're never going to paint my picture with an old duster on my head?"

"I'm going to paint you *just like that*," he declared firmly.

Sue sat down on the chair which he had arranged for her. She was miserable and nervous. She had had her photograph taken at the Beilford Gallery and had hated it, but this was much worse.

"How will I sit?" she enquired.

"Sit naturally," he replied, moving his easel slightly, and gazing at her with a strange impersonal expression in his eyes.

Sue composed herself carefully and hardened every muscle into rigid stone.

"Good heavens!" Darnay cried, "is that a natural position for you to sit in? Would it be natural for anybody to look like that? Are you supposed to represent Marie Antoinette driving to the scaffold or what?"

Sue lifted her chin and replied with asperity, quite forgetting about her pose. Darnay began to paint.

He had intended merely to make a few rough studies of Miss Bun's head, but he found his new subject so intriguing that his intentions vanished into thin air. It was not until he had started to paint her that he discovered she was beautiful—not beautiful perhaps by the usual canons, but beautiful in her own way. In most people of Darnay's world there are several strains, blending sometimes into beauty and sometimes not, but Miss Bun's ancestors were all Lowland Scots—a long line stretching back for centuries. He thought of this as he painted, and saw her pedigree written in the pure lines of her face, and he saw—or thought he saw—that this purity of race must produce beauty,

a beauty of its own which may or may not be attractive
to an alien eye. For instance, thought Darnay, we may
not admire the golden skin and slant eyes of the pure
Mongol, but who can dare to say that the Mongol has
no beauty of his own? If we do not believe that purity
of race is beauty then we deny God and God's hand in
our making—in the making of the races of the world.
Anthropology had always interested Darnay—anthropology from a painter's angle—it was a matter of
bones beneath that outer layer of flesh and skin which
produced certain differences of curve and contour
indigenous to the race from which the subject sprang.
Most of the people Darnay knew were mongrels in that
sense. His own wife Elise had a French mother, and
he himself a Norwegian grandmother (who had
probably contributed certain characteristics of her race
to his tall spare frame and the bony structure of his
head). Mongrels, thought Darnay, may be attractive,
or even beautiful in their early youth, but they seldom
age well. Miss Bun belonged to the soil upon which
she had been born and bred, she would grow into a
beautiful old woman—the sort that Rembrandt loved
to paint.

These were fascinating conjectures, but Darnay
could not pursue them as he wished, for as soon as he
left off talking Miss Bun became aware of her face.
The whole thing was a damned nuisance, he should
never have started on a portrait of Miss Bun, he should
have stuck to his trees and clouds as he had intended.
Now that he had started it was impossible to stop—
the beautiful faded blue of that thing on her head,
and the gorgeous hair, dark as chocolate with red
and gold lights, and the creamy skin—he must talk,

though, for again that Medusa look had petrified the delicious curves of jaw and neck.

"I shall make some studies of you first," he told her, "and then a proper portrait. Perhaps I'll paint you out of doors with one of your own hills for a background. Do you love your country, Miss Bun?"

"I like it well enough," replied Sue, somewhat embarrassed by the word.

"Have you ever been to London?"

"No, the only city I've been to is Edinburgh. Sometimes I've thought it would be grand fun to live in a city."

"It isn't," Darnay told her, dabbing at the canvas with his brush, "don't you believe it, Miss Bun. You need a hide like a rhinoceros to live in a city—and your hide is thinner than most."

"But why?"

"Because if you walk in a city you're jostled by hundreds of indifferent people with indifferent eyes which look at you as if you weren't there at all. You begin to feel you must be invisible. Hundreds and thousands of eyes, and not one pair really seeing you or caring who you are. I'd rather walk down Beilford High Street and know that everybody was saying, ' There goes the mad painter! ' It's better to be mad than invisible."

She wondered about that, and he painted her eyes, longing to say, "Hold it, keep like that for five minutes —or even for one," but refraining because he knew it would spoil everything.

"The city is impermanent," he continued, rattling on and hardly knowing what he said. "It is the country that goes on, for ever the same. D'you know Hardy's poem about the man harrowing his field? You've often seen men harrowing, haven't you? The words give you the actual feel of the earth turning over.

> 'Only a man harrowing clods
>   In a slow silent walk,
> With an old horse that stumbles and nods
>   Half asleep as they stalk.
>
> Only thin smoke without flame
>   From the heaps of couch grass,
> Yet this will go onward the same
>   Though dynasties pass.'"

It was twenty-five minutes to one when at last Sue said, "I must go, really. There will be no time for potatoes but there's liver and bacon for dinner."

"You'll go," he agreed, throwing down his brush, "but you'll go and rest. I've told you we're having bread and cheese to-day—it's been a splendid morning."

CHAPTER ELEVEN

It had been a busy day in Mr. Bulloch's shop, but now the stream of customers was slackening and Mr. Bulloch left Hickie in charge and mounted the stairs to his house.

"I'll be off now," he said to his wife. "Hickie will see to everything. I'll be back to supper most likely."

"I'll just expect ye when I see ye," replied Mrs. Bulloch comfortably, "maybe ye'll stay and take supper with Sue."

Mr. Bulloch put on his overcoat and took his soft hat off the peg, but he still lingered. "I'm wishing I knew what to say," he murmured, "it's difficult."

"Ye'll soon see what to say. I never knew ye to be at a loss yet and I've known ye forty-seven years come February. Away with ye, Thomas, or ye'll miss the bus."

"I wouldn't be weeping over it if I did," muttered Thomas as he shut the door and descended the front stairs to the street.

It was a fine evening, cold and starry, a thin film of ice was forming on the moist pavements as Bulloch walked down to the Market Cross. He caught the bus with a few minutes to spare and very soon he was well on his way to Tog's Mill. The bus stopped at the top of the hill for him to alight, and he stood—as Sue had stood that first night—and watched the lights disappear down the road, before descending the rough track to the house.

Mr. Bulloch had been pressed into this adventure by the importunities of his wife. He did not see what good could come of it, but he had no alternative suggestion to offer and he realised that something must be done. It was bad enough for Sue to take any sort of job, and this job was "queer"—they both felt that. Sue was too young to be shut up alone with a man, and Darnay, being an artist, was an unknown quantity to the Bullochs. He might be all right or he might not. The situation of Tog's Mill did not help to reassure the Bullochs—Tog's Mill was a queer place, deserted, solitary.

Mr. Bulloch had come to Tog's Mill as a pleni-potentiary. He was to see how the land lay and try to persuade Sue to come home. If possible he was to have a "wee crack" with Darnay himself and suggest that another housekeeper be found—it was a delicate mission.

Sue was very much surprised when she answered the door and found her grandfather standing on the step.

"There's nothing wrong, is there?" she asked anxiously.

"What should be wrong?" he enquired. "Can I not come and see ye without ye thinking something's wrong?"

Sue hesitated. "Come in, then," she said reluctantly.

He came in, well aware of her reluctance and considerably alarmed by it, and found Mr. Darnay sitting by the kitchen fire.

"This is my grandfather, Mr. Darnay," declared Sue, and washed her hands of the situation.

Mr. Darnay was quite equal to it—in fact he seemed unaware that there was a situation at all—he rose and shook hands with Mr. Bulloch and invited him to sit down.

"This is the only warm room in the house," he said, laughing, "so I'm allowed to sit here—it's a great privilege I can tell you. The fact is we're short of coal and the coal merchant has refused to deliver his black diamonds until the end of the week."

"It's a comfortable kitchen," Mr. Bulloch said.

"You two will want a little chat," declared Darnay, "so I'll just leave you to it."

"No, no!" cried Mr. Bulloch, "that'll never do, Mr. Darnay. There's no earthly need for ye to go and freeze in a cold room—I'm not staying long anyway."

"But you must stay to supper."

There was a good deal of argument about it, but eventually they both gave in. Mr. Darnay remained by the kitchen fire and Mr. Bulloch stayed to supper. The two men sat down in a friendly manner and Sue resumed her place at the table near the lamp, for she was mending the linen, and light was necessary for the task.

Sue had been considerably embarrassed by her grandfather's unexpected arrival, but now she saw that everything was all right for they were talking to each other in the friendliest way imaginable. She listened to their talk with a queer inner excitement, surprised to find that they had so much in common. She had known her grandfather all her life, of course, but she had never heard him talk like this—it was quite a shock to find that there was so much more in him than she had suspected.

Somehow or other they had plunged straight into an argument about faith. (It was not remarkable that Darnay should talk about faith, for he would talk about anything and his mind was packed full of information upon every subject under the sun, but that her grandfather should discuss such a subject with a perfect stranger was almost incredible—indeed, unless Sue had heard him with her own ears, she would not have believed it.) Darnay was swift and keen, he went straight at the root of things, and outran Mr. Bulloch; but Bulloch was very sure, he had thought a great deal, and, arriving at certain conclusions, knew his reasons for that arrival.

"You can't get anything worth having for nothing," Darnay declared, offering his guest a fill of tobacco from his pouch, "and faith is worth having—it's the only thing that can save us now, when the whole world has straws in its hair. Faith is worth working for."

Bulloch considered this while he filled his pipe.

"To some people it's a leap in the dark," Darnay continued earnestly, "to others a struggle, like the time Israel wrestled with God. To others it's a search (but I think you must have had it and lost it before you can search for it) like the woman who lost the piece of silver and had to sweep out the whole house before she found it."

"We've fought for it," Mr. Bulloch put in, "and it was more real then—more important to us."

"Your Covenanters fought for the right to interpret faith in their own way."

"That's what I was meaning. Ye've got to have freedom first. It's no use believing what other folks say, the only thing is for each man to fend for himself, Mr. Darnay. Each man standing on his own feet, finding his own path——"

"Grand!" cried Darnay with flashing eyes, "it's a religion of super men."

"It's a religion of free men," Bulloch replied.

Sue left them hard at it and busied herself with preparations for supper. She was surprised to find her hands trembling as she took the dishes from the shelf. How happy I am ! she thought suddenly, and stood there for a moment with one hand pressed to her bosom where her heart was beating fast. How happy she was—yet what was there to cause such a turmoil of happiness within her?

When she returned to the kitchen with her tray, Darnay was talking hard, and Bulloch, sitting forward in his chair, was listening intently to the flow of words.

". . . never a Scottish painter yet who had the insight to paint the soul of Scotland," Darnay was declaring. "You must look outside your own land for a man to do justice to the Scottish scene."

"But a Scotsman must surely understand his own land better than another."

Darnay laughed. "Does a chicken inside an egg know what the egg looks like?"

"No, no!" cried Bulloch, "it's not a fair comparison that. Who knows the house best, Mr. Darnay? I'm thinking it's the person who lives in it."

"Perhaps he knows it so well that he doesn't see it any more—that is possible, you know."

"Raeburn——" began Bulloch doubtfully.

". . . for portraits, yes, I'll give you Raeburn," Darnay interrupted with a generous wave of his hand. "He was influenced by Reynolds of course, and perhaps a little by Velasquez, but you can have Raeburn. He painted his own people well, I'll agree. He saw them and painted them."

"What are ye meaning by that?" Mr. Bulloch enquired, "when ye say ' he saw them.'"

"Raeburn was dignified and simple and these qualities belong to your race. Compare him with Rubens—a much greater painter but a less worthy man. Rubens loved life and enjoyed it. Even if we knew nothing about the man we could deduce these facts from his work. His women are plump and rotund, zestful and rosy, with pleasant curves and comfortable bosoms; compare them with the thin anæmic ladies of Burne Jones, and the coldness of Botticelli's saints."

"Ye mean a painter paints in his own nature," said Bulloch slowly.

"He can only paint what he sees and he can only see what he is capable of seeing."

At supper Darnay tried to control his tongue—which was apt to run away with him in the company of a sympathetic listener—and to allow Miss Bun and her grandfather a fair share of the conversation; but Sue did not want to talk. She could have talked to either of her companions separately, but she could find nothing suitable for them both together. Her position was difficult and she was glad when supper was finished and Darnay, who had already informed Mr. Bulloch that he was making some studies of "Miss Bun," suggested a visit to the studio.

Mr. Bulloch followed his host into the studio with mixed feelings. He was bewildered by Darnay, for the man was entirely different from what he had expected. The man had definite—if somewhat unconventional—ideas upon religious matters and could back his arguments with incidents from "The Book" and this was not Mr. Bulloch's preconceived idea of an artist. He remembered suddenly the reason for which he had come to Tog's Mill and found it more distasteful than ever. Mr. Darnay was a real gentleman in the highest sense of the word; he was blade straight, and Sue was perfectly safe with him (Bulloch was sure of it) but Bulloch saw another danger which was almost as fearsome—supposing Sue were to fall in love with the man, that would be a nice kettle of fish! The two of them were very much in harmony, he could see, and their expression when they looked at each other was kindly and understanding, more like the kindly look of folk long married than a lover's glance—but dear sakes! thought Mr. Bulloch, horrified to find where he was heading, dear sakes, what am I thinking about! The man's far above Sue as the stars, and married to boot. I'll need to take care what I say to Susan or she'll have the whole thing out of me before I know.

He was hoping that the pictures of Sue would help to solve the problem (for hadn't Darnay said that a painter must paint what he sees?) and he scarcely dared to raise his eyes and look at them in case Darnay had painted her in the Rubens manner, "zestful

and rotund " with a "comfortable bosom." If Darnay
had seen her like that he would need to speak—no
matter what it cost him he would need to take Sue
straight home.

"Well," said Darnay, "there you are, Mr. Bulloch.
It isn't a good light, of course."

"Well!" said Mr. Bulloch, "well, I never!"

"You like it?"

"It's Sue," declared her grandfather, "it's—well it's
just Sue. I can see her breathing, almost."

"You think it good?" Darnay enquired casually,
trying to hide the absurd pleasure he felt at the old
man's astonishment and delight.

"Man, it's wonderful!" cried Bulloch, "it's the
cleverest thing—I've seen her look like that a hundred
times! I've seen her turn her head and raise her chin
—she was affronted, eh?"

Darnay laughed. "I'm afraid I annoyed her on
purpose," he admitted.

"Vairry reprrehensible!" declared Mr. Bulloch with a
twinkle in his eye, "but maybe the end justifies the
means."

"How d'you like the other one?" Darnay asked.

"The other? It's a wondering look, Mr. Darnay.
I've not seen her like that somehow—Sue's too practical
for dreams."

"I saw her like that."

"I'm not saying ye didn't. I'm only saying it's not
the Sue I know," began Mr. Bulloch, and then he paused
suddenly; this was not the Sue *he* knew, but Mr.
Darnay knew her like that—knew her with that
wondering rapt look transfiguring her small determined face. I'll need to say it, he thought, and added

aloud and somewhat abruptly, "We're wanting Sue home, Mr. Darnay."

"You're what?"

"We're wanting her home," repeated Mr. Bulloch and left it at that.

For a moment Darnay was silent, and then he said, "Well, of course—Miss Bun must do as she pleases— I mean——"

"But it's not Sue," explained her grandfather, "it's ourselves—wanting her. She would not be pleased if she knew I had spoken about it."

"I think you must decide that yourselves," Darnay said, and all at once he was a thousand miles away.

Bulloch knew he had been put in his place, and perhaps he deserved it, for he had been admitted to Mr. Darnay's friendship, and had presumed upon it. He saw now that he should never have approached Darnay behind Sue's back. He would have liked to apologise for his error of judgment, but it was not in his nature to apologise, he was too proud, too independent to own himself in the wrong.

Bulloch stood there for a moment without speaking, and then he felt Darnay's hand on his shoulder. "I'm glad you like the portraits, Mr. Bulloch," said Darnay, in a friendly voice. "I'd like to give you that one if you will accept it."

"But Mr. Darnay——"

"It's just a study, you see, and when I've finished my picture I shan't want it, so if you'd care to have it——"

"But I couldn't!" cried Bulloch in dismay. "I couldn't take it—unless—unless ye'd let me pay for it. I couldn't accept it from ye."

"And I couldn't sell it," declared Darnay, smiling and shaking his head, "it's just a study and I don't in the least know what it's worth—precious little really. Perhaps you'd allow me to give it to Miss Bun's grandmother—how would that do?"

It made very little difference, Bulloch thought. He was most uncomfortable, and his discomfort was augmented by the knowledge that Darnay had no intention of heaping coals of fire upon his head. Darnay was impulsive and his offer was spontaneous and genuinely kind, but it put Mr. Bulloch in a very awkward position—there was not a doubt of that. It complicated the whole situation so that he could see no way of escape. To refuse the picture would be ungrateful and boorish, and yet, if they accepted it, how could they drag Sue away? He saw quite clearly that even if they didn't accept it there was no certainty of being able to drag Sue away.

"Well, it's good of ye, Mr. Darnay," said Bulloch at last, "the truth is I'm at a loss what to say. I'm thinking yon picture of Sue is valuable whether it's a study or a portrait or whatever ye call it. Mrs. Bulloch—well—I'll see what she says. I doubt she'll think the same as me."

"She won't if you put it to her the right way," Darnay assured him.

And that, as Bulloch found, was exactly the trouble, for no matter how carefully he explained the whole thing to Susan—and as a matter of fact he knew all the time that he was explaining it far too much and far too carefully—he could see that Susan thought he had been "got over" by Mr. Darnay; fed on the fat of the land, cossetted with good talk, and bribed with the picture he had so admired.

"A man need not be good for all he can quote the Scriptures," said Mrs. Bulloch at last with a sigh. "Look at David himself! I'd not have trusted Sue alone in a house with David five minutes."

There was nothing more to be said.

CHAPTER TWELVE

DARNAY began to appreciate his housekeeper more highly now that there seemed a chance of losing her—and he began to realise how comfortable he was. He was comfortable with Miss Bun not only in the sense of being well fed and well looked after but also in mind and spirit. She was exactly the sort of person he needed, a parcel of complements to his own nature. He needed her practical common sense, for it made him feel safely anchored to the earth, and he needed her admiration which, though perfectly obvious, was never merely silly. She had a flavour all her own, and Darnay knew that he would never find anybody else who suited him so well. It never crossed his mind that the girl's reputation might suffer through being alone with him in the house. His mind was keen and flexible, but he had the egotism of the peculiarly gifted, and the very brilliance of his vision blinded him to the small worldly problems of his neighbours.

Sue could have eased his mind if she had known what was troubling him, for she had not the slightest intention of leaving Tog's Mill. It was good for her to be here and she had never been so happy since her mother died. Looking back at her childhood Sue saw it as a mosaic of small unrelated pictures, or of pictures related only by one figure—her mother's—which could be seen in them all. Herself, the small Sue, seemed different in each picture—sometimes bold, sometimes shy, sometimes happy. She scarcely knew which of the pictures were real memories, and which were only stories kept green by her mother, for Mary had been so proud of her small daughter that she loved to tell stories about Sue's cleverness. Sue had worshipped her mother—there was nobody like her, there never could be. Mary had made life seem like a song, an old familiar song, a safe lullaby. She had danced through life but her very lightheartedness had made life safe. When Mary died the unthinkable had happened and life became dangerous and grim. It became grim in reality, for Will Pringle was strange and moody after the death of his wife; sometimes he was silent for days on end and at other times sarcastic and cynical. Sue, struggling with the house—which in her mother's lifetime seemed to run itself—had been an easy butt, and even when she had gained the mastery of housekeeping she was not safe from his caustic tongue.

All that was changed now and Sue had come out of the shadow into warm sunshine. Darnay, though he might ignore her when entranced with his work, was as frank and open as the day and had nothing but praise for his housekeeper.

"You do too much," he told her. "Honestly, you do. Who minds a little dust in the corners! The house is old and far too big—let the dust lie quietly and peacefully. All I want is my bed made, and an occasional meal."

It was perfectly true, Darnay was the most easily pleased man in the world, but Sue had been trained to fight dust—the battle was bred in her bone—and it was quite impossible for her to obey his command and let the dust lie; besides she loved the work and went about it with a glow at her heart; for no task, however monotonous or hard, is menial when one serves a King.

The new happy atmosphere and the daily contact with Darnay's mind was doing strange things to Sue. She felt the stirring of growth, not consciously, but more as a plant must feel its ripening. The river was a thread of melody, running through her life as a thread runs through beads, binding it into a harmonious whole. She heard it all day as she went about the house, but it was at night that she was most conscious of its song. Sometimes in the stillness the sound of the river would change with the rise in the level of its waters and she would hear it swell from a trickle, which splashed over the old wheel, into a turbulent roar like a giant, suddenly enraged—or she would go to sleep with the roar of a spate in her ears and wake to find it past.

Sue had not forgotten her desire to know more about the birds which frequented the place, and Darnay was quite ready to instruct her in their names and habits. In the little patch of garden outside the kitchen window there were dozens of birds which came daily for a largesse of crumbs: tits and wrens and chaffinches and countless numbers of sparrows and a cheeky robin which was Sue's especial friend. They would hop from twig to twig upon the branches of an old gnarled apple tree, or shelter in the beech hedge which still retained its copper coloured leaves.

"How nice it will be when we have apples!" said Sue one day, when they were leaning out of the kitchen window watching the birds.

"Apples!" exclaimed Darnay, "Oh, we shan't have any apples from that tree, it's too old. See how gnarled and twisted the branches are, and the little twigs are like an old man's fingers. If I were a proper gardener I should cut it down."

"I'm glad you're not a proper gardener," Sue declared.

"The hedge is nice," he continued—

> " '. . . deep in brambly hedges dank
> The small birds nip about and say
> Brothers, the Spring is not so far away . . .'

but they are wrong, of course," he added, "for Spring is still a long way off. They've got to weather the storms of winter first, poor little beggars!"

"Poetry," said Sue.

"Yes, poetry," he replied, smiling. "No, I can't remember any more. I've got a scrap-bag mind, Miss Bun. Just a little bit of this and a little bit of that—not big enough scraps to be of any use except, perhaps, to make a patchwork quilt."

Sue was silent; a patchwork quilt made of poetry was a strange idea. A few weeks ago she would have said it was nonsense, but she had learnt to see things in his way now.

"Do you like poetry?" Darnay enquired.

"We had it at school," said Sue thoughtfully. "The Lady of Shallott, and all that. I didn't mind it, but it was an awful waste of time getting it off by heart."

"What about Burns?" he asked.

"Oh, that's different—it's music," Sue told him.

"And the Lady of Shallott is a picture," Darnay

declared. "It's a sort of mediæval decoration—a frieze in scarlet and blue and gold. You can see the knights riding by, and the barge drifting down the river between the green waving reeds."

"Go on, I like it," Sue said.

"Here's another poem that makes a picture—a modern one this time—

' Why do you walk through the fields in gloves
    Fat white woman that nobody loves?'"

"I can't remember any more," he continued. "I told you I had a scrappy mind, but there you are. It's a problem picture, of course: why does she?"

"There might be lots of reasons," Sue said, a trifle breathless with following his flights of fancy.

"I can't think of any," Darnay declared, "no, not one. Give me three good reasons why she should do such an odd thing and I'll paint her for you, Miss Bun."

She thought hard, for she wanted the picture desperately. "Maybe she was on her way to church," she said at last.

Darnay nodded gravely. "That's possible," he agreed.

"Or she might have been going to tea with the minister's wife," cried Sue eagerly. "That's two reasons, Mr. Darnay."

"Hold on! It was in England, you know."

"The vicar's wife, then."

"I suppose I must let you have that," Darnay said doubtfully. "It isn't really very fair because your two reasons are much the same. She was 'dressed up' in both cases, wasn't she? What's your third reason?"

"It's dressed up too. She was the vicar's wife and she was going to call on the parish."

"No," he cried indignantly. "No, Miss Bun. You forget that nobody loved her. Do you mean to tell me that the vicar—a man of God—didn't love his wife after promising to love and cherish her until death did them part?"

Sue shook her head. "I'd forgotten that. Wait a minute, Mr. Darnay. Somebody had given her the gloves for her birthday and she was so taken up with them that she just had to put them on."

"Nobody loved her," declared Darnay firmly, "nobody loved her, so nobody gave her gloves for her birthday."

"She was vain, then," cried Sue in desperation. "She put stuff on her hands to make them white, and gloves over the top. She was going out to an evening party and wanted her hands to look nice—will that do?"

"It'll do," he said grudgingly. "I don't believe a word of it, really, but it's very ingenious. Come and see me paint her picture, Miss Bun?"

Sue followed him into the studio and watched with interest. He took a small wooden panel which was already prepared and set it on the easel near the north light. Then he began to paint.

The picture took shape before Sue's eyes: a field starred with flowers, a hedge, and a far-off clump of dark trees, and, in the foreground, the plumpish lady whom nobody loved, dressed in white and leaning against a stile. The face was turned away and half hidden by the hat, but there was dejection in every line of the figure and hopelessness in the droop of the fat white hands.

"Oh dear, she *is* miserable!" Sue said softly.

"Nobody loves her," muttered Darnay, painting away industriously.

"But maybe she doesn't mind."

"Of course she minds—there you are, Miss Bun. Take it away and never let me see it again. The damned woman has wasted my whole afternoon, and the light's going."

Sue returned to the kitchen with her prize. She stuck it up on the mantelpiece and made up the fire. Then she put the kettle on for tea. Every now and then she paused and glanced at the "White Lady" and smiled—it was her own—he had painted it for her—she would keep it always.

She was so happy over her latest acquisition that when the back door bell rang, and she found Grace standing on the steps, she welcomed her quite warmly. Sue was in love and charity with everyone to-day.

"Hullo Grace!" she said, "I was just going to infuse the tea."

Grace came in. She was looking very smart in a brown coat with a fur collar, and a red hat. It was a new outfit and Sue commented on it in a friendly manner.

"Are ye still liking it, Sue?" Grace asked when the subject of her new garments was exhausted.

"It's not so bad," declared Sue. "How's everybody at home?"

"Everybody's fine," replied Grace casually.

She said no more then, and it was not until they were sitting down to tea that she revealed the reason for her visit.

"Will sent me here. Ye're to come home, Sue," she said simply.

"I'm to come home, am I?"

"Yes," said Grace. "Will says it's not fit for ye to be here, yerself."

"Supposing I'm not wanting to come home."

Grace sighed gustily. "Will says yer to come. He says it's not decent living alone with a man."

"And how would Mr. Darnay manage without a housekeeper?" enquired Sue with dangerous sweetness. "How would he get his meals and keep the place clean?"

"He can get some other body. He can get an old woman—there's plenty would be glad of the job."

Sue laughed. "They'd not be glad long," she declared roundly. "It's no job, this, for an old done woman to tackle. I'd like to see what the place looked like when she'd been here a week."

"Maybe so, but that's no business of ours."

"It's my business, then," Sue told her, getting heated with the argument despite her efforts to remain calm. "It's my job, and I like it. I was miserable at home— you know that fine, and fine you know the reason."

"I know ye were hard to get on with," Grace said, keeping her temper with difficulty, "but maybe things would be better now, and maybe ye wouldn't be at home so long, either."

"So that's it!" cried Sue, her eyes flashing, "It's not that you're wanting me home at all. You're wanting me to marry Ben Grierson—I might have known that was the way of it if 'd had any sense. It's a pity Ben doesn't come and ask me himself like a man!"

"He would!" cried Grace eagerly. "Ben's mad for

ye, Sue. If I gave him the least wee hint he'd be out here like a shot."

"You can keep your hints, for I'm not wanting Ben Grierson nor any other man of your choosing."

They glared at each other for a moment or two, and then Grace sighed, more deeply than before. The interview was not developing in the way she had planned. "I can't think how we got on to Ben," she said in a propitiatory tone of voice. "Nobody's wanting ye to take the man. It was Will sent me here, and ye've to come home—he's yer father, Sue."

"So I've heard," declared Sue dryly.

"What do ye mean?"

"He's my father, and I've worked for him since I was fourteen years old—and never a kind word out of his head—I'm not owing him much."

"He's a difficult man," sighed Grace.

There was a little silence and then Grace rose. "I'll need to go," she said, "time's getting on and I've got stewing steak for supper—what will I say to him, Sue?"

"I've told you I'm not coming."

"My, he'll be awful mad!" said Grace apprehensively.

Sue was somewhat melted at the look on her visitor's face—she knew only too well that it was not without justification. "I'm sorry, Grace," she said, "I'm sorry, but it's no use saying one thing and meaning another. You're a great deal better off without me in the house."

Grace did not reply at once. She considered the matter. The fact was they were no better off without Sue. There were not so many open quarrels, of course, but the atmosphere was just as strained and uncom-

fortable as ever, and Grace still felt an interloper in
her husband's house. If she had been of an imaginative
turn of mind it might have occurred to her that the
house over the bakery was haunted by Mary's ghost,
but she was far too matter of fact to consider such a
possibility for a moment. The house was not haunted,
of course, it was Will who was haunted by Mary. He
had put another woman in her place but unfortunately
she could not fill it. Will never looked at his new wife's
heavy stolid face without seeing Mary's fair merry
one; he never heard her voice without hearing the
gentle tones of Mary's; he could not even take
Grace in his arms without experiencing a passion of
longing for Mary.

It was no wonder that Grace was unhappy in her
new life.

"What are you thinking?" enquired Sue at last.

"Nothing much," answered Grace. "It's just—we're
not so much better off. Yer father's hard to understand—he scarcely opens his mouth, and Sandy's
awful sulky."

"You should let Sandy do what he wants," Sue told
her. "He's miserable—that's what's the matter with
him."

"Sandy doesn't know what he wants," said Grace
promptly.

"He wants——"

"He wants one thing on Monday and another thing
on Tuesday," continued Grace. "If he'd speak out and
say what he's thinking there'd be some chance of
dealing with him. I declare I'm half crazy between the
two of them—I never had to do with dumb folks
before."

"You didn't like me speaking out and you don't like their dumbness—you're hard to please, Grace."

"Maybe I am," she replied hopelessly.

In spite of the hard words which had been said the two felt more friendly to each other at this moment than they had ever felt before. They had spoken with perfect frankness, and the bitter feelings which had been pent up within them for so long were eased away.

"I'm sorry," said Sue again, as they parted on the doorstep.

"Och, well——" said Grace resignedly, and with that she put up her umbrella and disappeared into the darkness of the night.

CHAPTER THIRTEEN

ONE morning in December Sue awoke to find the voice
of the river muted to a mere whisper in the grey dark,
and rising from her bed she looked out upon an
unfamiliar scene. Snow had fallen heavily in the
night, blanketing the hills, outlining every branch of
every tree, and crusting thickly upon the rocks which
lined the river bed. The sun had not yet risen, but the
sky was dove grey with the promise of dawn and the
light, instead of falling from above, seemed to rise
from below—a strange ghostly light like the winter
daylight of the Arctic wastes.

Sue was young enough to love the snow. The mere
fact that it threw everything out of gear and dis-
located the even tenor of existence was an adventure
not a nuisance to her. She raced through her work
for she wanted to go out; the country round about
Tog's Mill was familiar to her now in its bare winter
garb, but the snow would make it all different—Sue
wanted to see it and smell it, she wanted to walk knee
deep in the crispness of it. Darnay was pleased too,
and could hardly wait to eat his breakfast before
seizing his painting gear and sallying forth to find
a subject for his brush.

At eleven o'clock Sue filled a thermos flask with hot
coffee and arrayed herself for her walk. She tucked
up her skirt and tied a blue woollen scarf over her
head. The sun was shining now, but it was low on the

horizon and there was little heat in its rays; the air was like chilled wine, and the snow was crisp as sugar underfoot. The trees were finely etched against the whiteness of their background, their shadows were deep blue, and the little dells and depressions in the covering were dove grey. Over the fields the snow was as smooth as a blanket and the hedges and banks showed only as gentle mounds, and through it all— the only thing that moved in all that wide still waste —the river ran swiftly, like a dark green snake.

Sue had wondered whether she would be able to find Darnay—for sometimes he painted by the river, and sometimes on the hills—but there was no difficulty at all in finding him for his footmarks were clear and firm, leading her westwards along the river path. It was fun tracking him like this and Sue enjoyed the novelty. She tried to place her own feet in the marks but his strides were too long to be comfortable for her. Darnay's footmarks were the only human ones to mar the whiteness of the snow but there were dozens of tiny prints made by rabbits and river rats. Their padding feet had run over the snow this way and that as they sought their food so that their light trails crossed and re-crossed confusedly. There were bird-marks too, and, in one place near the river's edge, a scatter of ruby drops and a tiny heap of feathers showed where an owl or a hawk or some such bird of prey had made its kill.

Sue's eyes were very bright and the cold air made her cheeks tingle, she was so happy that she sang as she went. She sang some of the old Scots songs that she knew and loved: "The Bonnie Banks of Loch Lomond," and "Will ye no' come back again," and then suddenly she came round a bend in the path beside a great rock with crystal icicles hanging from its crown and found Darnay painting by the river.

He looked up and smiled at her. "Why stop?" he enquired. "It was the prettiest thing in the world to hear your voice coming nearer and nearer and nearer. I didn't know you had such a pretty voice, Miss Bun. Why have you hidden your light under a bushel?"

Sue blushed. "I was singing to myself."

"So I supposed—but you have no objection to other people enjoying it, I hope. What's that you've got?"

"Coffee," she replied. "I was thinking you might be a wee bit cold."

"You were wrong," he told her, and laughed when he saw how her face fell. "You were entirely wrong in thinking I might be a wee bit cold—I'm almost frozen to death. What a wonderful person you are!" he continued as he took the cup and warmed his hands upon it, and sipped the coffee with relish. "You really are the perfect housekeeper. How did you find me?"

Sue chuckled. "How do you think I would find you?" she enquired.

He thought for a moment, crinkling up his eyes and then he exclaimed, "Of course! You tracked my footsteps in the snow. How clever of you!"

"Savages are often good at tracking—so I've heard," declared Sue, dryly.

Darnay roared with laughter. "So you haven't forgotten that insult! Come and look at the picture, Miss Bun."

She came and looked at it, and this time she was

careful to look at it from a distance so that her eye would not be confused by the whorls of crude paint.

"Yes," she said thoughtfully.

"You like it?"

"Well, I wouldn't say that," she declared with absolute honesty. "It's too queer for me to *like* it and I can't see all those colours in the snow. Snow looks white to me."

"Only because you have a preconceived idea that snow is white," said Darnay seriously. "It is your brain tells you snow is white—not your eyes."

Darnay crossed the river at the weir above the mill and set off up the snowy slopes of the opposite bank. He was going to see Loch Beil, which Miss Bun had told him lay on the north side of the tree-clad hill. The loch would be frozen—perhaps it would be covered with snow—and Darnay thought he could find a subject there. He carried, besides his painting gear, a knapsack containing his lunch, for he intended to be out all day, but despite the load he strode up the hill with long easy strides. He felt fit and strong and happy, for he knew that he was doing good work—the "new medium" was going to be a success.

There was a fine view from the top of the hill and Darnay paused to admire it. The town of Beilford lay to eastward, a cluster of grey houses half hidden by a haze of smoke. All around were hills: small hills, rounded and glistening white in the winter sunshine, and big hills faintly opalescent, their more rugged contours outlined against the pale blue sky. Below him lay the loch, a smooth white sheet, surrounded by pine trees, tall and stiff as sentinels. Darnay noticed that, at one end of the loch, a patch of grey ice had been swept clear, and this patch was occupied by a group of dark figures which moved backwards and forwards in an apparently meaningless way.

Darnay watched the small figures for a few moments, crinkling up his eyes in the white glare, and suddenly he realised that there was a curling match in progress. He had seen curling in Switzerland, and it had not appealed to him in the least (it was foolish—so Darnay thought—to spend your days rolling stones upon a rectangular patch of ice when you could climb the mountains and rush down them on skis with the wind whistling through your hair) but here it was quite a different matter for these people were curling upon a real loch in natural surroundings, and the game was their own game—indigenous to their soil.

Darnay stacked his painting things behind a rock and went down to see the game. He would watch them for a little and see where the fascination lay. As he drew nearer he heard cries and shouts and a strange rumbling sound as the stones slid over the ice. It was an elemental sound, exciting as thunder, and was echoed back (as thunder is echoed) from the high cliffs to northward of the loch.

As Darnay reached the bank it seemed that a game had ended, for the players were standing in a little group, talking and laughing together. They were all men, he noticed, and they were dressed in the queerest assortment of clothes—old torn jackets and knicker-bockers which looked as though they had come out of the Ark. (Bulloch was the only one that Darnay knew —an outstanding figure with his tall, spare frame and silver hair.) He was sorry that the game was over, for he had wanted to watch them, and to hear that gorgeous roar at close quarters.

Suddenly Bulloch looked round and saw Darnay; he said something to one of his companions and came over to the bank.

"Would ye care to join us, Mr. Darnay?" he enquired. "We're a man short, ye see. The fact is the doctor was called away."

"I don't know the first thing about curling," said Darnay laughing.

Bulloch smiled, "It's high time ye made a start, then," he declared. "Come away now, we'll soon put ye in the way of it."

"I shouldn't be the least use."

"You'd wonder," Bulloch said, "maybe ye've played bowls now and then?"

Darnay had played bowls.

"Well then ye'll soon get into the way of it—come away, Mr. Darnay."

Darnay was led over to the rink, protesting feebly, and was received by the other players with unceremonious friendliness.

"Ye'll soon get into it," they told him.

"Never too old to learn."

"We'll make a curler of ye yet."

They showed him how to stand.

"Stand right, foot fair, look even"—and how to grip the handle of the stone, and swing it slowly backward and upward, and they impressed him with the importance of soling the stone—letting it gently off his hand at exactly the right moment.

At first Darnay found it difficult, he had a straight eye but the length bothered him and his stones either failed to reach "the hog" or went careering through "the house" and fetched up in the bank of snow which surrounded the rink, but after a little practice and tuition he was absurdly delighted to find that he really was beginning to get the hang of it. He would have liked to practice longer, but the others were eager to start and declared that Darnay was quite fit to take his place in the match.

By this time Darnay had managed to sort out his companions and to distinguish them by their names —or at least the names used by their fellow curlers. His own side interested him most: First was himself (for beginners usually play lead); second was "Hickie" a solid pleasant man of about twenty-eight years of age; third was "Bill," an old man in a green shooting jacket, very much the worse for wear; fourth was "Hornie" who was rather short and thick-set and walked with a nautical roll. Darnay put him down as a retired seafaring man, possibly a mate in the mercantile marine. He was the "skip" of Darnay's side, and took his duties seriously.

At first Darnay had been a little contemptuous of the excitement of his companions, but quite soon the game gripped him and he was shouting as loudly as anybody and "sooping" as though his life depended upon it. Time passed quickly, and he was quite surprised when it was decided to knock off for lunch. They were very friendly now, tossing jokes backwards and forwards as they ate their sandwiches—it was "Darnay this" and "Darnay that," and Darnay entered into the spirit of the thing and called his companions by the names he had learnt.

"I'm thinking we'll have to hold a court this year,"

Bulloch said. "It's three years and more since we had one and there's several folks to initiate."

"Darnay for one," suggested Bill.

"Aye, Darnay of course," agreed Hornie, "we'll make a fine curler of Darnay if only the frost lasts."

"What's all this?" enquired Darnay laughing.

"It's the mysteries."

"Aye, we canna tell ye."

"Wait an' see what's coming to ye!"

"High jinks, eh?"

They all laughed then, but refused to be more explicit, saying that it was a secret, and that only the initiated were allowed to know what "the mysteries" consisted of.

"Is it a kind of club?" Darnay asked.

"Aye, it's a club."

"The best club in the wurrld."

In the afternoon they curled again and Darnay improved considerably. Bulloch was far and away the best player—it was sheer joy to watch the effortless ease with which he sent up his stone—but Bill and Hornie were no mean performers, and the sides were so evenly matched that when they had played eight ends they were even.

"We're peal thirteen," Hornie said, and added for Darnay's benefit, "that's thirteen all, and only one more end to play. Try and sole your stone well, Darnay, and let it gently off your hand—you're doing fine."

Hornie had changed the order of play in the afternoon, putting Hickie lead, Darnay second, himself third, and Bill fourth. Darnay had grasped the principles of the game by this time and was aware that his duty was to put a guard on Hickie's well-placed stones. His first stone was too weak (he had tilted it slightly as it left his hand, and it failed to reach "the hog") but his second stone was better.

"Soop for yer lives, men," Hornie cried, "soop, soop, soop!"

Bill and Hickie seized their birch brooms and sooped industriously and the stone came to rest in its appointed place.

"It's a grand shot, that," cried Hornie, capering with excitement; "man, it's the very thing I wanted!"

The stones were well grouped in "the house" when Bulloch, who played last for his side, took up his stand on the crampit. There was a faint smile on his lips and he weighed the stone carefully in his hand before sending it down. The stone started so slowly that the others prepared to "soop" but Bulloch shouted the command, "Brooms up, lads!" The stone was wide, but, as it lost momentum, it curled inwards—curled and curled until Darnay could hardly believe his eyes, and finally slid in between the other stones and lay right upon "the pot lid."

Great was the excitement of Bulloch's men, they hopped about from foot to foot and waved their brooms in the air.

"A good shot, man!"

"Losh, it's bonnie!"

"You, for a curler—gie's a shake o' your hand."

It was a bad lookout for Darnay's side now, but Bill still had one more stone to play. He and Hornie discussed the situation somewhat ruefully—it might have been of European importance from the gravity of their expressions.

"It will need to be a thunderbolt, Hornie," declared Bill with a gleam in his bright blue eyes.

Hornie agreed reluctantly—he preferred the wily canny game of slipping between your opponents' guards to the forceful methods of scattering them— but alas, Bulloch's stone was surrounded on every side. The situation was desperate, and desperate situations require desperate measures.

"It's the only way," Bill pointed out.

"Aye, it's the only way."

Bill walked back to the crampit and took up his stand. He swung the stone well back and let fly with all his force. It roared down the rink like a torpedo and crashed into the little group centred round the pot lid. "Crack-crack, crack-crack-crack" went the stones, one against the other, and they shot away in all directions.

The whole situation was now completely changed, and everybody gathered round to see what had happened. Darnay saw that the stone which he had placed as a guard now lay upon the pot lid with Bulloch's a good two feet away—the others were scattered far and wide.

"We've won!" cried Darnay, throwing up his cap, "hurrah, we've won. Good old Bill!" and he slapped the doughty champion on the back.

It was getting too dark to play any longer, but they stood about for a few minutes discussing the fortunes of the game before taking the road home. Darnay knew them all quite well now, for curling is a game which begets intimacies, and he decided that next to Bulloch he liked Bill best. He was such a good fellow, so keen and yet so kind—applauding the good play of the other side as heartily as that of his own. He was interesting, too, quite apart from the game, and Darnay had arrived at the conclusion that Bill must be a gamekeeper or a forester on Sir James Faulds' estate. He had an "out of doors" look about him, and he was obviously interested in trees, for he had remarked to Bulloch, "Have ye seen my conifers, Thomas? They're doing well. I'm ordering another lot from Norway."

A forester, thought Darnay, looking at the ragged shooting jacket with the frayed cuffs, and, because Darnay himself was interested in trees—as indeed he was interested in most things—he spoke to Bill and asked him various pertinent questions about the climate and the soil, and what height was most suitable to the growth of Norwegian conifers, and he found Bill knew all about it.

"Who is he?" Darnay asked Bulloch as he helped to put the stones away in the shed. "Who is Bill? He's an interesting old fellow."

"Beil?"

"Yes, who is he?"

"It'll be the Laird ye're meaning," said Bulloch, straightening his back and stretching his arms to relieve his tired muscles.

"The Laird?" queried Darnay in bewilderment.

"Aye, Sir James Faulds of Beil—that's him."

Darnay was speechless—the Laird, Sir James Faulds, and he had slapped him on the back and called him "good old Bill."

"Curling's a queer game," continued Bulloch, with a glance at Darnay's dismayed expression. "Ye wouldn't understand the way of it maybe. Ye see, Mr. Darnay, we're all equals on the rink—the best man's the best player, but there's not one of us would presume on it. The Laird's a fine man, there's none finer."

"Yes," said Darnay feebly, "and who—who is Hornie, then?"

"He's Admiral Lang," replied Bulloch, his eyes twinkling with merriment beneath his bushy white eyebrows, "Admiral Sir Rupert Lang, that's him. He's called 'Hornie' on account of him having got a medal at Horne's Reef—it was a V.C. he got."

"Great Scott!" exclaimed Darnay. "Great Scott! and I suppose Hickie is a Cabinet Minister in disguise?"

"No, no, Hickie's an assistant in my business. He's my right hand is Hickie, and as reliable as the bank, but dinna' fash yersel'," he added, smiling, and laying his hand for a moment on Darnay's arm. "There's no harm done ye may be sure. They knew ye hadn't any idea who they were. They'll be laughing over it together, most like—for they're gey chief the pair of them and nobody enjoys a joke more than the Laird."

CHAPTER FOURTEEN

THE house above the Bulloch's shop was full of bustle when Sue opened the door and walked in, for it was three o'clock in the afternoon on the 31st of December.

"Granny!" called Sue, "Granny, where are you? Can I get any messages before I take off my coat?"

"I've sent the gurll," replied Mrs. Bulloch, appearing from the kitchen with a red face and white floury hands. "The daft limmer was a' to bits and no use to anybody. I was glad to see her back, and that's the truth. Come away ben, I'm real glad to see ye. Take off yer things, ma pet."

It was easy to see that Mrs. Bulloch was in a fine state of excitement and fluster over the preparations for her party and Sue hastened to take off her coat and get to work. The small kitchen was as hot as a furnace with the stove on full blast, and various delicious smells were blended together so that the very air seemed fit to eat. Mrs. Bulloch, though flustered, had by no means lost her head, and was in full command of the situation.

"If ye'd lay the table, Sue," she directed. "Here's the flowers, dearie. It would be a load off ma mind to feel the table was done. Thomas and me and you, that's three; and Mr. Darnay's four—dear knows what possessed Thomas to ask Mr. Darnay—and Will and

Grace and Sandy, how many's that, Sue? And Hickie, of course, and Jamie Waugh and Chairlie Anderson, he's the second fiddle, and puir wee Miss Mimms."

"It's eleven, Granny," said Sue, counting rapidly on her fingers.

"Are ye sure, dearie? I thought there was twelve— save us all, I'd forgotten Mistress Cowal!"

"Oh, Granny, that awful woman!" Sue cried, "you've not got her coming."

"She's a dejected sort of creature," Mrs. Bulloch explained apologetically. "I jest couldn't enjoy ma denner if I knew yon puir auld body was sitting moping by her lane. She's a bit dreich, but—ochwell—there'll be plenty of us to keep things cheery. It's Mr. Darnay I'm worried about, Sue—and that's the truth—Thomas means well, but he never should have bidden Mr. Darnay. I wish he'd said he couldn't come," she added with a sigh.

"How could he?" Sue asked indignantly, "he hadn't any excuse. Grandfather shouldn't have asked him. I was *dismayed* when he told me he was coming to-night." She paused a moment, thinking about it and wondering what on earth Mr. Darnay would think of her friends: of Grace, and Jamie Waugh, and old old Mrs. Cowal whose false teeth were a constant source of anxiety. "For pity's sake don't offer Mrs. Cowal any toffee," she added significantly, "you remember what happened last year."

"We're not having toffee at all," declared Mrs. Bulloch. "I thought it was safer not—and the denner will be fine, Sue, I can promise ye that. Maybe it'll no be so bad as we're thinking."

The invitation had been given and accepted the day of the curling match on Loch Beil, and, to tell the truth, both men regretted it when they thought it over in cool blood, but the thing was arranged and neither party could upset the arrangement without seeming ungracious—Bulloch could not withdraw the invitation, and Darnay had no excuse for cancelling his acceptance of it.

Darnay parked his car in a side street and walked along to the house. He had been asked to come at 7.30 and it was 7.25 exactly when he rang the bell. Mr. Bulloch opened the door to Darnay himself, and ushered him into the large and well-proportioned sitting-room. It was disconcerting to find the room full of people, for Darnay had hoped—by coming early—to be the first to arrive, and had brought the picture of Sue which Mr. Bulloch had admired. The picture, done up in brown paper, was too large to be hidden until a more suitable moment, so he was forced to present it to Mrs. Bulloch in front of an audience.

"It's just a little New Year gift," he said, putting it into her hands. "Don't open it now— *please.*"

But Mrs. Bulloch was already tearing the paper off and exclaiming rapturously over the picture.

"My, it's awful like Sue," she cried, "no wonder Thomas was taken with it. Look at that, Grace—it's just Sue to the life."

"It's real pretty!"

"The colours are awful nice."

"What's yon blue thing on yer heid, Sue?"

Darnay stood on one side listening to the remarks

and looking at the people who made them. His first thought was that they were a queer-looking collection, but, after a few moments, he discovered that, taken individually, they were not really queer. It was only because they were all so utterly different one from the other that they gave the impression of "queerness." In most gatherings people blend into one another— they are dressed in the same fashion and their faces wear the same sort of "party look"—but these people were so strong and rugged in personality that they always remain themselves no matter where they were or what they were doing.

Presently, finding himself seated at the table, which was positively groaning with Christmas fare, Darnay looked round and disentangled the various faces. He decided that Miss Bun's father (somehow one could not think of him as Mr. Bun) had a strange gloomy look and he wondered whether that was his natural expression. The new "Mrs. Bun" was fat and comely, but there were already faint lines round her mouth which would deepen into permanent wrinkles of discontent. Darnay thought it probable that she was already regretting her marriage to the saturnine baker. The old woman had an interesting face; he had never seen so many wrinkles in all his life. She was like an apple which has lain forgotten in a dry loft, and Darnay would have liked to paint her. He looked at Hickie next, for he knew Hickie, of course, and it was pleasant to see a known face amongst so many strangers— it was a good face, too, and well worth looking at with its firm jaw and well-defined chin—Hickie was talking to Miss Bun and the way he was looking at her gave Darnay an unpleasant jolt. So that was how the land lay! Well, and what of it? said Darnay to himself, it would be very suitable, very suitable indeed. Of course it would be suitable, why not? She would be safe with that man, his eyes are kind. *Safe*—did he want Miss Bun to be safe? Of course he did. He would like to see Miss Bun safely married to a good husband, and Hickie was obviously the very man. It would be eminently suitable, Darnay told himself firmly, and he wrenched his eyes away from Hickie's enraptured face and began to talk nonsense to his hostess.

Mrs. Bulloch was arrayed in black silk with a large cameo brooch which had belonged to her grandmother. Her face was shining so brightly with happiness that it seemed as if there must be a light inside. At the other end of the table sat Mr. Bulloch, with an enormous turkey before him—never had Darnay seen such a turkey, it was a king among birds. Bulloch was obviously in his element, slicing the pure white flesh from its ample breast; digging out mounds of pinky brown chestnut stuffing from the cavern of its ribs; ladling out brown gravy and snow-white bread sauce. When his guests were all helped Bulloch rose and served the wine himself, and Darnay, who knew a good deal about wine, was a little anxious when he saw that it was red; but his anxiety vanished with his first sip, for Bulloch was giving them Chateâu Lafite of an impeccable vintage.

"If ye'd rather have whisky——" Bulloch said suddenly, looking down the long table at his guest of honour. "I never thought to ask ye, Mr. Darnay."

"Have you so low an opinion of me?" returned

Darnay, leaning forward glass in hand and smiling at his host. "I may be only a poor benighted Englishman but I know a good wine—Chateâu Lafite—99, isn't it?"

"Man, ye're right!" cried Bulloch, delighted to find his claret appreciated. "I saw it vinted myself, and laid down a hundred dozen bottles—What a year, Mr. Darnay! What bouquet, what colour! Can ye beat it?"

"It's the queen of wines," agreed Darnay. "It has the true flavour of the grape, and of the sun and the good earth and the rain."

"I'd as lief drink whisky as any French wine," Pringle declared in a low vibrant voice, scowling at his plate as he spoke. "It's drumlie stuff at the best. We're not needing wines from France as long as we've our own barley growing in our own fields. Whisky's a man's drink."

"Each man to his own taste, Will," replied Bulloch pleasantly. "We'll not object to ye drinking whisky, and ye'll not object to our drinking claret, I'm hoping. Each man to his own taste, that's the thing."

"Ye can drink ink for all I care," muttered Pringle viciously.

There was a sudden silence and then a burst of talk, and the little incident was closed; but Darnay saw a glance pass between his host and hostess—a glance so full of sympathy and understanding that he was almost ashamed to have seen it. How beautiful, he thought, how marvellous to be so in tune with another soul—there would only be one thing in life to fear if one had that treasure.

There was talk and laughter and the good food disappeared rapidly. The shaded light flooded the snow-white damask cloth and shone on the polished silver and the gleaming plate.

Darnay talked to his hostess, and liked her immensely. She had the same direct gaze, and the same grave humour which he enjoyed in Miss Bun.

"Your granddaughter is very like you," he told her, smiling at her in a friendly way.

"Thomas thinks so too," she replied quickly. "It's funny that, isn't it? My daughter was different altogether—she was more like the Bullochs."

They both looked down the long table and their eyes dwelt on Sue. Darney thought his Miss Bun seemed different to-night, but perhaps that was the different dress. It was a pretty dress—of a soft shade of green which suited her colouring admirably—but Darnay preferred her in her neat overalls. He was glad that he had painted her in her working clothes. She was listening to Hickie's conversation with a vague look on her face as if she only half heard what he was saying, and her broad white brow was clouded. Darnay was certain that she was not enjoying the party and he wondered why. It was a good party, he thought.

Sandy Pringle was sitting on Darnay's right, and Darnay tried to draw him into the conversation. He had been somewhat annoyed with Sandy (the boy had come to him for advice and failed to take it, and this is always extremely irritating) but now that he saw Will Pringle and had sampled his mettle he realised that there was a good deal of excuse for Sandy. The boy was sensitive and nervous—you could hardly expect him to tackle that grim forbidding man.

Darnay sought for something to say. "Are you fond of music?" he enquired.

"Yes," said Sandy in a low voice.

He tried him again, with questions about his school, but Sandy would not be drawn. This was all the more strange because, at their previous interview, Sandy had been far from shy, and had responded to Darnay's friendliness with animation. The boy is miserable, Darnay decided, and it's no wonder—something will have to be done.

He would have to think of some way of helping Sandy, but he could do nothing now, so he turned and spoke to his hostess again and left Sandy to his own devices.

Darnay had been a little doubtful as to how he would get on with these people, but his doubts had vanished long ago; he was getting on famously.

There was one somewhat disconcerting incident during dinner, when old Mrs. Cowal leaned forward and said something to him in what sounded like a foreign language. Darnay could not make out what it was (for she spoke so broadly, and her teeth were too big for her mouth) but he decided that she was asking him to admire the plum pudding which had just arrived on the scene—a huge rich dark mound, covered with sugar almonds and surrounded by leaping flames.

"Yes rather. It's splendid," he agreed, nodding and smiling, "simply splendid."

He thought the old woman seemed somewhat

taken aback, and looked towards his hostess for help.

"Mrs. Cowal was saying did ye see about the awful railway smash on the posters," declared Mrs. Bulloch gravely.

CHAPTER FIFTEEN

DINNER was over now, but the chief purpose of the evening was still to come, and when everybody was comfortably settled round the fire in the sitting-room, the four performers produced their instruments. Their faces were very serious as befitted the gravity of their task, and there was a good deal of talking and moving of music stands and lights before they were ready.

Miss Mimms was playing the viola. She was a dried-up little spinster with long thin hands—the hands of a true musician—Darnay had scarcely noticed her before, for she was a mouse-like creature, but now he noticed her because she was aflame with excitement. There were two bright spots of red on her cheeks, and her eyes shone like stars behind the thick lenses of her spectacles. Mr. Waugh, the first violin, stood beside her with his fiddle tucked under his chin. His nostrils quivered and his iron-grey hair stood straight on end. Young Anderson was obviously nervous, his face pale, his brow beaded with perspiration. It was Bulloch who dominated the group; he sat in a low chair facing the audience with his 'cello held tenderly between his knees, and a faint smile upon his lips. It was the same smile that had curved his firm mouth when he had weighed the curling stone in his hand before sending up that champion shot of his.

What a picture! Darnay thought as he looked at

them. What a picture! If Rembrandt was here—
nobody else could touch it.

"It's Haydn's 'cello Concerto in E," announced
Bulloch, "and there's three movements."

Darnay did not expect very much from Bulloch and
his friends, but they had not been playing long before
he realised that they were good, in fact they were very
good indeed, and he thought they had chosen well
when they chose Haydn, for the music seemed to fit
them. It was slow music, rather simple and dignified—
even as they were—and it had a sort of undercurrent
of humour. There was purpose in it and calm sense.
You felt certain that it was getting somewhere, and
that it knew where it was going—even as they did.

Darnay did not know a great deal about music, he
liked it not so much for its own sake but because of its
human interest, and the pictures it made in his brain—
this music suited him to a T and he lay back and gave
himself up to the enjoyment of it.

The first movement opened with a haunting little
melody from the 'cello which was repeated louder and
more insistently with the other instruments joining
in. The 'cello solo, at the end of this movement, was
somewhat intricate, and Bulloch took it rather slowly
—but his tone was beautiful. Darnay liked the second
movement better, for it was more singing and tuneful.
It opened slowly, softly, sadly. At first it was muted
and restrained but afterwards it swelled and, mingling
with other harmonies, ended in a strain of hopefulness.
The third movement opened cheerfully. "Deedledy
deedledy dumpty dee," sang the 'cello and the other
instruments took up the refrain and echoed it with
shriller voices. The themes of the first and second

movement were blended with it harmoniously and, after another 'cello solo, the concerto ended in a fine burst of music.

There was tremendous applause, and many laudatory comments from the audience, and old Mrs. Cowal, who had listened in a state of trance, came to life and called out in a high piping voice, "Angcore, angcore. Could ye no play it through agen, Maister Bulloch, fer it wis a reel pleesure."

"Aye, play it again," agreed Hickie, nodding, "it was far too short."

Bulloch was clearly taken aback at this unusual request. He looked round at his fellow musicians, uncertainly. "Well, maybe later on," he said, "I'm thinking we need a wee rest first. Yon twiddly bit at the end of the first movement is awful hard work."

"Play the second movement again," Darnay suggested, "it was beautiful."

This suggestion pleased everybody, and the second movement was played again with great success.

After this Hickie was induced to sing "Annie Laurie," while Miss Mimms accompanied him on the piano. He sang it in a soulful tenor with his eyes firmly fixed on Sue. Mr. Waugh played a violin solo of Handel's Largo, and young Robert Anderson forgot his shyness and sang "A Man's a Man for a' that," with fire and spirit.

Darnay, prevailed upon to contribute to the entertainment, delved into the music cupboard and found a tattered copy of "Drink to me only," which Miss Mimms transposed into a suitable key and played without apparent difficulty, a feat which surprised Darnay a good deal.

The mystic hour was now approaching, indeed there were only a few minutes of the old year left. Bulloch threw open the window "to let the New Year in" and they all formed a circle—each person crossing his arms and holding his neighbour's hands. They waited thus until the clock on the church tower boomed out the strokes of twelve and then they sang:

"Should auld acquaintance be forgot . . ."

There were several verses of course, and Darnay did not know the words, but he followed as best he could and, when the last verse came and they all shook their clasped hands up and down, he "pump-handled" with the best of them. Old Mrs. Cowal was on one side of him, and Mrs. Pringle on the other. Mrs. Cowal's hand was hard and dry—a small bony withered appendage, rough with long years of dish washing—and Mrs. Pringle's hand was even less attractive for it was hot and moist, but Darnay squeezed them both and shook them manfully. He could not help wondering what Elise would say if she could see him, and hear him swearing eternal amity with two such strange neighbours; but the thought just passed through his mind, and there was no bitterness in it—a moment later he met Miss Bun's eyes across the charmed circle and smiled at her with his whole heart. These people were all very well, but Miss Bun was his own—perhaps the best friend he had ever had.

The bells were ringing now, and there was talk and laughter in the street, and Darnay saw that the party, which had been such a success, had come to an end. Some of the guests were going "first footing," and

others were going home to bed. He met Sue's eyes across
the room again, and this time she nodded gravely—
she was ready to go.

It was late when all the guests had departed, but
for the Bullochs the party was not over yet. Perhaps
this was the time they both enjoyed best of all, when
the guests had gone, and they were alone together
with so much to discuss. Mrs. Bulloch sat down by
the fire and pulled her black silk skirt over her knees,
and Mr. Bulloch looked at her and smiled tenderly
and reached for his pipe. He had smoked a cigar with
Darnay, but there was nothing like a pipe for comfort.

"It was all right, Susan," Bulloch said.

"Aye, it was all right—he's a nice man that Mr.
Darnay. There was no awkwardness in him."

"They all enjoyed themselves I'm thinking."

"Excepting Will," Mrs. Bulloch amended. "Such
an affront to put upon ye, Thomas! Yon man'll not
enjoy Heaven if he gets there."

"He'll maybe complain that the harps are out of
tune," agreed her husband, smiling. "It's a queer thing,
Susan, but I'm not caring these days what Will says.
He used to rile me, but I'm past that now, it's a fine
thing to be old."

Mrs. Bulloch sighed. "Are ye too old to be hurt?"
she asked. "I'm thinking ye'd best be. There's trouble
coming to us, Thomas."

"Trouble!" he exclaimed.

"I was watching Sue," Mrs. Bulloch continued in a
flat, tired voice. "Oh Thomas, she's changed! Sue's
changed to us. She's above us now and what's to come
of it? What's to come of it, Thomas, for she's neither
fish nor flesh—no good ever came of that."

"Did ye think so?" Thomas enquired in dismay. "I was thinking Sue was real nice—happier and sweeter than she's been this many a day. There's plenty of common sense in Sue—she's a homely creature, not the kind to have her head turned."

"It's her heart that's turned," declared Mrs. Bulloch sadly. "Maybe she doesn't know it yet."

But Sue did know. It was when Darnay stood up to sing that the knowledge came to her. She looked at him and a wave of loving tenderness swept over her heart, and, when he sang, his voice—a deep baritone, round and true and velvety—moved her so deeply that she had difficulty in restraining her tears.

Sue thought of this as she followed him through the crowded streets to the place where he had parked his car. I am his, she thought, but he is not mine—and never can be. But what does that matter, as long as I can work for him and see him every day. That ought to make me happy and indeed it does.

The streets were so full of merry-makers that it was difficult to get along and Darnay stopped and offered Sue his arm.

"Hang on to me," he said, smiling down at her, "I can't risk losing my housekeeper, you know."

She took his arm and they went on together—it was better like this. Sue felt his strength—a muscular, nervous strength, and liked the feeling of it.

CHAPTER SIXTEEN

THEY reached Tog's Mill without adventure, and Darnay put the car away in the shed. He came into the house singing softly, for he was happy. It had been a good party, and the knowledge that he had succeeded with these people and had made friends with them, gave him a glow at heart. They were worth while— very much worth while.

> "The rank is but a guinea stamp,
> A man's a man for a' that:
> For a' that, for a' that,
> A man's a man for a' that."

sang Darnay as he barred the door.

Sue was waiting for him in the kitchen, and he noticed that there was a worried look on her face.

"Hallo, what's the matter?" he enquired, breaking off in the middle of a bar.

"Do you ever smoke cigarettes?" she enquired.

The question was so unexpected that he could only stand and stare at her.

"You don't, do you?" she said. "I've never seen you smoking cigarettes."

"I don't like them," declared Darnay in a bewildered voice.

"No, you don't like them and you never smoke them, *somebody's been here*."

"Somebody's been here?" he echoed.

She opened her hand and showed him the remains of a cigarette—a twisted fragment of paper and tobacco with a charred end. "It was at the back of the fire on the ledge," she told him. "I saw it when I went to rake out the fire."

"Boy Scout!" said Darnay, but his eyes were grave. He took the fragment and smelt it and rolled it over between his fingers.

"What do you think he was like?" Sue enquired.

Darnay smiled at her. "My dear Watson, the man who smoked this cigarette was a small thin fellow of about thirty-five years old, dark and clean-shaven and dressed in a navy blue suit, black lacing shoes and a soft hat."

Sue laughed, she could not help it, for she was well acquainted with Sherlock Holmes.

"But really and truly, Mr. Darnay," she said.

"Really and truly," he replied. "The fact is I've seen a man hanging about the place for some days, and I found some of his cigarettes behind a rock near where I was painting—Turkish cigarettes exactly like this."

"What ever can he want?" cried Sue in alarm.

"Heaven knows."

"And I wonder how on earth he got in," Sue continued, looking round anxiously. "I snibbed the kitchen window before I went."

"Perhaps he came in through the door," Darnay suggested. "I left it open, you see—I suppose it was foolish," he added with a smile at his housekeeper's horrified face, "but the truth is I couldn't find the key, and I didn't want to be late."

"It was daft!" Sue cried.

"I suppose it was rather," he admitted apologetically, "but I didn't think anybody would bother to try the door—in fact I didn't think anybody would come near the place."

"He may be here yet," Sue declared, glancing over her shoulder.

"We'll see," said Darnay grimly.

It was an eerie business going through the dark empty house. The faint beam of Darnay's pocket torch seemed to make the darkness visible and no more. They went from room to room, searching behind the furniture, and in the cupboards, they even visited the rooms in the old wing—meal lofts which had been closed for years and smelt musty with cobwebs and damp. In one attic, where the window was broken and had never been mended, there was a heap of rubbish in the corner, and when beam of the torch reached it there was a sudden wild scrambling sound, and something blundered towards them across the floor.

Sue screamed aloud.

"It's a bat," Darnay said, taking her hand and pressing reassuringly. "It's only a bat. Poor brute, we disturbed it with the light. Don't be frightened, Miss Bun, there's not a soul in the house. I'm sure of it, I can feel it in my bones."

Sue was not so sure. They had looked everywhere it was true, but how easy it would be for a man to avoid them! He could have slipped from room to room, behind their backs, stealing along silently with stockinged feet. The light, though necessary to their purpose, showed only too clearly where they were, and its pale beam blinded them to the surrounding gloom.

Darnay was aware that she was frightened, and he was not surprised for the whole thing was mysterious and unaccountable. He was pretty certain that his papers had been tampered with, but a small heap of money in the same drawer was untouched.

"Come along, Miss Bun," he said kindly, "we'll search your room thoroughly and then you can lock the door. You can move your chest of drawers across it too, you'll be quite safe then."

"But you——" objected Sue, "if the burglar——"

"Don't worry," said Darnay grimly, "the burglar will be sorry if I lay eyes on him—funny sort of burglar," he added with a little frown.

They were in Sue's room now, and she had lighted her lamp. He looked at her and saw that she was very pale. A strand of dark red hair—the colour of old mahogany—lay across her white brow, and her eyes were shadowed with weariness.

"Is a man a burglar when he doesn't burgle?" Darnay enquired, smiling at her and talking in that gently mocking voice she knew so well. "Are we justified in calling our visitor a burglar when, so far as we know, he has taken nothing, but left us a little memento in the shape of a half-smoked cigarette?"

"But what did he want?" cried Sue. "Oh, Mr. Darnay, I don't like it. I wish he had stolen all your money."

Darnay chuckled. "And I wish he had stolen your fat white lady," he retorted, pointing to the little panel which hung on the wall opposite Miss Bun's bed. "We should have known then that he was an escaped lunatic," he added, and went out and shut the door.

Nothing more was heard of the thin man in the blue suit, nor did they find any more of his Turkish cigarettes. Darnay informed the police, and it was discovered that a man answering to his description had been staying at a respectable boarding house in the town, but had gone and left no address. If the man had stolen anything the police would have been more interested, but as it was they soon give up the quest.

"It's a strange thing and no mistake," Mr. Bulloch declared about a week later when Sue had dropped in to tea. "If the man had stolen something it would be a lot easier to understand."

"I wish he had," declared Sue.

"That's a queer thing to say!"

"No, it isn't," she retorted, "it isn't queer at all. I hate the mystery of it."

The Bullochs were delighted to have Sue to tea, but they declared that she only came when she wanted things from the shop and this was so near the truth that it was difficult to deny. On this particular evening Bulloch walked down to the bus with Sue when her visit was over saying that he wanted some exercise. It was a fine night, though somewhat cloudy, and the wind whistled eerily through the streets.

"Sue," said her grandfather, "there's something I'm wanting to ask ye."

"I'm not coming home," said Sue quickly.

"It's not that," he replied, for indeed he and Susan had decided that it was no use trying to make Sue come home. "It's not that, Sue, it's about the bills. They've been running on a long while now."

"Are you afraid you'll not get paid?" enquired Sue scornfully.

"It's not me so much. Some of the others have been at me: Alec Anderson, the butcher, and yer father, and a few more."

"Tell them they'll get paid in good time," Sue commanded. "I'm not going to worry Mr. Darnay when he's busy with his painting. They ought to be proud to serve him," she added, getting quite indignant at the thought of it. "He's a great painter and great painters ought to be considered and helped."

"They're only wanting their own money."

"It's money, money all the time."

"It's what's due to them, Sue," Mr. Bulloch pointed out. "They're not grasping folks at all. I'm not caring for myself; I know the man, ye see, and I'd take my oath he's straight—he's given us that picture, forbye, so it's not for me to complain—but it's a wee bit different for the others. Ye see that, don't ye?"

"They'll wait if you tell them," said Sue firmly.

CHAPTER SEVENTEEN

THE air-rifle which Sandy had acquired from the saddler was a great source of pleasure to himself and his friends, and for the first few weeks Sandy saved up his pocket money and paid his shilling ungrudgingly. The rifle was worth every penny he had spent upon it, there was no doubt of that. After a bit, however, the novelty began to wear off and the drain upon his resources became a nuisance. The rifle cost a good deal more than a shilling a week—so Sandy found—for unless he bought ammunition it was useless. This meant that he could never spend money on anything else and must deny himself sweets and apples and a host of small luxuries to which he was accustomed.

Sandy was not used to self-denial and gradually he began to fall behind with his payments, and Mr. Hogg, who had been so pleasant and accommodating became very unpleasant and grasping. Unfortunately for Sandy he was obliged to pass the saddler's shop daily on his way to school, and Mr. Hogg knew the hour of his passing and would lie in wait for him, and, pouncing out of his shop, he would seize Sandy by the arm and enquire grimly when Sandy proposed to pay up his arrears. It was all most unpleasant and Sandy had come to hate the sight of the saddler's long sallow face.

By the middle of February he owed Mr. Hogg five shillings—an immense sum—and could see no way of raising the wind. He had tried to borrow money from everybody he could think of, but, as this was by no means the first time he had found himself in financial straits, his friends and relations were aware that money lent to Sandy was money lost.

It was Saturday morning—a holiday of course—and the day dawned clear and bright. Sandy had arranged to go up to the moors and shoot with David Brown. They had not been out together for some weeks for the weather had been bad and Sandy had not been able to face Mr. Hogg to obtain the necessary ammunition for his rifle, but now the weather had cleared and the ammunition had been procured from the saddler by the simple means of bribing one of Will Pringle's message boys to fetch it—a means so simple indeed that Sandy was annoyed with himself for not thinking of it before. After a good deal of thought Sandy had decided to explain his difficulties to David, and offer him a half-share of the air-rifle in return for the money which he needed to pay Mr. Hogg—David was never very flush, but he might be able to raise five shillings at a pinch— it was worth trying. The position was really desperate by this time, for Mr. Hogg had come to the end of his patience and had told Sandy that he would speak to his father unless the money was paid on Monday morning. The threat alarmed Sandy considerably for he was aware that his father would be furious if he heard about his transactions, and, to make things worse, he had already involved himself with Will Pringle on the subject of the air-rifle. Will had seen it in his room. "What's that, eh? Where did ye get that from, Sandy?" Will had enquired, and Sandy, taken aback at the sudden question, had replied, "It's David Brown's air-rifle. I'm keeping it for him."

"David Brown's, is it?" grumbled Will. "I thought Brown had more sense than to give the lad a thing like that. Ye needn't come asking *me* for money to buy one. . . . See and not shoot yourself, nor any other body either."

Sandy had quailed before the glowering look, and had taken care to hide his treasure more carefully than before.

It was obvious to Sandy that he would get short shrift if his father discovered the truth, and he had lain awake for hours trying to find a way out of the mess. He was now eating his porridge, or rather he was toying with it distastefully, for his trouble loomed so large that it had taken away his appetite. David *must* help me, he thought, it's the only possible way. I'll have to explain——

"What's wrong with the porridge?" enquired Grace.

"What's wrong . . . nothing," replied Sandy, waking from his unpleasant dreams.

"Ye've been swishing it round yer plate for the last five minutes," declared Grace indignantly; "yer getting so nice over yer food there's no pleasing ye."

"I'm not hungry, that's all."

Will, who had been glooming silently over his bacon and eggs, suddenly looked up and said, "Hurry up with yer breakfast for any sake. I'll be needing ye this morning."

"You'll be needing me!" echoed Sandy in dismay.

"Aye, I'm short-handed. Two of them are off with colds—'flu, they call it—I'll 'flu them. Folks are soft as butter these days; they take to their beds every time they sneeze, damn them."

"I was going off on my bike with David," objected Sandy with a courage born of sheer desperation.

"Well, ye can't then. I've told ye I'm needing ye," said Will.

Thus it was that Sandy's last hope disappeared, and he found himself doomed to spend his holiday serving out scones and cookies, and crusty loaves of bread, and counting out change to fat women with market baskets instead of pedalling off to the moors with David Brown. He was angry and rebellious—his holiday had been filched from him at the last minute without the slightest compunction—he was also very frightened, for unless he could pay up the arrears which he owed before Monday, Mr. Hogg was going to speak to his father. All this grumbled away at the back of Sandy's mind as he served his father's customers that fine Saturday morning.

At half-past twelve the other assistants went home to lunch, and Sandy was left alone in the shop. The morning rush was over and there were very few customers between the hours of half-past twelve and two. Sandy opened the till to find change for a pound note for Mrs. Anderson, the butcher's wife and, when he tried to shut it, the drawer stuck. Mrs. Anderson left the shop and Sandy returned to the till. He jiggled the drawer this way and that, trying to make it work, but without success. There was a lot of money in the till, Sandy noticed—pounds and pounds—and he needed money so badly. That pound note of Mrs. Anderson's would pay off every penny that he owed and he would be perfectly clear to start afresh. Perfectly clear ! No more worry ; no more need to slink past Mr. Hogg's

shop like a murderer; no more need to pinch and save
. . . perfectly clear. . . .

The temptation to take the money was sudden and
absolutely irresistible; Sandy hesitated for a moment,
glanced round to see if he was alone, and slipped the
note into his pocket.

"So ye're a thief, Sandy!" exclaimed a voice from the
back of the shop.

"Grace!" cried Sandy in dismay.

"Aye, it's me," said Grace grimly. "Ye weren't
expecting to see me, were ye? I was coming to call ye
to yer dinner. I saw ye take the money. It's a fine thing
to steal from yer own father—a fine thing! Wait till
I tell him about it. *You'll* catch it, my lad!"

"I'll put it back," Sandy cried.

"Aye, ye'll put it back and take it some other time,"
declared Grace, her eyes blazing with anger. "I'm
sick of yer soft sa dering ways, and that's the truth.
It's a right good thrashing ye need, and ye'll get it too.
I'm away this minute to tell yer father the whole
thing. . . ."

Sandy seized her arm. "Grace!" he cried. "Please,
Grace. . . . I'll promise—anything."

"I know that fine," she replied, throwing off his hand.
"Ye'll promise anything, Sandy; ye never spoke a truer
word." And so saying, she turned and vanished
upstairs.

Sandy stood there for a moment, petrified with
horror, and then he turned and fled from the shop.

His first idea had been to go to the Bullochs for
protection but when he reached the West Gate he
changed his mind for what could he say to the Bullochs
to explain his arrival? There was nothing he could say.

He hesitated for a moment at their door and then sped on westward along the river path into the open country.

When he had left the town behind him Sandy dropped into a walk and began to consider the situation in which he found himself. It was a ghastly situation. Nobody could save him from his father's wrath, nobody would want to save him, for they would all be against him, every one of them. They would not listen to him if he tried to explain how the thing had happened. Sandy looked back along the road he had travelled since that fateful day in November when Mr. Darnay had given him the five shillings, and he had decided to buy the air-rifle. It had all started then—all the trouble—it wasn't his fault at all, it was just bad luck. One thing had led to another until there was absolutely no escape. He had been forced by circumstances to take the money, and if only Grace hadn't seen him it would have been all right. It was just like Grace to go snooping round where she wasn't wanted.

By this time Sandy was very tired and exceedingly hungry. He thought longingly of the piles of scones and cookies in his father's shop, and wished he had had the foresight to fill his pockets before leaving. He was not far from Tog's Mill now. If he called there, Sue would give him food, but she would want to know why he had come and what he was doing. People were all so inquisitive about one's affairs and Sue was no exception; besides, if there was any search, or hue and cry, Tog's Mill would be one of the first places they would visit.

Sandy had just decided to give Tog's Mill a wide berth when he saw his sister coming towards him

along the path. She was walking slowly and her eyes
were fixed upon the ground, and Sandy had time to
leap behind a convenient rock before she saw him. He
was lucky in his choice of a hiding-place for there was
a crevice in the rock, and in front of the crevice grew a
small fir tree. He crept in and lay there waiting for
Sue to pass.

She was so long in coming that Sandy began to think
she must have turned back, and then he heard a stone
rattle on the path and she came round the corner of
the rock. He could see her quite clearly between the
branches of the fir tree, and it seemed to him that she
looked different. He had always seen her as a matter-
of-fact sort of person, brisk and business-like, but this
Sue was sad and dreamy. She stood for a few moments
looking at the river as it splashed by, her head bent in
thought, and suddenly Sandy felt a rush of affection
for her—she was the only person in the whole world
who really cared for him.

He crawled out of his hole and stood up. "Sue,"
he said.

She turned and looked at him in surprise. "What a
fright you gave me!" she exclaimed.

"I didn't mean to speak to you," Sandy told her;
"but then I felt I couldn't go away without saying
good-bye."

"Go away?" she echoed in amazement.

"I'm going away. I can't stand it any more—Grace
and Father," declared Sandy, and somehow or other it
seemed to him that this was the truth. He saw himself
as a patient and long-suffering individual who had
borne injustice and persecution for months and had
now come to the end of his tether. "It's dreadful," he

added. "You can't call your soul your own with Grace snooping round the house. It was bad enough when you were there——"

"Oh, Sandy!" she cried. "I thought you'd get on better without me."

"I've nobody now," he told her sadly. "Nobody to talk to. Everybody's against me. I'm on my way to Edinburgh to enlist in the army. It's the only thing for me to do."

The idea had only just this moment occurred to him, but he spoke as if it had been in his mind for weeks, and indeed, no sooner had the words left his lips than it seemed to him that this was what he had always intended, for Sandy was such a master of deceit that he was able to deceive himself.

"Sandy!" cried Sue aghast.

"It's the only thing," he repeated. "It's the only way to escape from Father. Promise me you'll not tell a soul where I've gone."

"But Sandy——"

"Promise," he cried, seizing her arm. "Promise that whatever happens you'll not tell. You *must* promise, Sue. If they follow me to Edinburgh and try to get me, I'll kill myself—I swear I will——"

"But supposing they're anxious——"

"No, you've to promise, Sue. I needn't have spoken to you at all and then you'd not have known."

"I'd have been demented if you'd disappeared without a word," she exclaimed.

"I knew that," Sandy replied, squeezing her arm. "You're the only person in the world that cares a hoot what becomes of me."

Sue was touched. She loved Sandy in spite of his

faults, but she was aware that nobody else cared for him very deeply—even the Bullochs were more apt to see his faults than to appreciate his good points. She also saw that what he said was true, and that he need not have spoken to her at all—how dreadful that would have been!

Sandy was watching her face. "I'd never have gone without saying good-bye to you," he continued, quite oblivious of the fact that this had been his intention. "Never in this world; I wouldn't have thought of doing such a mean thing, so you must promise, Sue."

"All right, I'll promise," Sue said. "I won't tell anybody, but you must write and tell me how you get on—maybe they'll not take you," she added hopefully.

"They'll take me," Sandy declared. "I'll not tell them my real age of course, and I'm big and strong. Oh, yes, they'll take me all right. I'll soon make my way in the army and maybe I'll get a commission—you never know."

Sue had heard this sort of talk before, and her heart misgave her. "Don't be too—too sure of yourself," she said, aware as the words left her lips that this was not what she had intended to say at all. It was a good thing to be sure of yourself, and if only Sandy would continue being sure of himself in the same sort of way he might make something of life. Sandy's aims were too unstable, he was blown this way and that with every breeze; and he embarked upon every project with a high heart and soaring ambitions.

"Don't worry," said Sandy confidently, "you'll be proud of me yet, Sue. Just you wait."

"I'm sure I shall," she replied, taking his arm and

looking up into his fair boyish face, "and I believe the
army will be good for you—only you must stick to it,
Sandy, and work hard, and not expect too much at first.
There will be lots of things you won't like, but we've
all got to put up with things we don't like——"

"I must get on now," said Sandy, interrupting the
lecture. "I'm just wasting time here. I'll walk across
the hills and get the train at Langtown."

"Have you got money for your fare?" she enquired.

"Yes," said Sandy shortly. He was annoyed with Sue
for mentioning money, for it reminded him of the
unpleasant scene at the shop. It was a scene he wished
to forget.

Sue was surprised at his reply for she had never
known Sandy refuse money. "But, Sandy——" she
began.

"Don't fuss," he said. "I'm not a child. I know what
I'm doing. It will be grand to be on my own and not
have people after me from morning to night nosing
into my affairs. I don't mean you," he added generously;
"you've always been decent to me."

"Oh, Sandy, I don't like you going like this."

"It's the only way. Father's determined to have me
in the bakery and I couldn't stand it. I want a man's
life; I want to travel about and see the world."

He was feeling a man already, for his little talk with
Sue had encouraged him tremendously. It was not so
much what she had said to him, but what he had said to
her. No longer did he feel a fugitive from justice but a
bold adventurer setting forth to make his fortune. He
saw himself leading a forlorn hope against over-
whelming odds, and could almost hear the plaudits of
his comrades and the quiet commendation of the

Colonel. "Pringle is the sort of fellow we want," the Colonel would say. "He must have a commission— perhaps I should recommend him for the V.C." They would all be sorry then, thought Sandy; sorry for the mean way they had treated him.

Buoyed up by these dreams of the future Sandy said good-bye to Sue and crossed the river, and set off at a good pace up the hill. He paused once or twice and waved to her, and Sue waved back.

CHAPTER EIGHTEEN

No sooner had Sandy vanished than Sue began to regret her part in the interview. He had taken her so by surprise that she had absolutely lost her wits. I should have asked him if they had a row, thought Sue, and why on earth didn't he take his coat—he'll be starved with cold before he gets to Edinburgh—and it's Saturday too. What will he do when he gets there if the recruiting office is shut? And I wonder if he's thought of this for long—maybe it's just one of his sudden hare-brained schemes. Oh, dear!

She was still standing on the path, thinking it all over and wondering whether she had been mad to encourage Sandy in his plan, when she saw Darnay approaching. He waved and beckoned to her, and she turned to meet him.

"Your father's here," he said. "I'm afraid it's trouble for you, Miss Bun."

"Trouble?" she asked, taking care not to meet his eyes.

"It's about Sandy," Darnay explained. "Your father's furious. He says Sandy took a pound note out of the till and disappeared."

"What!" cried Sue aghast. "He took—money——"

"It's all right," said Darnay, seizing her arm and trying to comfort her with the first words that came to his lips. "Sandy's only a child; don't worry too much. . . ."

"Worry!" she cried.

"I know how you feel," declared Darnay, and indeed it was true, for he knew his Miss Bun inside out by this time.

"Nobody knows how I feel," she murmured faintly.

"I know," he said. "You feel it's the end of the world because he stole money out of the till, but the boy was in some sort of trouble—I'm sure of that—I felt certain that he was in trouble. . . . I ought to have done something about it."

"There's no excuse——"

"Oh, but there is," Darnay interrupted. "There's every excuse. Sandy isn't like you, and you mustn't judge him by your standards. Your father should never have had a sensitive son." He had been talking rather wildly, for Sue's distress had frightened him; her face was as white as chalk and her whole body trembling. He saw now that she was a little comforted by his words. "Sit down for a minute," he continued. "We must go back and talk to your father but there's no hurry."

"You're kind," she said, looking up at him gratefully; "but why should you have all this—bother? You had better let me go back myself."

"Perhaps you're right," admitted Darnay thoughtfully. "Perhaps you should see him alone. It's nothing to do with me, and I don't want to meddle with your affairs. Go back yourself and see what he has to say— don't talk, but just listen. I have a feeling that his bark is a good deal worse than his bite."

"I'll go now," said Sue, getting up from the rock where she had been sitting.

"No, wait for a minute; wait till you feel better."

"I'm all right," she declared. "Really I am—it was

just the—the shock. I can't possibly sit here . . . Oh,
Mr. Darnay, it will be dreadful!"

Darnay realised that it was her nature to take her
fences at a gallop and he let her go. He sat down and
thought about it very seriously, for he was deeply
interested in the lives of these people, and it did not
seem strange to him that he should waste a whole
morning of his precious time in considering their
problems. How strange it was, thought Darnay, that
this brother and sister, brought up in the same atmosphere, should have "come out" so utterly different.
Will Pringle was a tyrant—there was no doubt of that
—but his tyranny had affected his two children in
exactly opposite ways.

Meanwhile, Sue had reached Tog's Mill and had
found her father striding about the studio like a caged
beast. It was an unpleasant interview, but not really so
appalling as Sue had feared. Perhaps she had outgrown
her fear of Will, or perhaps Darnay's suggestion that
"his bark was worse than his bite " had given her
courage. He raged and stormed at her, and she sat and
listened, and after a little she actually began to feel
sorry for him. How foolish it was to expend so much
energy raging at an innocent person—he was foolish,
and impotent.

"What will folks say?" cried Will, striding up and
down the room, and pausing to shoot out the question
at the silent figure of his daughter who sat at the table
resting her chin on her hands. "What will folks say—
tell me that. Are ye dumb, Sue?"

She looked up at him, but made no answer,
and Will's eyes fell before her straight unflinching
gaze.

"The whole of Beilford to know that my son's a thief!" he cried.

"They needn't know," Sue pointed out, "nobody need know unless you tell them."

He looked at the floor. "I was going to the police," he said doubtfully.

"Everybody will know then," she replied, trying to hide her dismay and to speak in a matter-of-fact tone.

"Aye, that's true enough," he said. There was silence for a few moments and then he added, "Maybe I'd better keep it to myself."

"That's for you to decide."

"Aye, that's true." He hesitated a moment, and gazed out of the window with his hands in his pockets. "Maybe I'll just wait till he comes home—and then thrash him," added Will, with relish.

Ten days passed before Sue received the letter which Sandy had promised, and she was beginning to wonder whether his determination to enlist had lasted long enough to carry him to the recruiting office. She tore the envelope open with shaking hands and straightened out the flimsy sheet of paper. It was not a long letter, but it told her all she wanted to know. Sandy had enlisted and was comparatively happy in his new life. It was hard work, and there were a good many draw-backs, but he had no regrets. There was one sentence which comforted Sue a good deal, for she thought it gave a clue to Sandy's nature. "They are very strict here," he wrote; "but if you do your best they give you credit for it. They never jump on you for no reason and frighten the life out of you."

Sue could read a good deal in this, for she knew who

it was that had jumped on Sandy and frightened the life out of him. If Sandy was not afraid any more there would be no need for deceit. She took the letter to Mr. Darnay and showed it to him—it was the least she could do after all his kindness to her, and Sue did not feel that she was breaking her promise to Sandy in letting him into the secret, for Mr. Darnay was in a different category from other people—or so she felt.

"You knew about this before," said Darnay, looking up at her and smiling. "Oh, yes, you did. You can't deceive me, Miss Bun. If you hadn't known where the boy was you would have been far more anxious and worried over him—and so should I."

"What *do* you mean?" she inquired.

"You were a little anxious about him, but not unduly," Darnay pointed out, "so I took the hint and didn't worry too much. I'm fond of Sandy, you know, and I'd like him to have a chance to make good. He's got it now."

"You really think so?"

"It will be the making of him," said Darnay confidently. "He's feeling better already—you can see that." ,

"Yes," she agreed; "yes, if he sticks to it."

"He must stick to it. He has no choice," Darnay pointed out. "You can write a nice little lecture to him about his disgraceful behaviour and tell him that his father is waiting for him with a big stick. It will do him good, Miss Bun, for Sandy is obviously one of those fortunate people with a very short memory for their own misdeeds."

"Yes," said Sue again.

"And you can cheer up," continued Darnay. "Sandy

will be all right, so you needn't worry about him any more."

Sue smiled a little sadly and went away. She was aware that the advice to "cheer up" was necessary, for she had been feeling very miserable indeed. The anxiety about Sandy was bad enough, but she had troubles of her own which were even harder to bear. She had been so happy at Tog's Mill, happy in her work, and happy in her daily contact with Darnay, but, since her discovery that she loved him, her happiness had gone. It was foolish, of course, for everything was going on exactly the same, it was only her feelings that were changed. It was foolish to be miserable, to lie in bed at night and wonder how she would be able to bear it when he went away and left her. He would go away—for this was only an interlude in his life—he would go back to his own world, and forget all about her, and she would be left.

But why *think* about the future, she would ask herself, beating her pillow and turning it over so that the cool side was against her hot cheek; why think of the future and be miserable about it? He's here now, so why can't I be happy? I don't know what's come over me. I used to be so sensible, and now I'm just a fool.

CHAPTER NINETEEN

It was March, and spring was coming slowly but surely to the lands of Beil. The rooks were beginning to build in the trees at the other side of the river—or at least they were busy looking for suitable sites for their nests. They had their own way of alighting upon the trees, quite different from that of other birds. Other birds hopped up from branch to branch inside the tree, but the rooks hovered in the air and sailed downwards, choosing a high branch and alighting upon it daintily. Their movements were a poem of balanced rhythm; a speck in the sky, a hovering, a sailing earthwards, and lastly the swaying branch.

Sue watched them from the window of Darnay's room, while she was dusting his dressing-table. This was a labour of love, and she lingered over it, taking up each object in turn—his brushes and comb, his stud box, his razor-case and the manicure scissors in their tiny sheath, and tidying up as she went. Darnay was painting near home to-day; he was down near the weir, and she could see him standing there with his easel in front of him—it was like a little picture seen through the wrong end of a telescope, and her heart turned over in her breast.

To-day she was even more miserable than usual, for Darnay had received a letter from the Laird asking him to dine at the castle. Darnay had told her about it casually, and had added, "I suppose I had better go. It's nice of the old boy to ask me."

Sue did not know about the incident at the curling match, so she could not understand the faint smile which accompanied Darnay's remark; she did understand, however, and only too well, that Darnay took the invitation lightly—it was nice of the old boy to ask him! All of a sudden she saw more clearly than ever before the frightful gulf that lay between them. Darnay was free and easy, he was able to descend to her level and to play his part quite comfortably at the Bullochs' hospitable board, but his real level, his real place in social life, was at the dinner-table of the Laird —and she could never rise to his level however hard she tried.

I ought to be glad, Sue told herself, I'm a selfish, horrible creature. It's nice for him to be asked to the castle; he'll meet other gentlemen and talk to them and enjoy himself with his own kind. It's only right and natural; I ought to be glad.

Darnay was very pleased at receiving the invitation to dine at the Castle, for it showed that the "old boy" bore him no grudge. In spite of Bulloch's assurance that all would be well Darnay could not help feeling that Sir James had every right to be annoyed. The Laird had been "incognito," of course—you might almost say disguised—but there were certain limits, and Darnay felt he had overstepped them.

Darnay whistled gaily as he put on his dinner-jacket— the dinner was quite informal—and came down to the kitchen to have his collar brushed.

"I may be late," he told Sue. "Don't wait up, Miss Bun."

"No," she said shortly.

He looked at her and saw that she was very white,

and her lips were pressed into a straight line. "What's
the matter?" he asked. "Don't you approve of me in
this kit? It's pretty silly, isn't it?"

"You suit it, Mr. Darnay."

"I suit it, do I?" laughed Darnay. "Well, it doesn't
suit me. . . . I'm much more comfortable in grey
flannel slacks and a pullover."

Sue was silent, and he was surprised to see her
compressed lips quiver. "Why, Miss Bun!" he cried.
"What's the matter?"

"Nothing," said Sue. "Nothing at all . . . it's
getting late," she added significantly.

"Good heavens, so it is!" he cried, snatching up his
coat. "I musn't keep Sir James waiting for his dinner
—that would be adding insult to injury, wouldn't
it?"

Sir James Faulds was a widower. He had two sons,
both of whom were in the army. The only other guest
was Admiral Lang. They were drinking sherry in the
library when Darnay arrived, and toasting themselves
in front of a roaring fire. They greeted Darnay
cordially and invited him to pull in a chair.

"Have you seen my conifers?" inquired the Laird
with twinkling eyes. "You know a good bit about
them—unless you've forgotten the lesson you had at
the curling match."

"That wasn't the only lesson I learnt," declared
Darnay, smiling ruefully.

"Good old Bill," murmured the Admiral, with a
mischievous look in his eyes.

It was obvious that the two gentlemen had enjoyed
the joke. Bulloch had been right about that, and he

had also been right in saying that they were "gey chief." (This expression had puzzled Darnay at the time, but he had found out from Miss Bun that it meant very friendly—or, perhaps "thick" was a better translation.) There was a very pleasant harmony between them, a harmony which can only exist between men who have known each other from boyhood's days, and even when they disagreed with each other—as they frequently did—their fundamental friendliness was undisturbed.

In spite of this friendliness, however, Darnay was not made to feel an intruder, but rather that he was giving them both a great deal of pleasure by his company and by his different views and ideas of life. This feeling excited him and went to his head (for it was so long since he had spoken to anybody of his own world) and he found himself talking a lot, and knew that he was talking well.

The three men dined at a small round table set in the middle of the vast shadowy dining-hall. The curtains were drawn and a huge fire burned in the old-fashioned fireplace. Two menservants moved about, soft-footed as shadows behind their chairs, offering them the conventional dishes in the conventional way. It was so different from his mode of life at Tog's Mill that Darnay could have laughed.

"What do you do with yourself when you're not painting?" inquired the Laird.

Darnay tried to tell them. There was not much to interest them except the Bullochs' dinner-party, so he made the most of that for their benefit.

"They're grand folk," Sir James said, "and I see you have discovered it—and they have discovered you.

Well, I think you're going the right way to paint Scotland, for these folk are the real Scotland."

"Now you're getting beyond me, Jamie," declared the Admiral. "I can see Darnay would have to know the people before he could paint them, but why must he know the people before he paints the hills?"

"I never knew such a man for argument!" cried his host. "Darnay's told us he wants to paint the real Scotland——"

"He should paint you, then."

"I don't want my ugly face immortalised," declared Sir James somewhat ruefully; "but I wouldn't mind a good portrait of Jean. How about it, Darnay, would you like a commission to paint my niece?"

"I'll wager he would!" cried Sir Rupert. "If he saw Jean there would be no holding him."

"I would like to," said Darnay eagerly. "There's nothing I'd like better. But I wonder if *you* would like it."

They asked what he meant by this, and Darnay explained about the "new medium." He found himself telling them the whole story. How he had suddenly felt that everything had gone flat and stale, and that he was not progressing in his art, and how it had seemed to him that the only thing to do was to "get away from it all."

"Yet your pictures were selling—you had made a name for yourself," the Admiral pointed out.

"I wasn't satisfying myself," Darnay declared.

"You must paint Jean," said Sir James. "I'd like to see what you make of her."

"I'll paint her," agreed Darnay; "and if you don't like it we'll burn it. How will that do?"

"That's certainly a fair offer," declared Sir James, laughing. "Have some port, Darnay, and pass the decanter."

Darney did as requested.

"Your name is very unusual," the Admiral remarked. "Is it English or what?"

"It's Norman," replied Darnay. "D'Arraigné was the old form. Our crest is a spider."

"Battle of Hastings, 1066," put in Sir James. "That and Bannockburn, 1314, were the only two dates I could ever get into my head."

After dinner they played billiards; Darnay took on the Admiral, while their host marked for them. They talked in a desultory fashion as they played, and the two old friends chaffed each other pleasantly.

"A wife in every port," declared Sir James, as he marked a break of eleven for Darnay. "Everybody knows that."

"It's a libel," replied his friend, with a smile. "The fact is sailors have no time for wives—I never had. Besides, the ladies are all such darlings, it's impossible to limit oneself by marriage."

"You've never been in love?"

"No, never."

"What, *never*?"

"Well, hardly ever."

They all laughed.

"I knew a man," continued the Admiral, "who disliked his wife so much that he went and lived on the top of a mountain to get away from her. It was a Swiss mountain, and they kept their cows in the house all winter. Now, if that man had been a sailor——"

"Tog's Mill . . ." began Darnay, and then he stopped, for he had been on the point of say~ng that the man might have lived at Tog's Mill—a place which seemed to be as distasteful to wives as a Swiss mountain top.

"Tog's Mill," said Sir James, taking him up. "How do you manage about servants, Darnay? I've sometimes wondered about you."

"I've got Bulloch's granddaughter."

The Admiral, who had been chalking his cue, looked up quickly. "You have, have you?" he said.

"I'm in clover," Darnay continued, with a smile. "She's most capable and very attractive. There's something very charming about her."

"Her mother was a lovely creature," declared Sir James. "D'you remember her, Rupert? What was her name again?"

"Mary," replied Sir Rupert shortly. He took up his position and potted the white.

"What on earth did you do that for?" his host inquired. "Your game was in off—it was an easier shot too."

"Was she really beautiful?" Darnay asked. "And, if so, why did she marry the baker?—not a very attractive specimen, I thought."

"Women do these odd things," said Sir James; "and do them for the oddest reasons."

"It's raining," declared the Admiral. "I can hear it on the window. We're in for a wet night."

Darnay left early, and when he had gone the two old friends sat down by the fire for a last chat before parting.

"I like that fellow," said Sir James, pouring out a generous measure of whisky as he spoke. "There's something very attractive about him. You feel he's absolutely straight—and I like his enthusiasm. There's too little enthusiasm about young people to-day. Even if you don't agree with his views, which are a bit peculiar to an old stick-in-the-mud like me, you've got to admit that he——"

"Listen, Jamie," his friend interrupted. "There's something I want to tell you—it's about that girl."

"What girl?"

"Mary Bulloch's daughter—she might be mine, Jamie."

"What?"

"I said she might be mine; I never really knew; I don't know now. It's an old story, of course. Mary and I were in love—deeply—and I meant to marry her. Mary could have taken her place in any sphere of life. And then the war came and I was sent to the Dardanelles. You remember that, Jamie; it was a secret mission. I was in submarines then."

"I remember."

"When I came home she was married—and a mother."

"Great Scott!"

"That's all," Sir Rupert said. "I said nothing, I did nothing, for I thought it was better to leave it. I was sore and wretched as hell about the whole thing. What am I to do, Jamie?"

"Do? You can't do anything."

"I want to do something for the girl."

"You can't. You don't know anything—you said so yourself—and the girl doesn't need anything done for her."

"How d'you mean?"

"I mean she's Bulloch's granddaughter. He can look

after his own. Why are you bothering now, after all these years?"

"Because I'm lonely, I suppose," said Sir Rupert slowly. "Because I'm old and lonely and selfish. He said she was very charming, didn't he?"

"Leave it alone, Rupert; leave it alone. You'll only make trouble if you begin to stir up the mud."

Sir Rupert sighed. "I suppose I must," he said; "but I'd give a lot to know . . ."

CHAPTER TWENTY

SUE was not best pleased when she heard that Miss Faulds was coming to the studio to have her portrait painted. She had had Darnay to herself for so long that she viewed with dismay the prospect of another woman coming daily to Tog's Mill. She was therefore very proper and polite, and exceedingly stand-offish when she opened the door in answer to Miss Faulds' ring.

"Mr. Darnay is in the studio. Come this way, please," she said, eyeing the visitor appraisingly, and taking in her whole appearance at a glance. She's pretty, thought Sue, grudgingly, and her clothes are lovely. He won't paint *her* with an old duster on her head.

Darnay thought she was pretty too, with her dark wavy hair and brown eyes, but her clothes did not please him so much.

"Shall we go for a walk along the river?" he inquired, when he had greeted her in a suitable manner.

"A walk!" exclaimed Miss Faulds in surprise.

"I want to get to know you a little," said Darnay, smiling. "I can't sit down and paint you straight off—at least, I don't want to—and I'm not going to paint you in that dress."

She was a little taken aback at this. "Don't you like it?" she exclaimed.

"It's very pretty, but it's not you," replied Darnay. "What do you usually wear? What sort of clothes do you feel most comfortable in?"

"Tweeds and a jersey," said Jean Faulds promptly.

"Then I'll paint you in tweeds and a jersey," he declared.

Sue saw them go out together, talking and laughing like old friends, and she was torn by the fiercest emotion she had ever experienced. She rushed into the kitchen like a whirlwind, seized a pail and a scrubbing brush, and proceeded to scrub the floor as if her life depended upon it.

Meanwhile Darnay and his prospective sitter were walking up the river path. Jean was not clad for such an expedition, but there was something about this man that compelled you to do what he wanted—or so she felt—and soon she was so interested in his conversation that she forgot about her clothes. Darnay was watching her carefully and making up his mind about the portrait. She was not so interesting as Miss Bun—from a painter's point of view—but she had an engaging personality, and he was glad that he was going to paint her. She was a friendly creature and soon she was telling Darnay about her affairs.

"I live with Uncle Jamie mostly, and keep house for him," she said; "but I've been staying with friends—that's why I wasn't there when you dined at the castle. I was awfully excited when he said you were going to paint me. I've seen some of your pictures. By the way, there was a Mrs. Darnay staying at Fulham Park; is she any relation, I wonder?"

"Perhaps it was my wife," Darnay said.

Jean was silent, for she did not want to pry into private matters.

"She knows a lot of people," Darnay added. He was aware that a constraint had arisen between them, and, although he did not want to bother her with his personal affairs, he felt that he must give some explanation. Miss Faulds would think it odd that he did not know more about his wife's movements. "It was too dull for her here," he explained, "so she went home for a little."

"I see," said Jean.

"I wonder if it *was* my wife," he continued, trying to speak lightly. "Had she a leopard-skin coat?"

"She had," replied Jean, smiling. "A most wonderful skin—we were all wild with envy."

"That would please her," he declared.

Jean did not answer this for she was embarrassed by his bitter tone. The woman had been pleased, of course, and had shown her pleasure so openly that they had laughed at her behind her back and called her "My Jungle Love." She was a rotten sort of woman—they had all thought so. What a pity she was married to this charming man!

"I suppose you make a lot of money by your pictures," she said, uttering the first words that came into her head in order to change the subject.

"I did at one time——" he began.

"Oh, yes, of course," cried Jean. "Uncle Jamie told me about it. I think it was a wonderful thing to do."

"Anybody who felt as I felt would have done the same."

"They might not have been able to," she answered quickly, "if they hadn't got private means."

They were on a narrow path now—so narrow that Darnay had gone ahead. He stopped suddenly as if he had been shot, for the words were like a flash of lightning illuminating the dark places of his mind.

He saw suddenly that he had been living in a dreamer's paradise: eating, sleeping, painting, and talking nonsense to Miss Bun. *Money*—he had never thought of it. What on earth had he been living on all these months?

Jean had stopped too, for she could not pass him; he was standing in the middle of the path.

"What is it?" she asked.

"No," he said, answering her previous remark. "No, I haven't got anything except what I make myself. My father lost all his money in the Wall Street crash. Fortunately, I was established by then." He could say no more, for his throat felt dry and stiff. He tried to calculate how much money he must owe to Miss Bun, and to the Beilford shops, but it was impossible—he had no idea at all. Why hadn't they sent him bills? It seemed odd that they should be willing to give him unlimited credit—a stranger of whom they knew nothing.

These thoughts took but a few moments to pass through his mind, and he came to himself to hear Jean's voice. "Uncle Jamie nearly got caught," she was saying, "and some friends of ours lost everything. It was dreadful, wasn't it?"

"Dreadful," agreed Darnay.

Jean was sure that something was the matter, for Mr. Darnay's manner had completely changed. He had been gay and friendly, and now, quite suddenly, he was aloof and grave. She wondered if she had offended him, and if so, how. They were now on their way home, and they walked on in silence, busy with their own thoughts.

"What *is* the matter, Mr. Darnay?" said Jean at last.

"The matter?" he enquired. "Oh, yes. I'm sorry I'm so dull. The fact is I've just thought of something rather worrying—something you said. . . ."

"I didn't mean——"

"It's just as well. I ought to have thought of it before."

They said no more, but walked on till they came to the old mill; it was getting dark now and beginning to rain. Jean's small car was waiting in the drive.

"Won't you stay and have some tea, or a glass of sherry?" he asked.

She shook her head. "I had better go back. Shall I come to-morrow morning—in my oldest and most disreputable clothes?"

Darnay hesitated before he answered. He was standing at the window of the car and he had to stoop to look in and speak to her. "I don't know," he said doubtfully.

"You don't know what?" she asked in astonishment.

"I do apologise," he continued in a low voice. "I know I'm behaving in a most extraordinary way. We may have to postpone the portrait—I may have to go away."

"It doesn't matter," she replied. "You can paint me when you come back."

"You've no idea how——"

"I wish I could help," she cried impulsively.

"That's nice of you," he said. "You ought to be angry with me for being so dull, but I'm afraid nobody can help."

It was all very mysterious, and Jean pondered over it as she drove home. She came to the conclusion that it was something to do with his wife, for they had been talking about her when his manner had suddenly changed. She tried to remember what she had said about the woman. I said we were wild with envy, she thought, as she turned into the castle gates, but surely he could see it was meant for a joke. Even if he had taken it seriously Jean did not see how the words could have disturbed him so profoundly.

Meanwhile, Darnay, after ringing the bell, and pounding on the door without any result, had decided that the house was empty. He remembered that Sue always left the key of the front door under a stone when she went out, and lifting the stone found it and let himself in. The house felt empty and deserted, and Darnay knew the moment he crossed the threshold that Sue had gone. He went into the kitchen and found a note on the table. "Back at ten," said the note tersely.

Darnay was surprised at this sudden desertion, for it was most unusual. Miss Bun never went out of her own accord, and he was obliged to use persuasion when he considered that a visit to the Bullochs was overdue. He was surprised and somewhat annoyed, for he wanted to talk to her. She might have waited till I came in, thought Darnay. He sat down to his supper (which had been left ready for him on the table) in a thoroughly bad humour, but after a few minutes he saw how unreasonable he was and became annoyed with himself instead of with Miss Bun. He was always telling her to go out more, to go and see the Bullochs, or those Graingers at the chicken farm with whom she was so friendly, and now that she had taken him at his word and gone he was as peevish as a spoilt child —and that's exactly what I am, thought Darnay, *a spoilt child.* I've done exactly what I wanted for months, and considered nobody but myself.

After supper he went into the studio and opened his desk. There were piles of letters in it, all neatly stacked and girded with elastic bands. Darnay sat down and began to go through them.

There were letters from Elise, and letters from Hedley, his agent, and one or two bills from London shops, but there were no Beilford bills amongst them —not one. Darnay remembered telling Miss Bun that he did not want to be bothered with letters, and he saw that she had taken him at his word. He waded through the letters and found that they were just what he expected. Elise wanted him to go back to London and paint pictures that would sell; Hedley wanted the same thing. They didn't understand.

It took him a long time to read the letters, and he had only just finished his task when he heard Miss Bun come in. I can't speak to her to-night, said Darnay to himself. I must think it over first. I must think what I am going to do.

He rose and stretched himself and went out into the hall to say good-night to her. "Did you have a good time?" he enquired.

"Yes, thank you," said Sue brightly. "Did you enjoy your walk?"

"Not very much," replied Darnay.

Miss Bun was half-way upstairs by this time. She paused and looked back. "Did you not?" she asked in a surprised tone. "I thought Miss Faulds so nice—and so pretty!"

"Yes, I suppose she is," he said.

Miss Bun smiled inscrutably; she looked pleased for

some reason. "Are you going to paint her in that pretty dress, Mr. Darnay?" she inquired.

"No. Perhaps I shan't paint her at all."

She hesitated a moment or two longer, and then, as he did not vouchsafe any more information on the subject, she said "Good-night," and ran upstairs to bed.

CHAPTER TWENTY-ONE

THINGS always seem worse at night, and any sort of trouble is magnified. The darkness, the stillness, the feeling that everybody else is safely and soundly asleep give rise to feelings of desperation. Darnay's case was no exception to the rule. At first, when Jean Faulds' words had opened his eyes to the fact that his financial position was unsound, he had thought of the whole affair as "a bore"—he would have to do something about it—but the more he considered the matter the more worried he became. He was in debt, he had no money to pay his bills, and he could see no way of making money to pay them—this was the situation, and the thought of it weighed upon him like an intolerable burden.

The truth was that Darnay had never had to think about money or trouble his head about it, for he had always had enough for his needs: his pictures had sold well and his wife had money of her own, but now the position had changed, for his new pictures would not sell, and his wife had left him.

He thought of Jean Faulds' portrait, but he could not depend upon that for the money which he required. He had promised to burn it if it did not please the Laird —and it wouldn't please him, thought Darnay, I knew that from the beginning; he would hate it.

There was Elise, of course, but he would not accept a penny from Elise. He would rather die than crawl back

to Elise and ask her for money. Elise wanted him back
—on her own terms, for she had no use for failures—
but could he ever go back to Elise? He visualised her,
with her painted mouth, and her hard eyes, and,
remembering all the deceits and subterfuges which
were part of her nature, he suddenly shuddered. *How
could I have borne it?* he asked himself.

Darnay paced to and fro in his room, listening to
the rain which beat against the windows, and to the
eerie whistling of the wind. The old house rattled and
creaked and groaned like a soul in pain, and the river
rose rapidly and roared down the glen.

What a fool I was! Darnay thought. Did I imagine
that food fell from the skies like manna? No, I never
thought at all. I was so wrapped up in my painting
that I let everything else slide. Selfish, egotistical, vain
—that's what I am—dishonest too, for I've been eating
food that I can't pay for. I've been living in dreams,
but the world isn't made for dreamers. A man must
stand on his own feet; Bulloch said that; but it isn't
any use thinking of the past. What am I to do? That's
the question. . . .

It was four o'clock in the morning now—a dark
and desperate hour—and to Darnay it seemed the
darkest hour of his life. He had believed in himself,
believed that what he was doing was worth while,
believed that eventually the world would acknowledge
his genius, but now for the first time he began to have
doubts. Perhaps Hedley was right after all, and the
new medium was worthless—a mere freak. Perhaps
he, Darnay, had thrown away the substance for the
shadow. . . .

Suddenly Darney stood still and gazed at his reflection

in the streaming window-pane. He saw what he must do. He must go to London and see Hedley, and tell him the whole thing and, if Hedley could not sell the new pictures, he must paint some "pot-boilers," that was all. The prospect sickened his soul; it was a betrayal of his art to go back to the technique which he had rejected and outgrown. It was an acknowledgment of failure.

He fought against the decision for, although it was his own decision, it was so alien to his nature that he felt as if it were being forced upon him by an influence outside himself. He was literally torn in twain; the one Darnay, sensible, matter-of-fact, logical, pointing out the only way out of the mess, and the other Darnay resisting, and protesting almost hysterically that some other way must be found.

"What other way?" enquired the sensible Darnay. "You can't make money any other way. You aren't trained."

"I would rather sweep a crossing," declared the hysterical Darnay.

"And how much money would you make by that?" demanded the sensible one.

Darnay dragged a suitcase from the box-room and began to pack. He gathered up his belongings and flung them into the case, stopping every now and then to curse himself, or to reflect upon another aspect of the situation. What would he do if he found it impossible to go back to the old outgrown technique? If he painted pot-boilers and Hedley couldn't sell them ?

"Oh, heavens, I shall go mad if I think of all this!" cried Darnay aloud. "I mustn't think at all. I must act. I must go to London and find out what I can do. . . ."

It was daylight now, and the skies were grey. Rain still fell slantingly in the wind. Darnay heard sounds of activity in the kitchen premises and knew that Miss Bun was starting her day's work. He put on the grey lounge suit which he had decided to wear and went down to speak to her.

She was busy cleaning the range when he went into the kitchen, that dreadful old range which she had always declared was inhabited by an evil spirit.

"Miss Bun," he said, "I'm going to London."

"To London!" she cried in amazement. "You don't mean—you don't mean *now*?"

"I shall start immediately after breakfast. I'm going in the car——"

"But why——?" she began.

"Why? Because I've wakened up—that's why. What's been happening here while I was asleep?"

She gazed at him wide-eyed.

"How much do I owe in Beilford?" he asked in a strange bitter voice. "How much—eh? Who has been paying for my food? Tell me that."

Sue couldn't speak. She couldn't answer him to save her life.

He walked up and down the kitchen once or twice and then came to a halt and stood looking out of the window at the drizzling rain. The day was grey—all grey—and so was his heart—clouded over with misery.

"The truth is," he said. "The truth is I haven't had to—to bother about money. I made enough by my pictures—and then my wife—my wife has—money. She managed everything; she liked doing it. When she wanted money for the house she asked me for it and I wrote a cheque. I'm telling you this, but it isn't an excuse, of course. There is no excuse for dishonesty, is there?"

"Dishonesty!" she echoed in dismay.

"Yes, dishonesty. If a man goes into your father's shop and takes a loaf of bread that he can't pay for—that's dishonest, isn't it? He's put into prison for stealing, isn't he?"

"It's all right," cried Sue. "You'll pay it all. . . ."

She thought she would die if that hard, bitter voice went on any longer. It was like a knife twisted in her heart. She loved him so, and she had taken such care to shield him. She saw now that she had made a mistake in shielding him from trouble—but she had done it for love, and because she believed that he needed peace to develop his genius—and because she wanted this quiet life to go on. It was over now.

"What do I owe?" he asked in a quieter tone.

"I don't know."

"You don't know?"

"Not the exact amount. It doesn't matter, Mr. Darnay. The bills can wait. You'll pay them when the pictures are sold."

"*If* the pictures are sold," he amended; "and they won't sell. Hedley told me that and Hedley knows. . . . Why, in heaven's name, didn't you speak to me about it?"

"I wanted to spare you trouble."

"And you," he continued, brutal in his bitterness. "What about your wages? Why didn't you ask me for them?"

"I wasn't wanting money from you," said Sue in low tones.

He turned and looked at her. She was still kneeling

on the floor in front of the empty range; he saw that her face was white and drawn as if she had been ill for a long time, and there was a smudge of soot across her cheek.

"Oh!" cried Darnay. "Oh, heavens, what a selfish brute I am—and how blind! Can you ever forgive me?"

He was crossing the room towards her with his hands outstretched, and Sue half-rose to meet him—and then, before he had reached her, his hands fell to his sides and he turned away.

"What is it?" asked Sue. "Oh, Mr. Darnay, what is the matter?"

"Nothing. I've just remembered . . ." he replied in a queer husky voice that she scarcely recognised.

He did not say what it was that he had remembered, and Sue did not ask. There was a constraint between them now; they avoided each other's eyes, and talked lightly, and rather feverishly, of the preparations to be made for Darnay's departure. She was vaguely aware that something had nearly happened, but she did not know what it was. She only knew that Darnay had been on the point of saying something, and had refrained.

"I don't know how long I shall be away," he told her, aware as the words left his lips that this was a lie. He must never come back to Tog's Mill. It was good-bye to Tog's Mill, where he had been so happy—and good-bye to Sue.

"I'll write when I get to London," he continued. "I'll tell you how I get on. Don't you think it would be a good plan to shut up the house?"

"I'd rather not," she said quickly.

"The Bullochs would be glad to have you."

She shook her head.

"I'll write," repeated Darney. (It would be easier to write and tell her that he could not return, easier and safer. He must be very careful . . . she must never suspect . . . she would marry Hickie eventually, of course.) "I shall know what I'm going to do when I've seen Hedley," he continued. "I must take some of the pictures to show him. Could we do them up in paper, do you think?"

Sue thought they could. She followed him into the studio and helped him to put out the pictures so that he could choose which to take. A great many of them were mere studies, but there were about a dozen finished pictures of trees and hills, and clouded skies.

"Mr. Hedley is sure to like them," she declared with conviction.

Darnay smiled. "You think so?" he asked. "But remember you didn't like them much yourself."

"Not at first," she admitted. "They were so different from anything I had ever seen, but I like them now. They're like olives, I think."

"Olives!"

"You get to like them more and more," Sue explained gravely. "Grandfather once gave me a bottle of olives and I thought they were horrid, but he laughed at me so much that I went on eating them, and quite soon I began to like them; I like them better than chocolates now."

"Olives," repeated Darnay thoughtfully. "You're a most encouraging person, and the beauty of it is you're absolutely honest."

"Well, of course."

"Of course," he agreed, looking into her frank eyes

for a moment, and then turning quickly away, "I'll take the willow tree," he added, in a different voice, "and those two pictures of the snow."

"Will you take me?" she inquired, pointing to the picture of herself which had now been finished.

"No," said Darnay shortly.

"But it's so good."

"I shall keep it," he declared. "Put it back in the cupboard. I'll take this one of Beil Hill and that cloudy sky. . . ."

His voice died away and he stood for a moment or two, silent, visualising a future of clouded skies. Sue saw the far-off look and thought: He has gone already —his spirit has gone on before him to London.

There was little left to do when Darnay had gone and all the time in the world to do it. Sue locked the door behind her and set off for a walk, taking the hill path. It was still raining in the wind, but she did not mind that, for the rain was in tune with her mood and therefore more welcome than bright sunshine. She walked slowly and heavily, for there was no spring in her body, and wound her way wearily towards the hills. Part of her saw and noted the rain, the birds, the brownish-red buds on the bog myrtle, and part of her was withdrawn, suffering in a sort of dark, dumb misery. This was not the first time Sue had suffered mental agony, for she had suffered the same kind of loss when her mother died. Then as now, the whole light of her life had been extinguished in a moment— the whole light of her life.

She scarcely knew where she walked, and she was too wretched even to choose her path. She splashed through boggy places where the sphagnum was pink and spongy, she climbed rocks and tore her way through thickets of thorn. It was late afternoon when at last, for sheer weariness, she could walk no more and stood still, looking about her on the very top of the hills.

It had stopped raining by this time and the wind, blowing up from beyond the world's end, was scattering the last remnants of the clouds. They fled before its thrust like a woman in rags. Then the sun shone—at first in dim watery fashion, but soon with warmth and splendour, so that the drops of rain on the coarse grass looked like scattered diamonds. Sue heard the curlews crying, and saw a pair of them winging their way across the shoulder of the hill, they were harbingers of spring to these deserted moors.

Sue wandered about a little longer—she passed near the Graingers' cottage, but she had not the heart to go in and talk to May—and at last when the light began to fail she went down from the hills by the side of a little burn and found herself at the river's edge about two miles above the mill.

It was a lonely landscape now that dusk was falling. Light came from the horizon, chilly yellow light, but more clouds had blown up and obscured the greater part of the sky. They were deep purple in hue, like a stain of purple ink on yellow blotting paper. As Sue came home down the river path she saw the trees on the hilltops stand out against the light in delicate outline, and she thought they looked like a cavalcade trudging wearily along. There were trees like men, walking bent and twisted beneath heavy loads, and another cluster looked like a coach with horses. The river was loud in her ears, it was running down now but still brown and drumlie and turbulent. She noted the broken branches of the trees and marked how the coarse grass at the river's edge was smoothed and flattened, all in one direction, like well-brushed hair. Between the rocks were matted lumps of twigs and straw and mud, caught there and cemented into place by the weight of water pressing upon them.

At last she came to the willow which Darnay had painted and she saw that the spate had torn away the bank so that the little tree had fallen. It was half in and half out of the water, draggled and broken and sullied by the mud. . . .

Suddenly she was overcome by the tears which she had fought against all day, and, with a little wail of misery like a wounded animal, she sank down upon the ground and wept.

CHAPTER TWENTY-TWO

MR. BULLOCH was walking down the hill to Tog's Mill. He walked slowly, for he could not think what he was going to say when he got there. It was nearly four months since the first time he had visited Tog's Mill; he had had a delicate mission then, he had a much more delicate mission now.

He was standing on the doorstep, wondering what he should say, when the door was opened by Sue. "I saw you coming," she explained. "Why didn't you ring?"

"I was just going to," Mr. Bulloch declared, and then he added, "Sue, I came . . . ye're alone here, my dearie."

"How did you know?" she asked.

Somehow or other her voice sounded strange in his ears, it was a hard voice, and the vowels were different. He thought, She *has* changed. Susan was right.

"How did you know I was alone?" she repeated.

"Darnay wrote me," he replied. "He's sent me a cheque to pay off all his debts in the town; he's not coming back, Sue."

"I know that," said Sue.

She was leading the way into the kitchen and Bulloch followed her, wondering what to say. He wanted to find out the reason for Darnay's unexpected departure. Had there been a crisis? Had the situation, which had seemed so dangerous to an outsider, suddenly become impossible to themselves. Was Darnay running away, and, if so, what was he running away from, and what was Sue feeling about it?

"Ye'll come home now, Sue," he said at last. "Home to Granny and me—we're wanting ye badly."

"Yes," said Sue in a low voice. "Yes, I'll come. It's good of you, Grandfather. I've had a letter too. We are to shut up the house—he says so."

"Aye, it's the best thing," declared Bulloch with forced cheerfulness. "There's no sense in ye staying on here yerself. Ye'd like to see my letter, maybe," he added, taking a large square envelope from his pocket.

He was pleased and surprised when Sue after a moment's hesitation produced another envelope (which might have been its twin) and handed it to him, saying, "Here's mine—you can read it if you like."

They read each other's letters in silence.

REDMAYES HOTEL,
LONDON.

DEAR MR. BULLOCH,—You were so good to me when I was at Beilford that I am going to ask you for more kindness. This is what often happens, I am afraid. The fact is I left Beilford suddenly and unexpectedly because I found the necessity for raising money to pay my bills. I have got a commission for a portrait and am starting work on it to-day. I enclose a cheque which I have received in advance, and I should be very grateful if you will pay what I owe in Beilford. Miss Pringle knows the amounts due to the various shops. If there is any residue it would make me very happy if Miss Pringle will accept it as a small token of my appreciation of all she has done for me. When the portrait is finished

I shall go abroad. I know that I am asking a great deal when I ask you and Miss Pringle to take so much trouble on my behalf, but I have no other friends in Beilford—nor in any other part of the world for that matter.

This has been a difficult letter to write. I have so much to say, but it is better that I should not say it. I have done enough harm. Please find enclosed my cheque for 100 guineas.

Yours sincerely,
JOHN DARNAY.

•　　•　　•　　•　　•　　•　　•

REDMAYES HOTEL,
LONDON.

DEAR MISS BUN,—London is a big noisy place after Tog's Mill, and I am feeling rather dazed, but I must not complain for I had nearly four months of peace. The pictures have not met with much success here, and Mr. Hedley does not think they will sell. It seems that Londoners do not care for olives. However, the money difficulty is solved which is the main thing. I am to paint the portrait of a lady. She is a fat white lady, but her husband loves her so much that he is willing to pay a hundred guineas to have her immortalised. I think a hundred guineas should clear off all my Beilford debts. I am to paint the lady in full evening dress, and I am to paint her in my old manner —all this for a hundred guineas in advance. When the portrait is finished I shall go away—perhaps to Italy or Germany, or perhaps to Timbuctoo. I am leaving you a lot to do, but your grandfather will help you. Will you shut up the house and pay off all my debts so that Beilford will think charitably of the mad painter?

You must not go on living alone at Tog's Mill—not good for you, Miss Bun—and your grandparents will love to have you, so that will be all right. The London sparrows are dirty and bedraggled, they have not a fine beech hedge to shelter in, nor a kind Miss Bun to give them crumbs.

You will notice I have not said, "Thank you for all you did for me." The truth is it would be quite absurd to try to thank you, I have not words. Besides, I know you hate gratitude.

Good-bye, Miss Bun. Forget about me.

JOHN DARNAY.

"Well," said Mr. Bulloch when he had finished reading the letter. "Well, that's settled then; that's fine. Ye'll come to us, Sue. There'll be no holding Granny when she hears." He spoke with forced heartiness for the situation was no clearer to him than before. He realised that there was a good deal "between the lines" in Sue's letter from Darnay, but he could not read it. (All that about London people not liking olives. What did it mean?) Sue was upset, of course—that was obvious—but he could not tell to what extent she was upset. His one idea now was to get her home to Susan —Susan would know how to talk to her.

Sue had finished reading the other letter now. She folded it up and handed it back to its owner.

"When will ye come, Sue?" he enquired anxiously.

"I'll pack now," she said; "there's no use staying on. I'll come back with you if you'll wait."

"Fine," declared Mr. Bulloch. "Fine, Sue. I'll help ye to go round the house and snib the windows."

Sue left Tog's Mill in a hurry for she felt that if she waited she would never have the strength to leave it at all. They went through the house together closing the windows and drawing down the blinds. Far in the distance she could hear her grandfather's voice talking to her in cheerful tones, and, more strangely still, her own voice replying quite sensibly, but the real Sue was not there at all, she was withdrawn from the world, sunk in a pit of misery.

The Bullochs were very kind to Sue—they were almost too kind—they spoke to her cheerfully, and fed her on the fat of the land. In fact, they treated her as if she were recovering from a serious illness. Mr. Bulloch explained to her that the business was to be hers when he retired. "And there's no need to thank me," he declared, cutting short Sue's protestations of gratitude, "for there's nobody else I could leave it to when I leave this world, and it's certain I couldn't take it with me."

They were sitting in the office, for Mr. Bulloch had called Sue into his sanctum to discuss the matter thoroughly, and Sue looked round at the laden shelves and sniffed the fine odour of spices that filled the air—and pinched herself to make sure she was not dreaming.

"All mine?" she asked increduously.

"All yer very own," he replied, smiling. "Once I'm dead ye can do what ye like with it."

"Well, I hope it'll be a long time, anyway," she said in her matter-of-fact way.

He laughed at that. "I hope so too," he told her. "I'm in no hurry to leave this world—it's not a bad world when all's said and done—but it's as well to have things settled."

"I'll have to learn . . ." Sue said thoughtfully.

"Aye, ye'll have a lot to learn," agreed Bulloch, "and that's why I'm wanting ye here. Hickie will help ye, Sue—he's a good man, is Hickie—and ye could trust him with anything, for he's safe as the bank." He hesitated for a moment, wondering if he had said enough. If Sue would only marry Bob Hickie the safety of the business would be assured. Sue and Hickie together would run the place as it should be run, and Bulloch could retire with an easy mind. It was no new idea, this; he and Susan had often talked about it and had decided that it was the best thing for everybody concerned. Hickie was just the man for Sue; steady and reliable and thoroughly good; he had been in love with Sue for years, and had never looked at anybody else. Such faithfulness should be rewarded—or so the Bullochs thought—but Mr. Bulloch was the last man to want to coerce Sue, she would have to come to it of her own free will.

"I'm wanting ye to see the whole thing," continued Mr. Bulloch after a little pause. "Ye can help in the shop, and ye can help me with the ordering, and ye can help Hickie to unpack the cases. But ye must get out too, for the fresh air's good for ye, Sue, and there's plenty of time to learn everything. I'm not wanting to retire just yet."

It was all arranged. At first Sue felt too miserable to take a real interest in the working of Mr. Bulloch's business, but she was so grateful to her grandfather that she simulated an interest she did not feel, and after about a week the thing gripped her and she began to see the fascination of it. Sue might have settled down quite comfortably if it had not been for Hickie.

Bob Hickie had been patient for a long time. He had been content to wait for Sue, and to hope that some day she would look his way, but, now that she was actually here and he was seeing her constantly, his patience began to wear thin. He loved her more than ever and wanted her as he had never wanted her before. Sue was aware of his devotion, and it made her uncomfortable because she could not return it, and because she did not know how to behave to him. If she were kind to Bob he immediately responded and jumped to the conclusion that she was "coming round," and if she were cold and distant he went about looking like a whipped dog.

The other assistants watched the game with interest, for the progress of Hickie's love affair had a direct bearing on the future of the business, and therefore on their own lives. They had not been told that Sue Pringle was Mr. Bulloch's heir, but they were aware of it all the same, and if Sue married Hickie then he would be the boss when Mr. Bulloch retired. It was an added discomfort to Sue to know that the staff were watching her treatment of Bob, and she was fully aware of the smiles and nods which were exchanged between them whenever she spoke to him. They thought she was playing fast and loose with Bob, and this was the last thing she wanted to do. She was far too kind-hearted, and far too fond of Bob to take pleasure in his discomforture. The whole affair was extremely complicated and Sue did not know what to do, for she was afraid that if she was obliged to tell Bob plainly that she could not marry him, he would leave Beilford altogether, and this would be most inconvenient for her grandfather. Mr. Bulloch had always depended upon Bob Hickie, and now that he was getting old he depended upon him more and more. "I don't know what I would do without Hickie," was a phrase that fell almost daily from Mr. Bulloch's lips.

CHAPTER TWENTY-THREE

ONE day when Sue had been at the Bullochs for about a fortnight Mr. Bulloch received another letter from Darnay. It arrived just as he was going upstairs to tea, so he took it with him to read at his leisure.

"Where's Sue?" he enquired as he sat down at the table, and smiled at his wife.

"She's away to Tog's Mill to air the house," Mrs. Bulloch replied. "I offered her to take the girl, but she said she'd rather go herself. Are ye wanting her, Thomas?"

"It's a letter from Mr. Darnay," said Bulloch, and he slit the envelope.

Mrs. Bulloch sat down and poured out the tea. She glanced at her husband's face and saw that it was grave and frowning.

"Is there something wrong?" she enquired anxiously.

"Wrong? Aye, there's something very far wrong. . . . By heaven, I wish we'd never laid eyes on the man!"

"I've wished that a long while," declared his wife. She waited a little, watching his face as he read and re-read the crackling sheets of paper, and at last she could be patient no longer. "Thomas, what's in it?" she inquired.

"Read it for yourself, woman," he replied, and put the letter into her hands.

She found her reading spectacles, and put them on,

but by this time she was so upset and frightened that the clear black "painter's writing" danced up and down before her eyes. "I canna' make head nor tail of it, Thomas," she said in a trembling voice.

"It's clear enough. What's the matter with ye that ye cannot read it?"

"I don't know; it's queer writing, Thomas. I think ye'd best tell me about it in plain words. I'm awful stupid. . . ."

He took the letter away and patted her shoulder, for her pathetic admission had melted his heart. "It's me that's stupid," he declared. "Here's what it is in plain words. Mr. Darnay's wife is wanting to divorce him."

"That's awful," she agreed; "but what has it to do with us?"

"She's fixed the blame on Sue."

"The blame!" cried Mrs. Bulloch in horror-stricken tones. "Thomas! Does that mean . . . Oh, Thomas, it doesna' mean——"

"It means nothing, but what I've said," Bulloch declared. "She's wanting to divorce him and she's fixed the blame on our Sue. Here's what he says, Susan. 'I need not tell you that the whole case is absolutely false, for that would be an impertinence on my part, but I am afraid we must face the fact that we have no proof of its falsity. The man who visited Tog's Mill, and whom we thought to be a burglar, was a private detective employed by my wife. I have consulted my lawyer, and he agrees that the man overstepped the law in entering the house in our absence, but we have no real proof that he did enter the house except the cigarette end which was thrown away. I think you should consult your lawyer. If you and he and Miss

Pringle decide that we should fight I shall fall in with your wishes (money need be no object as I have had several orders for portraits. I refused them, but they are still open to me). I want to do what is best—or least bad—from Miss Pringle's point of view. If the suit is undefended my lawyer says it will go through the courts with little or no publicity. If we defend the suit there will be more publicity. On the other hand, you may think that we ought to defend ourselves from the calumny, and that it would be wrong not to do so. I shall abide by your decision.' That's the gist of it," declared Bulloch. "The man goes on to call himself every name under the sun, but that doesn't help us much."

"Not defend themselves," Mrs. Bulloch cried. "But that would be awful, Thomas. They ought to tell the judge that they did nothing wrong—he would see they were innocent then."

"How would he see that?" enquired her husband in a dry tone.

"He would see when he looked at them of course. Nobody could think ill of our Sue."

Bulloch laughed mirthlessly.

"Thomas!" she cried. "What are you thinking on? The judge would see justice done, wouldn't he?"

"He would see the facts, Susan, and the facts are that the two of them lived alone at Tog's Mill for four months and more. He wouldn't look further than that. I'll go down and see Mr. Henderson, of course, but I'm thinking he'll say the same."

"What will folks say!" cried Mrs. Bulloch, wringing her hands.

"Nobody need know a thing about it. I'll see what

Mr. Henderson says, but that's my view. We'll keep the whole thing dark—we'll not tell Will, even . . ."

"Will!" exclaimed his wife. "If ye tell Will he'll tell Grace, and it'll be all over Beilford by nightfall."

"I said we'd not tell Will," repeated Mr. Bulloch patiently. "We'll tell nobody—nobody except Mr. Henderson, and solicitors are paid to keep their mouths shut. Dinna' fash, woman," he added tenderly, laying his hand on her thin shoulder; "we know our Sue and that's the main thing."

She caught his hand. "Wait," she said. "Wait, Thomas, could we not do anything? Could we not go to Mrs. Darnay herself? Maybe the puir soul's miserable about it; she'd be glad to know it was all a mistake. Maybe she's fond of him yet."

"Ye'd not think ill of the devil, Susan."

"Why should we think ill of her?"

"Because of the facts, woman, because of the facts. The whole thing is Mrs. Darnay's fault, she went off and left her man in the lurch. Does that look as if she's fond of him? I can't see *you* traipsing off to London and leaving me to fend for myself. . . . Ye're not thinking of it, by any chance, are ye?"

"Ye're daft, Thomas. What would I do in London?"

"Ye'd enjoy yerself," he told her. "Ye'd be going out to the pictures and the theatres—or maybe to one of these night clubs."

"Ye're clean daft," Mrs. Bulloch declared, smiling in spite of herself at the absurdity of the idea.

"Well, well," he said, patting her shoulder again. "Well, well, it's a great relief to my mind that ye're staying on here, for there's no other body can cook bacon to my taste."

He left her laughing, which was perhaps his intention, and, taking his hat from the peg, went off to speak to Mr. Henderson about the disaster which had befallen them.

Sue was already so miserable about Darnay that the new development made little difference to her. She had answered his letter but had not heard from him again, and he seemed to have disappeared completely out of her life. The new development did not bring him any closer for it was so extraordinary that she scarcely believed it; she knew, of course, that people did divorce each other—just as she knew that people sometimes flew to America, but both were equally incredible to Sue. The fact that she was a co-respondent in the case of "Darnay v. Darnay and Pringle" made no difference to her life; she rose at the same hour, she helped in the shop, she ate her meals and went to bed at night.

Mr. Bulloch replied to Darnay's letter in terms dictated by Mr. Henderson, saying that his solicitor advised that the case should be allowed to go through the courts undefended, but he added a little bit at the end on his own responsibility. "Sue says she stayed on at Tog's Mill on her own," wrote Mr. Bulloch in his old-fashioned copperplate hand. "She says you told her to go home and she would not go. She says will you please remember this, and not feel too bad about what has happened. We are not telling anybody about it, and Mr. Henderson says it is not likely anybody here will get to know. When Sue settles down and gets married I will need to tell the man, but it will make no difference to him for he knows Sue as well as we do. It matters little what the world says if your friends know you have done nothing wrong, so ' dinna' fash,' Mr. Darnay, and remember none of us bear you ill-will."

Mr. Bulloch hesitated for a moment before he dropped his letter into the box, for he wondered suddenly if he had done right to mention Hickie. . . . Nothing was settled yet between Sue and Hickie, of course. . . . But I didn't actually mention him, thought Mr. Bulloch, frowning with the effort to remember his exact words. The letter dropped into the empty box with a thud.

Although Sue had so much to occupy her mind she had not forgotten her friends the Graingers, and sometimes on a Sunday afternoon she would walk up to their cottage on the moor and spend the evening with them. It was more difficult for May to visit her, for the chickens could not be left, and now when the hatching time had come it was necessary for somebody to be constantly on the spot, watching the incubators and testing the temperature of the "foster mother." The Graingers had their troubles as well as Sue—for the moors were wild and hawks and stoats took toll of their stock, but they met adversity with courage and were not dismayed. The brother and sister were devoted to each other, but they had been parted for years—May had been working in Glasgow as a typist, and Alec as a clerk in Birmingham. A small legacy had enabled them to train themselves in chicken farming and to start a farm of their own, but they had very little money left and they began to realise that unless they could make a success of their new venture, and do so

within the next year, they might have to give it up
and return to their office stools.

Sue understood all this, and she approached her
grandfather on the subject, suggesting that he should
buy the Graingers' produce and make a special feature
of it, and Mr. Bulloch agreed.

"Away up to the cottage and see them about it,"
he said, smiling at her kindly. "Ye can put through
the deal yerself, Sue. It will be good practice for
ye."

Sue walked over to see the Graingers that very afternoon. She was glad to be the bearer of good tidings.
It was a fine day, sunny and bright with a strong breeze
which fluttered her skirt like a banner and blew roses
into her pale cheeks. Sue took off her hat, for it was
pleasant to feel the cool wind flowing through her hair.
She felt like a speck upon the moors to-day for they
were deserted and the clouds were high—there was no
mist or vapour to hide the spacious emptiness of the
hills.

The Graingers were digging in their garden when
Sue came down the rutty track to the gate. She called
and waved to them from afar off and May relinquished
her spade and ran to meet her like a child.

"Sue, where have you been?" she cried breathlessly.
"We thought you'd forgotten us."

Alec followed more slowly. He was a well-built,
solid young man with a pleasant open face, but he had
not the verve or the vitality which made his sister so
attractive.

They all three leaned on the gate while Sue unfolded
her plan. "Grandfather will pay you market prices,"
she told them; "and he can lift the eggs when he sends

up your order from the shop. That will save you the expense of carriage, won't it?"

"Oh, Sue, it's a splendid plan!" cried May.

Alec was silent for a few moments, his face was grave. "We'll have to think it over," he said dubiously.

"Think it over!" echoed Sue. "Why should you need to think it over? I thought you'd be pleased."

"There's a lot to think of," replied Alec. "For one thing, Mr. Bulloch would have to get the eggs cheaper if he lifted them himself. May and I are not going to take advantage of our friendship with you."

"What use are friends——?" began Sue, but she got no further, for May seized her arm and dragged her down the path towards the cottage.

"You had better finish the digging, Alec," she said over her shoulder. "You'll just have time to finish the row while I get the tea."

Once they were in the kitchen with the door shut May proceeded to explain her brother's attitude to the new plan. "Alec is so independent," she said. "You mustn't mind if he seems ungrateful. It's because he won't accept favours from anybody."

"But it's not a favour," Sue declared. "Grandfather will be glad of the eggs—and the honey too, when the time comes for it—he would need to pay market prices wherever he got them."

"Leave it to me," said May. "I'll manage Alec all right. The plan is an absolute godsend—almost too good to be true—things are not going too well for us at the moment."

"You're so brave!" exclaimed Sue impulsively.

"Not really brave," replied May with a faint smile. "I'm an awful coward at night. I think of the bills, and try to calculate how much money we've got left, but it's no use going about with a long face and moaning over our bad luck for that would only make things worse. I've got to think of Alec and keep him cheerful and that's a great help. It's when you've only got yourself to think of that it's difficult to smile through troubles."

Sue digested this philosophy in silence for she saw that she could apply it to her own case. And May's troubles are worse than mine, Sue thought as she walked home across the moor, for I'm sure of a roof over my head and plenty to eat. My troubles are imaginary, they are all in myself and the best thing to do is to pull myself together and make the best of life. She determined to cease brooding about Darnay. She had got to do without him, so she must try to do without him cheerfully and find what pleasures she could in small things. She had a comfortable home, and kind friends and interesting work; it was ungrateful to be dissatisfied with life.

CHAPTER TWENTY-FOUR

"Could ye spare Sue this afternoon?" Mrs. Bulloch enquired one day as they were sitting down to dinner.

"Could I?" said Mr. Bulloch, smiling. "I see by the gleam in yer eye that I'll *need* to spare her, whether or no. What's on this afternoon, Susan?"

"The Bonnywall Gardens are open," replied Mrs. Bulloch, "and I was thinking Sue and I might go over and have a look at them. The rhodies will be lovely, Thomas. Could ye not come yerself?"

"I could not," declared her husband firmly; "but that's no reason why you two shouldn't go. I suppose ye'll take the bus?"

"I suppose so," replied Mrs. Bulloch without much enthusiasm.

Mr. Bulloch roared with laughter. "What a woman!" he cried. "Ye know perfectly well I'd not let ye take the bus. As a matter of fact, there's an order going over to the Admiral this afternoon, and I'll send the big van. There's plenty of room for the two of ye on the front seat."

Sue was aware that the expedition had been planned for her benefit, and she was very grateful to her grandmother for the kind thought. She put on her best hat, and powdered her nose and was ready at the appointed hour. Mrs. Bulloch was ready too, and was looking very smart in a new spring coat; it was a great outing for her, and Sue could see that she was filled with the determination to enjoy every moment of it. They drove over to Bonnywall House very comfortably in the big van, and on the way Mrs. Bulloch and Dunn, the vanman, discussed the march of progress. She reminded him of the days when it took over an hour to drive to Bonnywall; that was before motors came in, of course.

"Aye, it was old Prince we had," agreed Dunn. "He was a fine old horse was Prince. I was gey sorry to part with him when Maister Bulloch bought the Ford van."

"We had to walk up the hill," Mrs. Bulloch said, settling herself comfortably in the padded seat. It was evident that she preferred modern transport and had no sentimental regrets for old Prince.

"Aye, it's changed days," continued Dunn. "I mind one day—it was very like this—when I drove you an' Miss Mary over to Bonnywall House. They were having a bazaar or something. Folks never thought on opening their gardens to the public then."

"I remember it too," declared Mrs. Bulloch. "We were late coming home that day, for I lost Mary in the crowd and never found her until the whole affair was over."

Sue scarcely listened to the talk. The beauty of the country made her heart ache and despite all her good resolutions she could not help thinking of Darnay. If he were here now there would be plenty of subjects for his brush. Winter had fled and spring was so beautiful; a slow awakening, sunshine gilding the hills, fat buds on the chestnut trees, and a scatter of yellow primroses in the sheltered hollows.

There was a long hill up to the gates of Bonnywall House, and when they reached the top they turned into an avenue between high stone gate-posts carved with the arms of the Lang family. Dunn slowed down here for the avenue was crowded with cars and pedestrians who had come from far and near to inspect the Admiral's rhododendrons.

"We'll get out," said Mrs. Bulloch who had no desire to drive up to the front door in her husband's van. "We'll just get out here, and ye can meet us at the big gates at six."

"Any time suits me," agreed Dunn pleasantly. "I'll maybe take a wee stroll round the rhodies mysel'."

Mrs. Bulloch and Sue got out of the van and walked up to the house. It was well worth a visit on its own account for parts of it were very old, dating from the fourteenth century. It was set on a slight eminence surrounded by lawns and trees and its old square tower looked solid and permanent as a rock.

"It's a fine old place," said Sue, looking at it with interest. "Wouldn't it be splendid to own a place like that?"

"It would be hard to keep," replied her grandmother dubiously. "I wouldn't like it, myself."

"But you'd have servants, Granny."

"Aye, a regiment of them, eating their heads off," retorted Mrs. Bulloch. "No, no, Sue, one girl is enough for me. A wee cosy house and one girl to do the scrubbing—that's all I want, and all I've ever wanted. It's lucky too," added Mrs. Bulloch thoughtfully, "for it's all I'm ever likely to have."

They stood and looked at the house for a few moments longer, and then Mrs. Bulloch shook herself out of her trance. "Come away, Sue," she said briskly. "The gardens are round at the other side. I've been here often, so I know the way. It's a pity the Admiral never married, isn't it? The place goes to a nephew when he's dead."

"Why did he never marry, I wonder," said Sue as she followed her grandmother down the path.

"Dear knows," declared Mrs. Bulloch. "He was a fine young fellow with a joke for everybody. All the young ladies were mad about him. He used to come over to Beilford in his wee car—before the war it was—but yer grandfather and I were better pleased when he stayed away."

"I thought you said he was nice, Granny!"

"He was a bit too nice," replied Mrs. Bulloch enigmatically.

Sue was about to enquire further into this mysterious pronouncement when a party of people came round the corner of the house and met them face to face. It was the Admiral himself with Mrs. Murray of Greenkirk and several other ladies. Mrs. Bulloch would have turned back if there had been time, for she was rather shy of "gentry" and preferred to give them a wide berth when possible, but there was no time to turn back.

"Mrs. Bulloch!" exclaimed Sir Rupert, stopping and holding out his hand. "How are you, Mrs. Bulloch? I haven't seen you for ages."

"I'm well enough, thank ye, sir," she replied, her thin face somewhat pink with excitement.

"That's splendid," declared the Admiral heartily. "I'm glad you've come over. And is this——"

"My granddaughter, Sue Pringle," Mrs. Bulloch told him.

Sue held out her hand and felt it taken in a firm

grip. She was conscious of a pair of keen eyes searching her face, searching it so intently that her own eyes dropped before the glance.

"How d'you do, sir," she said in a soft, low voice.

"I'm very glad . . ." he said, a trifle incoherently. "The rhodies are early—and the daffodils. I'd like to show them to you——"

"But yer friends!" exclaimed Mrs. Bulloch, nodding towards the ladies who had passed on and were now waiting indecisively at the corner. "Sue and I'll manage quite well," she added. "I know the way."

Sir Rupert took no notice of her protest, he had begun to talk to Sue and was leading her towards the sheltered wood where his early rhododendrons were in bloom.

"This way," he said, opening a little gate. "Tell me what you're doing now. Are you still with Darnay?"

Sue hesitated and looked back at her grandmother, for she was a little shy of the Admiral, and besides it seemed somewhat rude to go off and leave Mrs. Bulloch in the lurch.

"This way," said the Admiral again, smiling at her kindly. "I'd like to take you round myself."

There was nothing for it but to walk through the gate which was being held open so invitingly, and leave Mrs. Bulloch to follow—which she did with all speed.

"I'm afraid we're going too fast for you," said Sir Rupert with solicitude. "There's a sheltered seat here. and one or two rugs. Perhaps you would like to sit down for a few minutes."

"Sue and I will be fine and comfortable here," declared Mrs. Bulloch somewhat pointedly, but unfortunately her host did not take the hint; he placed a rug over her knees and led Sue away to see the rhododendrons.

This was not at all what Mrs. Bulloch had intended. She had felt slightly uneasy at the way in which Sir Rupert had singled out Sue and carried her off, but she was now quite alarmed. Anchored to the seat by the rug—which had been firmly tucked in by Sir Rupert's own hands and was therefore, in some strange way, as immovable as steel shackles—Mrs. Bulloch watched her granddaughter disappear into the wood.

"But it's nonsense," said Mrs. Bulloch to herself. "I'm just daft; the Admiral's old enough to be her father."

This reflection, though it comforted her a good deal, did not entirely allay her anxiety, for she had always been a little dubious about Rupert Lang. In the old days, when Mary's loveliness was turning the head of every man in the district, Mr. Lang had been a constant visitor at the shop. It was impossible—so the Bullochs decided—that any young man should find himself in need of odd pounds of sugar and butter, or even of peppermint balls in such enormous quantities, and they had come to the conclusion that he had designs upon their one ewe lamb. They talked it over together and Mr. Bulloch decided—most reluctantly—that he must speak to Mr. Lang and have it out with him, but the interview had never taken place for the war started, and Mr. Lang disappeared, and Mary married Will Pringle. Once Mary was safely married, and the somewhat wild and irresponsible young man had become a captain and, later, a distinguished Admiral in His Majesty's Navy, Mrs. Bulloch's feelings had changed and she had felt proud of Rupert Lang—as all Beilford was proud—for it was a great thing to have known and spoken to Admiral Sir Rupert Lang when he was a mere lad and as full of mischief as a terrier pup.

All this flashed through Mrs. Bulloch's mind, and her old fears returned. Sir Rupert was not young any longer of course, but once a rip, always a rip. . . . "Oh, dear!" exclaimed Mrs. Bulloch in dismay. "Oh, dear, why didn't I say I would go too; but I couldn't, somehow."

The minutes passed on leaden feet, and at last she became quite desperate—they would have had time to inspect a whole forest of rhododendrons by now—she threw off the rug and rose to her feet, determined to pursue the couple into the wood and see what was happening.

At this moment Sir James Faulds appeared from the direction of the house. He strolled in through the little gate, looking very neat and dapper in a grey flannel suit and a soft hat.

"Hullo, Mrs. Bulloch!" he said, smiling at her in a friendly manner. "How are you? Everybody seems to be here to-day. It's lovely, isn't it? Have you seen the rhodies yet?"

"I was just going to, sir," replied Mrs. Bulloch, somewhat flustered by his sudden appearance.

"Have you anybody with you?" he enquired. "Is Bulloch here?"

"No, sir. At least . . . yes . . . I mean, he's not here to-day but my granddaughter, Sue, came with me."

"Where is she?"

"In the wood," replied Mrs. Bulloch. "They've been

a long time, and I was just thinking I'd go and look
for them. The Admiral is showing——"

"What!" cried the Laird. "Is she there—alone—with
him?"

These extraordinary words, and the obvious dismay
of the speaker frightened poor Mrs. Bulloch out of
her wits.

"Maircy!" she exclaimed. "Are ye thinking . . .
But surely . . . Oh, maircy, we'll need to find them."

The Laird was obviously of the same opinion, for he
seized Mrs. Bulloch's arm and propelled her forcibly
down the path. "It's perfectly all right," he declared
incoherently. "He'll not have had time. Besides, he
practically promised . . . I mean it's quite all right,
there's nothing to worry about—nothing at all. Still,
you never know. You'd like to see the rhododendrons,
wouldn't you?"

Mrs. Bulloch was too breathless to reply—even if she
had been able to find any rational reply to such ravings.

"They're beautiful, aren't they?" he continued,
dragging her past bush after bush of blazing blossoms
without so much as a glance in their direction. "Such
colour! But they've no scent—or none to speak of—
and that's a pity."

She was far too frantic to care whether or not
rhododendrons had any scent. "Oh, dear!" she gasped.
"I never should have let her go with him—but I never
thought . . ."

It was warm, for the wood was sheltered and the sun
streamed down like a golden shower. Mrs. Bulloch
was not suitably clad for running races in the heat.
Her face was crimson when at last Sir James stopped
dead and pointed through the bushes.

"There they are!" he exclaimed.

Mrs. Bulloch stopped too, and peered through the thick shining leaves. She saw the two figures standing on the path deep in conversation. At that moment Sue's laugh rang out through the wood. It was a merry laugh, and brought a good deal of comfort to her friends.

"It's all right, he hasn't told her," said the Laird, with a sigh of relief.

"Told her what?" enquired his companion.

She received no answer, and the words were so strange that afterwards, when she thought it over, she decided that she must have misunderstood the noble gentleman. She followed him round the bushes, trying to compose herself—mopping her face with her handkerchief, and putting her hat straight—for, now that her fears had proved groundless, they seemed utterly ridiculous and shameful. Despite her efforts to improve her appearance, however, she did not fail to notice Sir Rupert's face when he saw who it was arriving to disturb his tête-à-tête. He looked annoyed, and perhaps that was natural, but he also looked uncomfortable and a trifle guilty. In fact, he looked for all the world like a little boy who has been discovered in the act of stealing jam.

"Hallo, Rupert!" said the Laird. "You're wanted at the house. I've been looking everywhere for you. How are you, Miss Pringle? It's a lovely day."

"What do they want me for?" enquired Sir Rupert irritably.

Sir James did not reply to the question, he said good-bye to Mrs. Bulloch and her granddaughter, slipped his hand through the Admiral's arm and led him reluctantly away.

"Well, I never did!" exclaimed Mrs. Bulloch, sub-
siding into a convenient seat. "Of all the queer set
outs . . . Maircy, I'm hot!"

"What *have* you been doing?" enquired Sue anxiously.
"Poor Granny, your face is like a beetroot. Are you
feeling all right?"

"All right!" echoed her grandparent. "It's a wonder
I'm alive. What with the fright and the Laird rushing
me down the path like a fire engine . . ."

"What on earth frightened you?" Sue demanded.

Mrs. Bulloch hesitated for a moment, and then she
smiled. "Maybe it was a lion," she said.

The whole affair was absolutely inexplicable to Sue,
and Mrs. Bulloch refused to clear up the mystery, or
indeed to make any addition to the absurd statement
she had already vouchsafed.

"But, Granny, it couldn't have been a lion," Sue
declared, perplexed beyond measure by the extraordinary way Mrs. Bulloch was behaving. "Did you
see it in the bushes? Was it a big dog or what?"

"Maybe it was."

"Was he frightened too?"

"He ran hard enough," declared Mrs. Bulloch; "but
never mind that now. We'll take a walk round and see
the rhodies. What was the Admiral telling ye about
them?"

Apparently the Admiral had told Sue very little
about the rhodies, and Sue found it difficult to say
what it was they had talked about. "He was very nice,"
she declared in answer to Mrs. Bulloch's searching
enquiries. "He asked what I was doing and all
that. I like the Admiral, he's a fatherly kind of
man."

"Fatherly, is he? That's grand," said Mrs. Bulloch, with a sigh of relief.

Meanwhile, the Admiral was being led firmly in the direction of the house, his anger rising at every step. "What the hell!" he was enquiring. "Really, Jamie; can I not have a chat with a young woman in my own garden without interference from you."

"Not that young woman," declared the baronet firmly.

"She's a very nice young woman. Very nice indeed. In fact, she's charming."

"All the more reason——"

"But I wasn't saying anything at all—not a blessed thing. I wanted to have a good look at her, and see what she was like."

"Who she was like, you mean."

"Well, perhaps," admitted Admiral Lang.

"Did you think she was like you?"

"God forbid!"

"She's like her grandmother," declared Sir James. "That's who she's like. You think she's like your mother because your mother had red hair."

"Auburn," interrupted the Admiral. "It's exactly the same colour, James; that rich, dark auburn——"

"For pity's sake! How many of us have hair like that? I could name half a dozen straight off."

"And her hands——"

"Rupert," said his friend sternly. "You've a bee in your bonnet about that girl. You'll raise hell if you're not careful. The old woman suspects something——"

"She doesn't!"

"She does indeed. She was scared to death when I found her."

"Great Scott!"

"Promise me you'll leave the girl alone," adjured Sir James. "I'll never have a peaceful moment if you don't."

"I'll promise, Jamie," said the Admiral meekly.

CHAPTER TWENTY-FIVE

THE warehouse was closed for the night, but there was still work to be done, and Sue was helping Bob Hickie to unpack some cases which had arrived in the afternoon. There were two cases from China, with queer lettering marked upon them in jet black ink, and one from Marseilles, larger but less romantic. Hickie had opened the Chinese cases first and now he was busy unpacking jars of ginger, and handing them to Sue to put away on the shelves.

"Sue," he said, pausing for a moment and looking up into her face with his soft brown eyes. "Sue, are you liking it here?"

"I like lots of work," Sue told him.

"You're a good worker," he agreed. "I like work too, and this is interesting work. I like to see the cases arrive and all the good things come out and fill up the shelves. I've been here nine years now."

Sue nodded.

"It's nine years since I saw you first," continued Hickie; "you were just a wee girl."

"I was fourteen," Sue told him in a matter-of-fact voice.

"Fourteen," he agreed. "That's not very old, but you were always awfully serious. You were never one to tease the life out of a person like some I could name."

Sue was busy wiping the jars and polishing them. She arranged several on the shelf with great care before she answered, "I could never see the fun of that."

"You're so kind-hearted, Sue," he told her earnestly.

Sue was touched by his words, and by the dog-like devotion in his eyes. She liked Bob immensely—he was so good and kind, and hard working—and she knew that he loved her dearly. It would be the best thing for everybody if she married Bob; it would solve all her problems and her grandparents would be beside themselves with delight. She was so tired of battling with her misery, of trying to be cheerful and bright when her heart was breaking. It was no use thinking of Mr. Darnay any more, for he had gone out of her life for ever. Why shouldn't she just say yes to Bob, and make him happy? *I'll do it*, she thought, and she turned and smiled at Bob; she was aware that a very little encouragement would bring Bob to the point.

Bob Hickie was groping in the crate so he did not see the smile which had been produced for his benefit. "What a pretty colour!" he said, holding up a pale-yellow jar with little blue Chinese figures painted on it. "I like it's shape too. It's queer to think the crate was packed by a Chinese man and it's being unpacked by you and me."

"Very queer," said Sue. The smile of encouragement had faded now, and she could not produce another to save her life.

Afterwards as she lay in bed and thought about the incident, Sue was aghast. I'm crazy, she decided. I'm fit for a madhouse. I ought to be locked up. Fancy if I had taken Bob; we'd be engaged this minute, and I would be lying here wondering how on earth I was going to get out of marrying him! She thought about it for a long time, pitying Bob out of the pain in her own heart, and suddenly she saw her way clear. Bob could not be allowed to go away, for he was necessary to the business, but she could go herself; there was absolutely nothing to prevent her from leaving Beilford. Why hadn't she seen that before?

Sue broached her new plan to the Bullochs next morning and met with less opposition than she had expected.

"Maybe a wee change would do ye good," Mrs. Bulloch said thoughtfully.

"Why not go to Bella for a while?" added Mr. Bulloch. "I'll miss ye badly, of course, but Granny's right, and a wee change would do ye no harm."

She had not thought where to go, and one place seemed as good as another. There was no reason why she should not go to London and stay with Aunt Bella. If Aunt Bella would have her.

"Bella will be glad to have ye," declared Mrs. Bulloch with conviction; "and it's so nice and near the station if ye're wanting home. Do ye remember her, Sue?"

Sue remembered Aunt Bella—a cheerful, bustling woman who occasionally came to Beilford to stay with the Bullochs. "She's not very like Grandfather, is she?" Sue remarked.

"She's only his half-sister," said Mrs. Bulloch. "Thomas's own mother died when he was born. . . ." And she launched forth into a long and detailed account of the Bulloch family.

Miss Bulloch kept a small hotel in London not far from Euston Station. The hotel was situated in a pleasant square and, as it was very comfortable and well kept, it was a flourishing concern. Miss Bulloch welcomed Sue with open arms, she had lived in London for twenty years but she still felt an exile, and it was

a great pleasure to be able to talk to Sue about her
own people and to hear the lilt of her own language on
Sue's lips. Miss Bulloch could speak "English" with
the best of them—so she declared—but the Scots fitted
her tongue like a comfortable shoe. She gave her great-
niece a little bedroom at the top of the house—a strange
little slip of a room rather like a ship's cabin. There
was a fixed basin in one corner of the room and a built-
in wardrobe in the other, and the divan bed—which
was a great deal more comfortable than it looked—hid
its real use beneath a gaudy chintz covering. Sue liked
the room. It was very small—so small that you could
hardly turn round in it far less swing the proverbial
cat; but it was fresh and bright, and contained everything necessary to her comfort. The window opened
on to a balcony, and gave her a vast view of sky and
chimney stacks. She put away her belongings tidily in
the cupboard, hung her "White Lady" on the wall
opposite her bed, and settled down to her new life.

Darnay had not written again, and Sue did not know
whether he had gone abroad or not. She knew nothing
about his movements and she found this hard to bear.
If he had written occasionally and told her how he was
and what he was doing it would have been so much
easier—or so she thought. She found it difficult to
visualise Darnay now—the lean figure, the tanned face,
the keen eyes—and sometimes she felt as if she must
go back to Beilford so that she could *see* Darnay again.
She knew that she would be able to see him very clearly
at Tog's Mill, for everything would conspire to bring
him before her eyes.

Sue had not been able to speak to her grandparents

about her feelings for Darnay, but strangely enough she found that she was able to confide in Aunt Bella.

It was one evening—a warm May evening—when they were sitting together at the open window in Aunt Bella's own private sitting-room. Miss Bulloch had been busy all day, for the hotel was very full, but now she had done everything necessary and was taking her well-earned rest. She sat in an old basket chair, filling it comfortably, and put her feet on a footstool.

"That's better," she said. "My, it's been a day! You've been real useful, Sue. I don't know what I would have done without you."

"I like helping you," Sue told her.

"I wish you'd stay. I'd be glad to have you and that's the truth. It isn't only that you're useful, but it's having somebody of your own that's nice, somebody you can trust. I'd give you a reasonable salary if you'd consider it."

"It's good of you, Aunt Bella," Sue declared. "I don't know what to say. Grandfather wants me to go home soon and help him with the business, but . . ."

Aunt Bella waited. "But what?" she said at last. "What's keeping you back from going home and helping Thomas?"

Sue told her. She told Aunt Bella all about Bob, and when she had finished that story, she found herself speaking quite naturally of Mr. Darnay, and of her time at Tog's Mill. Sue did not speak of the divorce, for she had promised her grandfather to tell nobody about that, but she told Aunt Bella everything else, and Aunt Bella listened enthralled. She nodded and sighed, and asked the right questions in the right places, for she was a romantically minded woman for all her bustling practical common sense.

"Well," she said at last. "Well, it's no use telling you to take Hickie; that would be the sensible thing. Maybe you'll come to it in time."

"No," said Sue in a low voice.

"No?"

"No, Aunt Bella. I've known Mr. Darnay, you see, and nobody is any good after that. I love him," continued Sue, lured into this extraordinary confession by her great-aunt's sympathy and the twilight hour. "I'll always love him. I know he doesn't think of me any more, but I'll think of him till I die."

"Another woman's husband!" commented Aunt Bella, not shocked, but shaking her head sadly.

"She doesn't want him!" Sue cried, sitting up very straight in her chair. "She treated him badly. She went away and left him. Besides, I'm doing her no harm in thinking of him."

"It's yourself you're harming," Aunt Bella said, sighing. "For what good can come of it, Sue?"

"Nothing. . . . I don't *want* anything except to see him sometimes. I'd be satisfied with that."

"That's poor comfort. Are you going to give up your life to thinking about the man? It's a man by your side you're needing, a flesh and blood man to bear the burdens of life with you, and share your sorrows and joys. Dreams . . ." said Aunt Bella in a low voice. "Dreams are useless, Sue. It's living that matters, everyday living."

"I've thought that too, sometimes."

"I've lived in dreams," continued Bella Bulloch softly. "My man was killed in the war and I never fancied another, so I just stayed single and worstled through alone, but it's a lonely road, Sue, and I wouldn't recommend it to anybody."

"I didn't know."

"It's a long time ago. I was young then, and not bad-looking either," declared Aunt Bella more cheerfully. "I could have had my pick of one or two—though you may not believe it—but it's *your* life we've to think of now, and it seems a real pity that you couldn't make up your mind and take Bob."

There was silence for a few minutes and then she added, "Och, well, it's no use. I'm not telling you to marry one man with the other in your head. There would be no good in that."

"What are you telling me then?" asked Sue in bewilderment.

"I'm telling you to put the man *out* of your head," said Aunt Bella firmly, "and the way to do it is to fill your head with other things. I'll take you to the theatre to-morrow."

CHAPTER TWENTY-SIX

Sue liked London. She was seeing it at its best, for the sun shone and the trees were green, their new leaves as yet ungrimed with soot. The chestnut trees with their waxy flowers were beautiful—more beautiful than flowers that grow upon the ground, for their background was the soft blue sky. Sue wandered about London by herself, she liked looking at the shops and the people, and she watched the children in the park— beautiful children, beautifully dressed, who sat in their prams like kings and queens or ran about playing and calling to each other in tiny shrill voices. She remembered what Darnay had said about cities, but, unlike him, Sue did not mind being invisible, in fact, she found it rather amusing and she wondered why Darnay had hated it so. These people, all so busy with their own small affairs, did not look at her, but she looked at them and wondered about them, and made up stories about their lives. It was not only the people who interested her, the city itself was fascinating. She went and looked at the river, and saw the ships pass up and down, she visited the docks and wandered down side streets into little old-fashioned squares and terraces where the roar of London could be heard afar off—like breakers on a distant shore. Sue enjoyed this solitary wandering even more than the round of "sightseeing" which Aunt Bella inaugurated for her entertainment.

One day when she was exploring in the vicinity of St. James's Palace she came across a shop window full of pictures, and, because she was always interested in pictures, she stopped and looked at them. How strange they were! How vivid in colour! How entirely unlike the objects which they were supposed to represent!

Sue looked at them all carefully, and then, just as she was turning away, she saw the name on the wrought-iron grill below the window—"Hedley"—it was Mr. Darnay's agent! She hesitated for a moment, wondering whether she should go in. It would be "rather awful" of her, of course, for she had no intention of buying a picture, but perhaps Mr. Darnay's pictures would be inside, and if so she would see them. Suddenly she felt that she must see those pictures again—they were a part of him. She pushed open the door and went inside.

She had expected to find herself in a shop, but this place was not like a shop at all. It was a large room with a thick fawn-coloured carpet, and walls of the same hue. On the walls were a few pictures—not many —and they were all vividly coloured and queer. There was nobody in the room except a young man in a lounge suit who sat at a table writing. He was so busy that he took no notice of Sue.

She stood for a few moments looking round timidly, and then she walked across the thick carpet and stood in front of one of the pictures. It was a very odd picture, Sue thought. The painter had chosen for his subject a china frog and a lemon, and an ugly blue glass vase with one tulip hanging out of it sideways. What a funny collection it was! She was still looking at it and wondering about it when she was startled by the young man's voice at her elbow (he had approached so silently that she had no idea he was there). "Very interesting, isn't it?" he said.

"Very," agreed Sue politely. Perhaps it *was* interesting when you really thought about it; interesting that anybody should bother to paint an ugly vase and a frog and a lemon, and should paint them in that queer way so that it looked as if they were all tumbling forwards out of the picture.

The young man was busy pointing out the especially "interesting" features of the picture in extremely technical terms and Sue listened and agreed with him. She agreed with everything he said, and the young man —who was by no means as foolish as he looked— realised quite soon that she was not a potential buyer.

"Are you interested in the work of Masserage?" he inquired hopefully, pointing to another picture at the far end of the room.

"Not awfully," admitted Sue sadly.

"Is there anybody——?" he asked, waving his hands as if he were offering her the World of Art. "Is there anybody at all——?"

"Well, I'm interested in . . . in John Darnay's work."

"You are, are you!" he cried. "Now that's very—er —interesting. We have one or two Darnays here—er— perhaps if you wouldn't mind waiting for a few moments—er—I think—er—I think Mr. Hedley himself would like to see you."

"Oh, *no!*" exclaimed Sue. "I mean I couldn't think of bothering him," she added hastily. She was rather frightened now at what she had done, it was dreadful to have entered the premises on false pretences. The young man was not so bad, for it was easy to agree with all he said, but Mr. Hedley would see through her in a moment and would realise that she was an impostor, absolutely ignorant of everything to do with painting. She thought regretfully of the book which Darnay had burned, and so vivid was her recollection of it that she could actually see it burning—the blackened leaves curling up and withering in the flames—If only I had read it, Sue thought, I would know exactly what to say.

"Mr. Hedley will be delighted to speak to you," the young man reassured her. "It will be no trouble at all. The fact is we are very—er—*interested* in Darnay just now." And with that somewhat enigmatic statement he vanished through a door in the wall—a door which did not look like a door until it was open because it was covered with wallpaper the same as the rest of the room.

Sue was still gazing at it, and wondering why a door should be thus disguised when it reopened very hastily and a small fat man appeared. He had a round red face and a bald head, and his eyes were bright and sharp like the eyes of a robin.

"Good-afternoon, Miss—er——"

"Pringle," said Sue.

"Miss Pringle," repeated Mr. Hedley, smiling at her with his head on one side. "Miss Pringle; yes. You are interested in Darnay's work?"

"Yes," said Sue, "but I don't want to buy anything."

"Dear me, no, of *course* not," agreed the little man as if that were the last thing he expected or desired. "You don't want to buy anything, but you're interested; that's what we like to hear. We have got one or two Darnays in the gallery, but they're all sold. Fetch them down, Edward."

The young man departed on his errand with silent speed.

"They're sold?" Sue enquired.

"That's right," said Mr. Hedley.

Sue was surprised to hear that they were sold, but she tried not to show it, for she was conscious that the little man was watching her intently. There was something here that she did not understand, and she must get to the bottom of it without giving herself away.

Edward returned laden with pictures. He lifted one on to an easel which stood against the wall and stepped back with the proud air of a conjurer who has produced a rabbit out of a hat. "Very, very interesting," he murmured.

It was more than interesting to Sue, for it brought back Darnay and the life at Tog's Mill in a wave of remembrance. She remembered the day he had painted it in the snow, and how she had tracked him down by his footprints, and she could hear his voice, that lazy teasing voice, saying, "It is your brain tells you snow is white—not your eyes." The last time she had seen the picture was in the studio at Tog's Mill. She had helped to pack it (or rather she had packed it herself, for Darnay, like most men, was not much use at making parcels), and now here it was again—an old friend in alien surroundings.

"You like it?" Mr. Hedley inquired.

"Yes," said Sue. "Yes, I think it is wonderful." She hesitated for a moment, and then added, "But I thought —I thought you said——"

"You thought what?" prompted Mr. Hedley, his eyes watching her face.

"Only that I thought you said it was sold?"

"It is sold," Mr. Hedley declared. He made a sign to his assistant and the young man whisked the picture away, and produced another in its place. Sue stood before it in silence drinking in the beauty of the pale sky with its flying clouds, and the delicate tracery of the bare trees upon Biel Hill. Mr. Hedley was silent too, and even the tall Edward forbore to make his usual remark, for there was something in Miss Pringle's face which rendered him dumb.

There were five pictures in all, and each was displayed in turn, and it seemed to Sue that Darnay was here in the room with them—for there was a strange wild beauty in the pictures, a brave freedom, and a vitality which were typical of Darnay's self. It amazed Sue to think that there had been a time when she saw no beauty in these canvases. I must have been blind, she thought.

"Well," said Mr. Hedley at last, "that's the five pictures Darnay brought me, and I've sold them all." He looked at Sue piercingly as he spoke, and then, as she made no comment, he continued earnestly. "Miss Pringle, I can see you are surprised to hear that the pictures are sold. Does this mean that you know Darnay? Does it mean that you are in communication with him?"

"I know him," said Sue faintly.

"Do you know where he is?"

She shook her head.

"I don't know what to do," declared Mr. Hedley with a helpless gesture of his small fat hands. "I really am at my wit's end. It is quite against my principles to discuss the affairs of my clients, but I feel sure you know something about Darnay. Shall we be frank with each other, Miss Pringle?"

"We might be," said Sue cautiously.

He smiled. "I think I can be frank with you," he told her. "It is not every lady—but no matter. I only ask you most earnestly that you will regard what I say as being in strict confidence."

They sat down on a small sofa in one corner of the room and Edward returned to his writing. "Now, Miss Pringle," said Mr. Hedley, "I'm going to tell you the whole story, and all I want in return is your help. Is that a bargain?"

"I'll help you if I can," she replied slowly.

Mr. Hedley smiled again. "You're Scotch, aren't you?" he said. "It's another word for cautious—but no matter, it's better that way. Now, listen to me. John Darnay was a popular painter. He had developed a certain technique and a great many people were interested in his work. I was able to sell his pictures without the slightest difficulty. Suddenly, and without the slightest warning, Darnay gave up the whole thing. He went off to Scotland and started painting in an entirely different style. It was bad enough, from a business point of view, that he should change his technique, for the people who had been interested in his work were interested no longer—they wanted the old type of 'Darnay.' But even worse was the fact that the new pictures were so strange, so stark and cold and unsympathetic, that nobody would look at them. People like bright colours, you see. I wrote to Darnay several times begging him to return to the old technique but it was no good."

"I know," Sue said. "But how could he go back to something he had outgrown?"

"He did go back to it, and most successfully," declared Mr. Hedley.

"Yes, but he hated it," she replied. "It was a dreadful thing for him to have to do; he only did it because he needed the money so badly."

"Oh, well, if you know *that*!" Mr. Hedley exclaimed, considerably relieved to find that so far he had violated no confidences. "I got him the commission for the portrait because he wanted the money, and, as I said, it was a tremendous success. Personally, I thought he had flattered his sitter *too* much—a little flattery is permissible of course; but Sir Archibald was charmed, positively charmed with the portrait. I was very much relieved, I can tell you, because I was a little doubtful what Darnay would do—he was in a strangely bitter mood."

"You needn't have worried," Sue told him; "Mr. Darnay had got the money so he was bound to give them what they wanted."

"Well, yes; I suppose if you look at it in that way."

"It's the way he would look at it," declared Sue.

"H'm," said Mr. Hedley. "Anyhow, they were more than satisfied. Darnay was offered several other commissions—good ones—but he wouldn't look at them; he simply vanished," said Mr. Hedley, throwing out his hands. "Simply vanished; leaving me with the five pictures which he had brought from Scotland. I held out no hope of selling them (for I didn't believe they would sell), but I told Darnay he could leave them here if he liked. Last week a gentleman called in to see me; a very rich American who is celebrated for his interest in Modern Art, and has an amazing collection at his house on Long Island. He always calls on me when he comes over here to see what I've got. I told him about

Darnay's latest craze and had the pictures brought down to show him—just to see what he would say."

"What did he say?" asked Sue eagerly.

"He bought the lot," replied Mr. Hedley significantly.

There was silence for a moment after this remarkable statement, and then Mr. Hedley continued, "Perhaps you don't realise what this means. It means that Darnay is a made man. The fact that Hiram B. Tollemacher has bought five Darnays is News with a big N. America will buy as many pictures as Darnay can paint —that's what it means. But Darnay has vanished off the face of the earth. . . ."

"Oh, I'm glad!" Sue cried excitedly. "Oh, Mr. Hedley, we must find him and tell him about it. Surely we can find him."

"We *must* find him," Mr. Hedley agreed. "But how are we to do it, that's the question. I've tried his wife and his bank and his lawyer, and they all declare that they don't know where he has gone. I thought, perhaps, when I saw you were interested in Darnay, that you might have some idea . . ."

"He told me he thought of going to Italy or Germany," Sue said doubtfully; "but that's not much help."

"Very little. I might put an advertisement in the Italian and German newspapers, of course. Can you suggest anything else?"

Sue could not.

"I've had several people inquiring for him," continued Mr. Hedley, "and quite a lot of letters—I don't know what to do with them. I must just wait, I suppose. Perhaps he'll write."

Sue did not think it likely. Darnay might pretend

that he did care what the world thought of his new medium, but in his heart of hearts he was bitterly wounded, and it had been a further blow to his pride as a painter to have to return to his old style for the hundred-guinea portrait.

"Oh, why didn't you *believe* in him!" she exclaimed. "Why ever didn't you, Mr. Hedley? It would have made all the difference to him if you had given him a little encouragement. Surely you must have known that the new pictures were good!"

"You can't kick me harder than I'm kicking myself," declared Mr. Hedley ruefully. "I knew the pictures were good—of course I did—but I thought they were unsaleable. It seemed such a *waste* when I could sell the others so well. . . . I hoped that when he found it wouldn't work he would go back to the old technique."

"You don't know him if you thought that," said Sue firmly.

Mr. Hedley could find no reply to that. "I'm a business man," he said, throwing out his hands.

"Oh, I see! I thought you were an art critic," said Sue, with unconscious irony.

Mr. Hedley was somewhat annoyed. He thought of several cutting retorts but decided not to utter them, for it was to his interest to keep in with Miss Pringle. She might be useful in tracing Darnay, and he was extremely anxious to trace Darnay and lure him back to the fold. Mr. Hedley wanted the large commission on the sale of Darnay's pictures in America; he wanted to be the only British agent for the new type of Darnays. This being so, Mr. Hedley returned a soft answer to the insult which had been offered to him, and rose to show that the uncomfortable interview was at an end.

Sue took the hint and departed, leaving her address and promising to call in at the "galleries" next time she found herself in the neighbourhood.

"Now who is she?" enquired Mr. Hedley when Sue had gone. "Who is she, eh?" It was a rhetorical question, of course, for Edward could not be expected to know who the visitor was any more than Mr. Hedley himself. In fact, he was a good deal less likely to know, not having enjoyed the doubtful pleasure of a private conversation with Miss Pringle.

"Gaga!" declared Edward, waggling his head idiotically.

"Gaga!" cried Mr. Hedley indignantly. "Why on earth can't you speak English? Need we have Yiddish words foisted upon us? Listen to me, Edward, that woman is no more 'gaga' than you are, not so much, if the truth were told. Besides, I didn't say 'What is she?' I said, 'Who is she?' She knows Darnay well, that's obvious."

"Knew him in Scotland at that farm he took," suggested Edward in a meek voice.

Mr. Hedley stood quite still for a few moments thinking deeply. "Yes," he said at last. "Yes, that's it. Darnay told me he had met Sir James Faulds of Beil— said something about a niece too, didn't he?"

"Sir James wanted him to paint her," replied Edward, "but I don't see what that——"

"You don't see!" Mr. Hedley exclaimed. "Why, that *is* the niece, of course."

Edward could not help smiling for it was so like the boss to jump to conclusions of this kind—especially where the nobility was concerned. The boss was an unconscionable snob, and enjoyed nothing better than to see Lord This or Sir Somebody That strolling about the gallery and looking at the pictures. It mattered little whether they bought anything—and to tell the truth, they very seldom did—their mere presence gave him joy.

"You may smile, Edward," said Mr. Hedley irritably. "You may smile like the Mona Lisa if you like, but I shouldn't be here now if I hadn't been able to put two and two together, and make four. You've no *flair*, Edward, that's what's the matter with you—no *flair*. I knew that girl was Somebody the moment I laid eyes on her. These old Scottish families have a sort of natural dignity—it's unmistakable."

CHAPTER TWENTY-SEVEN

Sue did not feel bound to keep the story of her adventures from Aunt Bella, for Aunt Bella was as safe as the bank, and knew so much already about Darnay's affairs that it seemed absurd not to tell her of the new development. It was fortunate for Sue that she did not feel bound to secrecy; she was bursting with the news of Darnay's success, and she could hardly get home quick enough to recount all her adventures to her aunt.

Miss Bulloch was an extremely good listener as Sue was already aware. She nodded and smiled and exclaimed rapturously over the discomfiture of Mr. Hedley, and laughed heartily at Sue's description of "Edward."

"They're queer folk these English," she declared at last. "I've lived amongst them twenty years and they still divert me. Mind you, I like them, Sue, but there's something awful silly about them. You wouldn't like to take a course of French lessons, I suppose!"

Sue was used to Aunt Bella by this time, and the sudden change of subject did not startle her. She turned her mind swiftly from the vagaries of the English to the language of the French, and considered the proposal seriously. "Well, I wouldn't mind," she declared.

"That's settled then," said Aunt Bella (who understood her niece about as well as her niece understood *her*, and was therefore aware that when Sue said she "wouldn't mind" it meant she was enchanted at the idea of French lessons). "It's yon Frenchman in number thirty," she added. "He's wanting pupils, and I'm sorry for the man."

This bald statement put Sue in complete command of the facts. The Frenchman could not pay his bill, and Aunt Bella, who had a heart of gold, was quite incapable of turning him into the street.

"It would be useful," continued Aunt Bella, trying to justify herself, and to pretend that the kind thought was not a kind thought at all but sheer business acumen. "It would be awful useful, if you could talk French. I get quite a good few French folk here. I'll put in on my cards too, 'Içi on parle Français'—or whatever it is. I'm getting some new cards printed, so you had best start to-morrow."

M. Delbos was a tall thin man with greying hair. He had come to England to write a book which was going to make his fortune, but the book had taken longer to write than he had imagined, and he had run out of funds. Authors must sleep and eat like other people, so he was obliged to eke out his small income by taking pupils. It was a waste of his precious time, but it could not be helped, and although he was annoyed with his pupils, and uninterested in them, he was a conscientious man and took pains to instruct them well. He welcomed Miss Bulloch's niece with a tired smile and, sweeping his work aside, invited her to sit down and tell him how much she knew.

"I learnt French at school," replied Sue, looking at him with her straight gaze; "but I've forgotten every word of it, so we'll start at the beginning if you don't mind."

"I would rather a thousand times," declared M. Delbos. "We will start with the pronunciation and then we shall not get that distressing ' miaow, miaow ' —as if you were a little cat."

But Miss Pringle had no distressing ' miaow '; her vowels were perfectly clear, and they were able to progress rapidly from pronunciation to reading and conversation.

M. Delbos became interested in his new pupil, and gave her of his best. He liked her naïvete, and her clear straight eyes. She was not like a woman at all—this niece of Miss Bulloch's—but neither was she like a man.

"How well do I talk?" she enquired one day when she had been visiting his sitting-room for about a month.

He looked at her inquiringly. "How well?" he said.

"Yes," said Sue. "Do I talk horrible broken French like some people talk horrible broken English—the kind of English that gives you a pain?"

"No," said M. Delbos, smiling. "Your pronunciation is good. It is very nearly perfect. It gives me no pain to hear you speak my language—none at all. May I ask why you are so anxious to acquire a good pronunciation of my tongue."

Sue blushed. "It's not a very nice reason," she said.

M. Delbos waited for a few moments, hoping that Miss Pringle would disclose the "not very nice reason" for her anxiety to speak good French, but she said no more, and the reason remained a mystery for all time. It was one of those small mysteries that tease the mind at odd moments, and she would have been surprised if she had known how often her instructor thought about it, and wondered.

It was very simple really, and the reason was a human if not a very worthy one. Sue had never forgotten the way in which she had been tricked by Ovette—the memory of it rankled in her breast—and it seemed to her that if she learnt to speak the woman's language, and learnt to speak it better than the woman could speak hers, she would be wiping out part of the old score. If she ever saw Ovette again it would be very pleasant to be able to reply to her appalling English in reasonably good French, and even if she never saw her again—and she had no wish to renew the acquaintance—she would feel that she had won an advantage over her enemy. Sue did not reason it out in so clear and detailed a fashion, of course, she only thought: what fun it would be if I met her one day in the street or gazing into one of her beloved shop windows, and could start talking French to her!

The lessons were a great success. They filled her mind so that she had less time to think about Darnay, and she found as time went on that she was not only learning a foreign tongue, and learning it thoroughly, but she was also learning to speak her own language more correctly. This pleased her enormously, for like all true Scots she had the desire to better herself firmly planted in her breast.

The weeks slipped past with remarkable rapidity. She took over the marketing for Aunt Bella and found it an interesting business. She visited Covent Garden in the early morning and returned laden with fruit and vegetables and flowers. She helped with the linen, added up accounts, and made herself generally useful. During the summer months the hotel was full of visitors but, in spite of the work which this entailed,

Sue and Aunt Bella went to the theatre regularly twice a week. Miss Bulloch loved the theatre, it was her chief recreation (and Sue was an excellent excuse for going more often than usual). She laughed and cried, and lived so intensely through the vicissitudes of the hero and heroine that she was like a rag when the play was over.

"It's grand!" she would say, leaning heavily on Sue's arm as they sought their homeward-bound bus. "It's just grand. Oh, my, I do love a good play! How anybody in their sane senses can go to the cinema when they could see a good play is more than I can understand."

Aunt Bella scorned the screen.

All this time there was no word from Darnay, and Mr. Hedley's advertisements in the foreign press brought no reply. Sue visited the galleries several times and was received with so much cordiality that she was quite surprised, and she formed the opinion that Mr. Hedley and his staff had very nice manners indeed.

"It isn't as if I had ever bought anything from them," she declared to Aunt Bella in some perplexity. "You could understand it then. I've never bought anything at all, and I always tell them that I'm not going to buy anything, but they don't seem to mind."

Aunt Bella laughed. "It's business, Sue, just business, that's all. They're aye hoping!"

One morning Sue returned from her marketing to find Aunt Bella closeted in her office with a young man. Sue had opened the door, and was about to retire hurriedly when the visitor looked round and laughed.

"Sue!" he cried. "Don't you know me?"

"Sandy!" exclaimed Sue in amazement.

"Yes, it's me," declared Sandy, leaping from his chair and enveloping his sister in a bear's hug. "It's your very own little brother—six feet one in his stocking soles—what have you got to say to him, eh?"

"Oh, Sandy," cried Sue. "You've grown. Why, you're enormous, and how well you look!"

"He's a fine man," declared Aunt Bella, smiling at them both. "A fine well-set-up fellow, and that's the truth."

"I'm through my training now," said Sandy, sitting down on the sofa and pulling Sue down beside him. "I've been telling Aunt Bella all my news. I'm going to India with a draft, and that's why I've got leave. I came straight here to see you, and then I'm going home."

Sue looked up into his face, and he met her eyes squarely.

"I've got to see Father," he said, flushing a little beneath his tan. "I want to make everything right before I go away."

"Oh, I'm glad!" she said, in a low voice.

He squeezed her hand. "It will be all right," he told her. "I'm not afraid of him now."

"Maybe he'll be afraid of you," suggested Aunt Bella grimly, with a glance at her nephew's inches.

Sue and Sandy laughed; they could not imagine Will Pringle being afraid of anybody.

"You may laugh," Miss Bulloch said. "The fact, is I never could thole your father—a grim growdie, that's what he is. Maybe I shouldn't say it to you," she added complacently; "but I'm in the habit of saying what I think, and Sue knows it."

Neither of Will's children was inclined to take up the cudgels on his behalf; they looked at each other and smiled.

"What Mary was thinking of beats me," continued Aunt Bella. "She could have had her pick. She was like a fairy, the creature, and the men were all mad for her, so what on earth induced her . . . But maybe I'd best hold my tongue, it's a wee bit apt to run away with me. You'll stay here, Sandy," she added, with another admiring glance at her nephew. "Aye, there's a wee room at the top near Sue. Stay on for a few days anyway, and we'll go to the theatre."

The few days lengthened into a week and passed very quickly for Sue and Sandy had much to talk about. Sue heard the whole story of the air-rifle for the first time and listened to it sympathetically.

"I don't know what was the matter with me," Sandy said at last. "I was under a kind of spell or something. The fact is, when I look back and think over what I did it seems as if it was somebody else's life I was looking at, and not my life at all. Yet, it's only six months since it happened. I can't believe it, Sue."

"You're changed," she told him.

"You've changed too," he replied, looking at her with critical eyes. "I don't know what it is about you, but you seem to be more of a person—you're not so prickly now," he added, laughing.

Sue smiled. "I was rather a hedgehog," she admitted. "I thought everybody was trying to 'do me down,' and I had to fight to keep my end up, but now I've discovered that people are awfully kind if you take them the right way."

"Aunt Bella's a gem," said Sandy.

Sue nodded. Aunt Bella was a gem, but it was not only Aunt Bella who was kind—everybody was—in fact, the world was a delightful place. There was only one flaw in it, and that was the disappearance of Darnay.

Sandy was such good company that Aunt Bella was very loth to part from him when the day arrived.

"You'll come back and see us," she told him as she stood on tiptoe to kiss his cheek.

"I will indeed," he replied. "I'll be back as quick as I can. You've been so good to me, Aunt Bella; maybe you'll see me back sooner than you expect if Father kicks me out of the door."

Aunt Bella wagged her finger at him seriously. "Don't you let him put upon you," she said. "He's a bully, is Will, and the thing to do is to stand up to him. He was polite and pleasant to me once I had showed him my mettle."

Sandy went off in a calm and confident mood. He intended to walk into his father's shop unexpectedly, to ask forgiveness for his misdeed, and to pay back the pound which he had taken from the till. What happened next would depend upon his father's attitude, and Sandy could not imagine what his father would do. He could not envisage a scene of reconciliation with Will—it was out of keeping with his character—but the truth was, Sandy did not greatly care what happened —he would have done what he could to make amends and that was all that mattered.

He travelled north by night and timed himself to arrive at the bakery during the dinner-hour, for he was aware that this was his best chance of seeing his father alone. How queer it was to walk through the streets that he knew so well feeling like a stranger! He saw several people that he knew, but they hurried past him without a glance, for Sandy had grown so tall and looked so much older that they did not recognise him. Mr. Hogg was standing at the door of his shop and Sandy passed without a sign. He intended to visit Mr. Hogg later and pay what was due, but he wanted to see his father first and he was impatient to get the interview over.

He reached the bakery at half-past twelve exactly, and stood looking at it for a few minutes before going in. He had spent all his life here, but the place seemed unfamiliar to him. It looked small and somewhat insignificant, but perhaps that was because he had seen so much and grown larger himself in mind as well as body. Although it was only six months since he had left, running away in fear of his life with the stolen money in his pocket, Sandy felt like Rip van Winkle.

Presently he drew near and peered in through the shining plate-glass windows, and—seeing that his father was alone in the shop—he pushed open the door and went in.

"Sandy!" exclaimed Will in amazement.

"Yes, it's me," said Sandy. "I'm in the army, Father, and I'm going abroad. I wanted to see you before I went and pay you back."

He put the pound note on the counter as he spoke. He had not asked forgiveness, because, now that he was back in the old atmosphere, he knew that it was impossible to say the words.

"Well, ye've grown a lot," remarked Will.

"I'm six feet one."

"I'd have thought ye were more."

There was a short strained silence, and then Sandy said, "No, I'm just six feet one, that's all."

"It's quite enough," Will replied dryly. He took up the pound note and put it in the till.

Sandy said nothing.

"I suppose ye can stay a few days," Will continued. "Ye can give me a hand in the shop if ye like—I'm short-handed."

"I'll do that gladly," Sandy declared. There was a lump in his throat which made speech difficult, or he would have said more.

Will ruminated for a few moments and then he roused himself and glanced at the clock. "It's early closing," he said. "Away and fetch the shutters, Sandy, it's time we were going upstairs to our dinners."

CHAPTER TWENTY-EIGHT

IN September people began to come back to London from the sea and the moors. The houses, which had been in the hands of caretakers for so many weeks, began to brighten up, the shutters were opened, the windows were painted, and the doorsteps cleaned. Some of the babies reappeared in the parks, brown and fit after their holidays by the sea; the traffic in the streets increased and there was a cool air in the evenings, very welcome after the stuffy heat of the day.

Sue, calling one afternoon at the galleries, found Mr. Hedley up to the eyes in work, but he was never too busy to speak to Miss Pringle. He came down the stairs smiling somewhat ruefully and showed her his hands. "Look at the dirt," he said. "No, I couldn't shake hands with you, Miss Pringle. The fact is, I'm having a small exhibition of Moderns, and I'm looking out what I've got."

Miss Pringle declared that that was "very interesting" (it was really Edward's word, of course, but Mr. Hedley used it a good deal too, and Sue found that she herself worked it pretty hard when she visited the galleries. If you could find nothing else to say about a picture—for instance—if it were so hideous or startling that it almost stunned you, or even if it were so inane that you scarcely knew what it was meant to be, you usually had enough strength left to murmur, "Interesting; very interesting indeed," and that was all that was required).

"I'm sending you a card for my Private View," continued Mr. Hedley confidentially. "I *do* hope we may count on you, Miss Pringle?"

Miss Pringle answered graciously that they might certainly count on her.

"Good; splendid!" he declared, and then suddenly his face fell, and he added sadly, "If only we had a Darnay to show. . . ."

Sue shook her head. It did seem a pity.

"Just one Darnay," he continued. "Mr. Tollemacher has taken his away with him to America, so we haven't got a single specimen of Darnay's work in the place. . . . I suppose there aren't any more—anywhere?"

There was a little silence while Sue considered the matter. All those pictures put away so carefully in the studio at Tog's Mill—the portrait of herself, which she liked so much, and one, two, three—perhaps five— others. She could easily have them sent, of course, for she had only to write to her grandfather. But what right had she to do this—to take them out of their cupboard and give them to Mr. Hedley to display? No right at all. It was a great pity, of course, because it would have been lovely to have the pictures displayed, and to hear everybody talking about them, and admiring them, but it just couldn't be done. Sue decided to say nothing about them, for she did not altogether trust Mr. Hedley for all his nice manners.

"Just one," Mr. Hedley said persuasively. "Don't you know anybody who owns one of the new Darnays? Haven't you—perhaps—got one yourself?"

"Well, I *have* got a small picture," admitted Sue; "but I don't want to sell it, Mr. Hedley."

"Of course not, but if you would *lend* it, Miss Pringle.

It would be a good thing for Darnay's own sake to keep his name before the public eye. We shall take the greatest care of it, I can assure you, so you need not be afraid. The Duke of Hambourne is lending us two very valuable pictures, and we have three from Lady Millingworth as well."

"It's only a tiny picture," said Sue, who was a little impressed by the grand names.

"No matter——"

"And I don't know whether he would like it to be shown. You see, it's just a rough little sketch."

"In oils?"

"Yes, but——"

"We must have it. Please, Miss Pringle."

Sue wished she had said nothing about it for she did not want to part from her "White Lady" for three weeks—it was the only bit of Darnay she had got and she valued it accordingly. But Mr. Hedley was so insistent, and produced so many arguments in favour of showing it that at last she was forced to agree.

When the "White Lady" was removed from Sue's bedroom she left a patch on the paper, for the bright sunshine had streamed in at the open window all summer and faded the wall. The patch was a comfort to Sue—it was a token of the "White Lady's" existence and gave promise of her return—but Aunt Bella found no pleasure in it at all.

Sue pushed open the door of Hedley's Galleries and walked in. She walked in with great assurance, for she had met with so much encouragement from Mr. Hedley that she felt almost as if the place belonged to her. The large room was full of people, but not uncomfortably full, for Mr. Hedley had issued his invitations to the Private View with great discrimination. There was no sense in having the place so crowded that you couldn't see the pictures, because, if you did, the affair degenerated into a sort of At Home and no pictures were sold. On the other hand you wanted *enough* people or the gallery looked empty, and unkind friends were quite likely to say that Hedley's was on the wane, and that they'd looked in at the Private View and the place was a vacuum—nobody there at all.

To-day Mr. Hedley had struck the happy medium and perhaps he was aware of this for he was in tremendous form, bustling about and waving his hands and talking to everybody at once. He welcomed Sue with a judicious blend of familiarity and respect, and apologised for his inability to show her round himself.

"So busy," declared Mr. Hedley. "Must speak to everybody. . . . The Duke . . . that's the Duke in the grey lounge suit . . . be sure to ask me, or Edward, if you see anything that interests you."

Sue started to go round with her catalogue, looking carefully at each picture and trying to make up her mind which she would buy—if she had the money to buy any of them. She did not get very far on her tour of inspection before Mr. Hedley was back at her elbow with rather an extraordinary request. Would she mind if he were to introduce one or two friends? They were people who were interested in pictures, and were particularly anxious to make Miss Pringle's acquaintance. It was quite impossible to refuse, even if she had wanted to, for the people had followed Mr. Hedley, and were standing there, waiting.

The introductions were made, and a group formed, and a great deal of talk and laughter ensued. Sue was surprised at their friendliness, and a trifle embarrassed by it—they treated her as if they had known her for years—one woman especially, a certain Mrs. Leon Hunter, beautifully dressed, with ash-blonde hair, orange lips and a strange golden complexion, was so extremely friendly that she was quite a nuisance. She attached herself firmly to Sue, when the others had drifted away, and talked so much about the pictures that Sue could not get on with her inspection.

"I adaw them *all*," she declared. "So fwesh and bwight—don't you *adaw* them, Miss Pwingle?"

Sue was about to reply in the true Scots manner that she "liked them well enough," but remembering in time that she was in England, declared instead that they were "very interesting."

"Vewy, vewy inta-westin'," agreed her new friend, turning her back to the wall. "I always say we ought to be vewy, vewy gwateful to deah Mr. Hedley for takin' so much twouble."

Sue could not get rid of Mrs. Leon Hunter anyhow, she was like an old man of the sea, and now she started talking about Scotland, and asking about the shooting and fishing round about Beilford. Sue answered the questions faithfully, wondering how Mrs. Leon Hunter knew that she came from Beilford, and deciding in her own mind that the lady contemplated renting a shooting in the neighbourhood of Beilford, and wanted some inside information on the subject. Finally, to cap everything, she asked if "Miss Pwingle" would waive ceremony and come on to her sherry party after the show. It was the last thing Sue wanted to do, but she had not sufficient *savoir faire* to refuse the invitation. Her sudden rise to popularity puzzled her a good deal, it seemed so queer that perfect strangers should want to be introduced to her, and to entertain her without knowing in the least who she was. Perhaps she would have understood it better if she could have followed Mr. Hedley's progress through the room. "Have you seen 'The White Lady'? It's a Darnay in the new medium—tremendously interesting," declared Mr. Hedley, buttonholing everybody within reach. "No, it isn't for sale, it is just *lent* to the exhibition by Miss Pringle, a niece of Sir James Faulds of Beil. Oh, yes, she is in the gallery at the moment. . . . What? . . . Yes, over there in navy blue with the crimson wing in her hat. . . . Very charming indeed—very, very charming. What, the Darnay? . . . No, definitely not for sale. He painted it for Miss Pringle and of course it belongs to her. . . . Very good of her to let us see it, don't you think?"

It was not until the rush was over and most of the fashionable crowd had drifted away to have tea, that Sue was able to resume her study of the pictures. Many a woman would have given up the struggle and gone home long before this, but Sue was made of sterner stuff than most. She had come to look at the pictures and she intended to look at them all. She saw her "White Lady" in a place of honour and stood still for a few moments looking at her affectionately.

"She looks nice there, doesn't she?" said Mr. Hedley's voice in her ear. "She's a trifle sketchy, of course, but——"

"He did it in about *two hours*," said Sue, quick to

resent the slightest criticism; "and I watched him all the time. . . . It was wonderful!"

"That makes my mission even more difficult," Mr. Hedley declared. "The fact is I've had an offer for the picture—an American gentleman—he knows it isn't really for sale, but he wondered if you were open to an offer."

"I told you——" began Sue indignantly.

"I know, I know," cried Mr. Hedley. "You told me it wasn't for sale, but he is offering you a hundred pounds. It isn't worth a quarter of the money, you know."

"A hundred pounds!"

"It's fantastic," agreed Mr. Hedley; "but Americans are like that. If they really want a thing they don't mind what they pay for it. There aren't any other pictures in the new technique and Mr. Francks has set his heart on having one."

"Well, he can't have mine," said Sue firmly; "not for *two* hundred pounds." And she moved on to show that her decision was final. She could not think of parting with the picture, but all the same she was pleased, and more than a little excited to find that her "White Lady" was appreciated so highly.

A few minutes later she felt a touch on her arm, and, turning quickly, she found herself face to face with a tall thin gentleman with a pleasant, clean-shaven face.

"Miss Pringle, I think," he said, bowing gravely.

"Yes," said Sue.

"Francks is my name," he declared; "Harold Francks. Now I hope you're not going to be vexed with me, Miss Pringle, but I just felt I had to speak to you. Mr.

Hedley's been telling me about you, but he wouldn't introduce me."

"I'm afraid you can't have my picture," she told him.

"That's just too bad," he declared. "Couldn't I tempt you, Miss Pringle?"

She shook her head.

"I've got to go back to the States next week," he continued, "and I've set my heart on taking a specimen of Darnay's work with me." He paused for a moment and then added thoughtfully, "Mr. Tollemacher has got five."

"Perhaps he would sell you one of them," suggested Sue.

Mr. Francks smiled. "You aren't acquainted with Hiram B., are you, Miss Pringle? . . . No, I thought not."

"I'm sorry," said Sue again, and she *was* sorry, for she liked Mr. Francks.

"So am I," he replied. "It's just too bad."

He went away sadly, and Sue was once more at liberty to continue her inspection.

CHAPTER TWENTY-NINE

THERE were three rooms full of pictures, and, by the time Sue had arrived at the third, her energy was beginning to flag. The galleries were very hot, and she was tired and footsore and dazzled by the bright colours which seemed to shriek at each other from canvas to canvas. She had just made up her mind that she must leave the third room for another day when her eyes fell on a picture that really "interested" her. It was quite a small panel—the same size as her "White Lady"—depicting the bare branch of a tree with a row of little birds sitting on it. They were such perky little birds, bright eyed and cocky, and they were so real and fluffy looking that you could almost hear them chirping. The tone of the picture was cool and quiet, which came as a relief after the dazzling splashes of ochre and blue and scarlet, and Sue stood still and feasted her eyes upon it.

Gradually it dawned upon Sue that she had seen that branch before, or a branch very like it—a bare twisted branch with gnarled twigs upon it—twigs which resembled an old man's fingers. . . .

She reopened her catalogue and found the number. It was 203. There was no name to show who had painted the picture—no name in the catalogue and no signature on the canvas. She looked at it again, more carefully than before. It was Darnay's work, she was sure of it. The room rocked beneath her feet. . . .

When she recovered a little from the horrible giddiness which had assailed her, she went in search of Mr. Hedley, but before she found him she changed her mind, for after all she had no proof that it was a Darnay, and she was doubtful of her ability to convince him of the fact. She decided to manage the affair herself in her own way and to tackle Edward about it —Edward was so much easier to manage.

"I'm rather interested in Number 203," she said, speaking in the kind of language which Edward understood. "Can you tell me who it is by?"

Edward came and looked at the picture. "Oh, that? Yes, it *is* interesting, isn't it?"

"Who is it by?" enquired Sue again.

"There's no name, is there?" Edward said, looking at his own catalogue. "I rather think it came from Amsterdam; we have an agent there who picks up anything he thinks might interest us."

"How much is it?"

"Twenty pounds," replied Edward, consulting his list. "But I dare say Mr. Hedley would consider an offer from you. Shall I ask him?"

"Yes."

He sped away, light-footed as ever, and returned with the message that Mr. Hedley would be delighted to let *Miss Pringle* have the picture for seventeen guineas.

Sue closed with the offer immediately. She had not got the money, of course, but Aunt Bella would lend it to her; money or no money she had to have the picture, it was an absolute necessity to her.

"I'd like to know who painted it," she said, and added with consummate guile, "It makes a picture more—er—interesting if you know who painted it."

Edward agreed that it did. In his heart of hearts, he saw no interest at all in a picture unless you knew who had painted it—the name was everything.

"Would your agent know?" enquired Sue.

"You could write to him," suggested Edward, who saw a way of delegating to Miss Pringle a task which would otherwise fall upon himself. "You could write and ask him. His name is Mr. Van Kampen, shall I give you his address?"

This was what Sue had hoped for, but she hid her delight. She noted the address carefully and then turned back to her row of little birds. "I'll take it home with me," she said.

Edward was horrified. He explained that it would have to remain on its hook for three weeks—three weeks wasn't long, was it? There was no fear at all of it being sold to somebody else by mistake, for, even now, he was about to affix a round red disc to the frame; he showed her the box of round red discs to convince her of the fact.

"But I want it now," Sue said armly. "Fetch Mr. Hedley, please."

Edward sighed. He was afraid that Mr. Hedley would take it off the wall and give it to Miss Pringle, for Miss Pringle was the niece of a baronet and therefore entitled to her whims. (This would mean that another picture of exactly the same size would have to be found in the attic and brought down to fill the gap, and he was sick of groping about in the attic, he had had his fill of the place.) Edward was not mistaken, for Mr. Hedley, when told of Miss Pringle's desire to take her picture home then and there, threw out his hands, shrugged his shoulders, and smiled.

"These dear ladies!" he exclaimed, watching the impression that his words were making upon the little group which surrounded him. "These dear, dear ladies! We must let Miss Pringle have it, Edward. Take it down for her like a good fellow, and see if she would like you to call a taxi to take her home."

It was not until Sue was half-way home in the taxi, with her precious picture beside her on the seat, that she suddenly remembered Mrs. Leon Hunter's sherry party which she had promised to attend. Och, well! said Sue to herself, there will be a big crowd . . . she'll never miss *me*.

Sue went straight up to her bedroom and hung the new picture in the "White Lady's" place. She stood back and looked at it, and the more she looked at it the more she liked it, and the more certain she became that Darnay's hand had painted it. The "little brothers" in the picture were exactly like the little brothers at Tog's Mill. A merry lot they were, with a look in their wee beady eyes that was at once impudent and greedy, and Sue wished that she could give them the feast of crumbs which they most certainly deserved.

She was still standing there when Aunt Bella came in with her arms full of linen. "Sue," she said. "We'll need to get these sheets mended. . . . My, what's happened to you?" she added in surprise, for Sue's cheeks were pink and her eyes were starry with excitement.

"Happened!" cried Sue. "All sorts of things have

happened. "I've bought a picture, for one thing—there it is—but I can't pay for it."

"I'll give it to you, dearie," declared Aunt Bella promptly. The picture was worth a good deal to have had such a tonic effect upon her niece. "Don't you worry about that, for I'll give it to you gladly. How much is it, eh?"

"Seventeen pounds . . . no, guineas . . . but I can pay the shillings myself."

"My, that's awful dear!"

Sue laughed. "It's worth a hundred pounds," she declared; "at least, I could get a hundred pounds for it if I wanted to sell it. I was offered that for the 'White Lady.'"

"A hundred pounds for yon wee picture of the 'White Lady.'"

Sue did not reply, she had pulled her suitcase from beneath the bed and was beginning to pack, tossing her garments into it in a haphazard manner.

"What in the name of fortune——?" her aunt exclaimed in astonishment.

"I've got to go. I simply must. I know it's inconvenient leaving you in the lurch, but I can't help it."

"Sue, is it home to Beilford? You'll not get a train till——"

"It's to Amsterdam."

"Miss Bulloch looked at her niece with horror-stricken eyes. "Amsterdam!" she cried. "Sue, is it Mr. Darnay, or what?"

"I don't know anything," Sue declared. "I don't know where he is. I don't even know if it's him at all. . . ."

"For pity's sake!"

". . . But I'm certain that it is."

"Could you not be a wee bit more explicit?" demanded Miss Bulloch with unconscious irony.

"I might, if I wasn't so excited," cried Sue, and suddenly she dropped an armful of clothes and laughed, and flung her arms round Aunt Bella's neck—it was a most unheard of demonstration of affection. "Dear Aunt Bella, what a bother I am! If you weren't the kindest person in the world you'd throw me out of the door. Now, listen till I try to be sensible. I'm sure in my own self that Mr. Darnay painted that picture— certain sure—but it's not signed, you see."

"How can you know, then?"

"Because of the tree and the birds."

Miss Bulloch gave up the riddle. "Well, if you say so," she declared in a hopeless tone of voice. "But, Sue, you're never going after the man yourself! It's not quite the thing—you, traipsing over half Europe after him. Would you not tell Mr. Hedley?"

"There are two reasons," Sue replied, quite serious now. "One, Mr. Darnay may not want people to know where he has gone, and two, Mr. Hedley might not believe me."

"But, Sue——"

"Don't you see?" she cried. "If I tell Mr. Hedley about it he'll either believe me, and go after Mr. Darnay himself, and worry and bother him to death, or else he won't believe me and he'll do nothing at all. It wouldn't be any use telling Mr. Hedley."

When Aunt Bella saw that Sue was determined on her course she made no more objections. She found a time-table and looked out the sailings, and then she knelt down and repacked the suitcase. The picture of the birds was wrapped in paper, and tied with string.

"You'll wire me?" she adjured her niece as they waited in the hall for the taxi. "You'll be sure to wire me, Sue. I tremble to think what your grandfather would say if he knew what you were up to."

CHAPTER THIRTY

IT was the first time that Sue had left her own land, but she had set out upon her adventure so hurriedly that she had no time to be alarmed at its magnitude. The crossing was calm, and there were plenty of people on the boat who were only too pleased to give assistance, and advice to an inexperienced traveller. Wrapped in a thick tweed coat—for the wind was cold—Sue stood at the rail and marvelled at her first view of Amsterdam. It was a beautiful city, with a dignity all its own. In the foreground was a perfect forest of masts, and behind was a vista of towers and spires outlined against the blue unclouded sky. It seemed to Sue that the whole city must be made up of churches, and this illusion was intensified when the bells began to ring. The country was very flat, of course, but she had expected that, and although she missed the hills, she perceived that there was something to be said for a plain. The horizon was wider, here, and the spires and towers looked taller and more dignified rising from the level land and reaching into the skies.

Sue hired a car and drove through the town—through wide, clean streets lined with tall trees—and presently arrived at Mr. Van Kampen's shop. It was a curiosity shop, and the window was full of old Dutch furniture and prints of Dutch masters in dark-oak frames. She opened the door and went in and found the shop full of people. This was annoying—it was her first set-back since she had started her adventure—and it meant that she would have to wait until Mr. Van Kampen was free to attend to her. She sat down quietly and waited, watching the people and listening to their talk, and, despite her impatience, she was amused and interested to hear them, for it seemed to her that this language resembled the broad Lowland Scots which she knew so well.

The shop was full of pewter jugs and Delft pottery—lustrous white china with little pictures of Dutch scenes and decorations in blue; and there were framed prints of Amsterdam harbour and public buildings, and a few larger pictures of windmills and canals and tulip fields in bloom. Sue could see no pictures which resembled Darnay's work and her heart sank a little. She began to wonder if Edward had made a mistake, and the bird-picture had come to Hedley's galleries from some other agent.

There was plenty of time for reflection and observation, for Mr. Van Kampen's customers took a great deal of care over their purchases, and he did not hurry them. He was a dear old man, Sue decided, his bald head, with its little fringe of white hair, was shiny and polished like a billiard ball, and his clean rosy face was full of kindliness.

At last her patience was rewarded. The door shut behind the last customer and Mr. Van Kampen turned to Sue and bowed. "Good-day, madame," he said in excellent English. "What can I do for you?"

"You knew I was English!" Sue exclaimed in amazement.

"That is so obvious," he returned, smiling at her in a friendly way.

"And you can *speak* English," added Sue in a relieved tone.

"And I can speak English," he repeated, nodding. "It is necessary that I should, for I have many English customers. I regret that I have had to keep you waiting so long. What is it that you want? A pewter jug, a little picture of our great city, or perhaps an old chair. . . ."

"I don't want anything," Sue replied. "The fact is I bought a picture the other day at Mr. Hedley's galleries in London. It's a very nice picture, but it's not signed, and I wondered if you could tell me who painted it."

Mr. Van Kampen had listened carefully to this, and now he shook his head. "How should I know if Mr. Hedley does not? He is more experienced than I am, madame."

"But he got it from you!" she cried. "It was one that you sent him. I'll show it to you." She tore the paper off and produced the picture, propping it up against a statuette of the Venus di Milo which stood on the counter.

Mr. Van Kampen put on his spectacles and looked at it. "Ah, yes, I like that picture," he said. "I remember it quite well—the row of little birds. How impertinent they are!"

"Do you know who painted it?"

"Yes, yes, indeed. I wanted the painter to sign it, but he said no. Strange, wasn't it, for most painters like to sign their pictures."

"Who is he?" enquired Sue, striving to hide her excitement.

"It is a countryman of your own," declared Mr. Van

Kampen. "A poor painter who lives at Leyden. He has painted a great many pictures of little birds and I have sold them all—to London, to Paris, to Brussels— dozens of little pictures of birds and trees. It is for his bread and butter, you see, and to buy materials for other bigger pictures. These bigger pictures he does not sell, I cannot tell you why."

"What is his name?"

"I have had several interesting talks with him," continued Mr. Van Kampen in his slow, deep voice. "It is a pleasure to me to speak English, for some of the happiest years of my life were spent in your country. We have talked together a great deal about painters. He is an admirer of Rembrandt. We are very proud of Rembrandt, we Nederlanders."

"Yes, you must be."

"We are very proud," repeated Mr. Van Kampen complacently. "He is the greatest painter of all time. Such power, such delicacy, such inimitable draughts-manship, such colour, such imagination, such fire! Yet Rembrandt was a man of the people—his father a miller, his mother a baker's daughter."

"A baker's daughter!" exclaimed Sue with interest.

"A baker's daughter," nodded the old man. "And why not? They are useful people, bakers, and we could not do without them. Rembrandt's people lived at Leyden, and he was brought up there——"

"But about my picture," interrupted Sue, who could listen no longer to the history of Rembrandt. "You were going to tell me the painter's name."

"Let me see," said the old man. "Let me think. Names are so difficult to me—I cannot remember them like I used to when I was young. I think I shall have to look in my books for his name. Perhaps you could come back to-morrow."

"I'll wait," said Sue firmly. "It won't take you long, will it?"

Mr. Van Kampen sighed, for it was his dinner-hour, but his visitor looked so determined that he saw it would be impossible to get rid of her. He produced a large account book and began to look through it. Sue waited impatiently, her excitement mounting like a fever. At last he gave a little grunt of satisfaction. "Eureka!" he said, smiling. "Yes, here is his name. John Day—and the address he gave me in Leyden to which I was to forward my cheque. I will write it down for you so that there will be no mistake."

"John Day!" repeated Sue. It was not his real name, of course, but it was near enough to give her added hope. She thanked Mr. Van Kampen, and hurried away.

CHAPTER THIRTY-ONE

SUE went to Leyden (or Leiden) by a train which dawdled contentedly through flat country scenes. She saw canals with barges moving slowly along, she saw windmills with their sails spinning merrily in the breeze, but these sights, strange though they were, made little or no impression upon her, for her whole being was filled to the brim with impatience. The train was a slow one (it seemed to Sue that she could have walked faster), and the delays at every station where the country people got in and out were almost unbearable.

At last, however, the journey came to an end and Sue found herself walking in the streets of Leyden; she looked about her like a person in a dream. There were plenty of churches here too, and fine buildings and quiet sleepy squares and canals bordered by avenues of tall trees. At first she tried asking her way to the address which she had been given (asking in English and in French), but, finding that useless, she took out the paper and showed it, enquiring by signs which direction to take. The place was difficult to find, and, even when she had found it, Sue could scarcely believe her eyes for it was nothing more nor less than a butcher's shop, spotlessly clean like all things Dutch, but very small and insignificant and tucked away in a narrow back street. In the shop was a big fat butcher with a smiling face—it seemed to Sue that everybody in this land was fat and cheerful—he could not understand Sue's enquiries, but when she said "John Day" loudly and clearly he pointed to a little stair and motioned her to go up.

"Oop, oop, oop," he said, pointing higher and higher until he was standing on the tips of his toes with his arm outstretched to its fullest extent. And then he doubled himself up and laughed heartily at this funny way of explaining where his lodger could be found.

"Up, up, up," repeated Sue, smiling and gesticulating to show that she understood, and would mount three flights of stairs to the very top of the house.

She mounted. The stairs were old and narrow, but they were clean and bright for there was a tall, many-paned window on the stair, and through it streamed the late afternoon sunshine making a pattern of diamonds on the steps. At last she came to the top landing and hesitated, for there were two doors here, and she did not know which to choose; and while she was still hesitating she heard Darnay's voice.

He was humming softly to himself as he often did when he was painting. Sue had heard that strange tuneless humming in the studio at Tog's Mill. . . . Tog's Mill! It seemed a hundred years ago and a thousand miles away. Now that she was here and knew, without the slightest possible doubt, that she had found him, her heart failed her a little, and the excitement which had carried her forward ebbed away leaving her cold and trembling. Supposing he was angry with her for seeking him out?

"Oh, God!" said Sue reverently. "Oh, God, let it be all right—*please*." And she opened the door and went in.

Darnay was painting. It was a moment or two before he raised his head, and she saw that he looked ill—his eyes shadowed and sunken, his face haggard and pale. Then, as the door shut behind Sue, he looked up and saw her.

"You?" he said softly. "You? How on earth——"

"You're not angry!" cried Sue in a breathless voice. "Oh, Mr. Darnay, you're not vexed with me. I had to come. I had to find you. Please don't be angry."

"I'm not—angry."

There was silence for a moment while they looked at each other.

"I found you through Mr. Van Kampen," continued Sue. "It was the bird picture. The little row of birds sitting on the apple tree, and saying, 'Brothers, the spring is not so far away.' I knew directly I saw it."

"And tracked me down," he added, with a faint smile.

"You can't get away from a savage," she told him, trying to speak lightly and ease the tension.

"Perhaps I don't want to."

She hesitated for a moment and then she cried, "Oh, Mr. Darnay, why did you go away? Why did you hide yourself from everybody?"

"I had to," he said in a low voice. "I was down and out. I had no illusions left. I saw myself stripped naked—a failure in life and a failure in art—there was nothing for me to do but to go away and hide from the world, and try to recover my self-respect."

"But you're not a failure," she cried. "That's what I've come to tell you. That's why I had to find you. The pictures have been sold. I was offered a hundred pounds for 'White Lady,' but I wouldn't——"

"You were *what*?"

"The White Lady that nobody loved," Sue told him. "An American gentleman wanted me to sell it to him for a hundred pounds."

"He must have been mad," Darnay said firmly. "Mad or drunk—probably both. Why on earth didn't you let him have it? Sit down and tell me the whole story."

Sue was thankful to see a glimpse of the old masterful Darnay, she sat down on the window-seat and told him all her news. Darnay listened intently, walking up and down, and pausing every now and then to ask questions, or to throw back his head and laugh. She saw that he was pleased to hear of the purchase of his new pictures.

"Mr. Tollemacher bought them?" he cried. "Not Hiram B.?"

Sue nodded.

"Great heavens. No wonder old Hedley wanted me found. Go on, Sue; tell me everything."

She noticed that he had called her Sue in his excitement, and she wondered why the name had slipped from his lips, for he had never called her that before—never in all the months they had spent together at Tog's Mill. It gave her a strange feeling, half-pain and half-joy, to hear him call her Sue.

At last she finished her story and a little silence fell in the room, broken only by the sound of Darnay's steps as he paced to and fro. Sue waited patiently for him to speak; she felt quite happy now, happy to be with him again—which was all she had ever wanted—and happy to know that she had brought him acceptable news.

"But, Sue," he said, stopping and looking at her

curiously; "but, Sue, aren't you . . . when are you to be married?"

The question was so unexpected that it took her breath away.

"Married," she echoed incredulously.

"Married to Hickie," he explained.

"Oh . . ." said Sue, and she smiled a little sadly. "Oh, poor Bob! I'm not going to marry him—nor anybody," she added with conviction.

He looked at her keenly and saw that she meant what she said; indeed, Sue always meant what she said, he remembered that about her.

"Why did you think I was getting married?" Sue inquired.

"It was something your grandfather said in his letter," Darnay replied. "I thought it was settled." He paused for a moment, and then he added, "It would have made all the difference if I had known that."

"They wanted me to marry him," Sue explained; "but I didn't want to, you see."

"I see," Darnay said thoughtfully; "but I still don't understand—and I must understand this because it's the most important thing of all—I don't understand why you aren't absolutely disgusted with me. Why did you take all this trouble to find me? I thought you would never want to see me again."

"Why should I feel—all that?" asked Sue in a low voice.

"I dragged your name in the mud," he told her. "It was unpardonable of me to keep you at Tog's Mill—I was mad to do it, I was utterly selfish and vile. . . ."

"You never thought," she cried. "Neither of us thought——"

"I *should* have thought. Oh, Sue, you can't imagine how deeply I have regretted my thoughtlessness."

"I haven't," she replied quickly. "Not for one moment. We were so happy, Mr. Darnay. It was worth everything . . . just to have known you . . . and been with you . . . there."

"Oh, Sue!" he cried, coming over to the window-seat and sitting down beside her and taking her hand in his. "Oh, Sue, do you really mean it?"

"You're so—thin," she said brokenly. "So thin—and worn. I can't bear it."

"You shall take care of me—you will, won't you? I can't get on without you any more."

"Yes," she whispered, stroking the poor thin hand. "Yes, I'll cook nice meals for you and fatten you up. I'll mend your clothes; look at your cuff, it's all frayed!"

"Shall we go back to Tog's Mill some day?"

"Soon!" cried Sue. "Oh, let's go soon. We were so happy at Tog's Mill, Mr. Darnay."

"John," he told her, smiling into her eyes.

"John?" she echoed in bewilderment.

"Yes, my dearest. You can't call your future husband Mr. Darnay."

"But, Mr. Darnay!" cried Sue, pushing him away. "I can't marry you—you never thought of *that*!"

Darnay sat back and looked at her ruefully. "I most certainly thought of it," he declared. "In fact, I thought you had accepted my proposal. What did——"

"No, no, no," she cried. "I wanted to be with you like we were at Tog's Mill. I couldn't marry you—how could I?"

"Am I so utterly revolting?"

Sue did not heed the absurd interruption, she raced on. "How could you introduce me to all your grand friends? You'll have lots of grand friends now that you're so famous. . . . I could never entertain your friends, and I could *never* go to dinner with the Laird. . . . You needn't laugh about it," she added seriously. "I simply couldn't do it even if he asked me—and he wouldn't ask me; you would be cut off from all that."

"But I don't *want* all that."

"You would miss it—later," she declared. "No, no, it would never do at all. I'll stay with you and take care of you, and I'll do anything—anything you want," said Sue, her voice faltering a little at this comprehensive statement; "but I couldn't ever marry you, Mr. Darnay."

"Now, listen to me," said Darnay gravely. "It's my turn now. I have no friends that I value so much as the tip of your little finger. Dear Sue, I love you so much. I've loved you a long time. I never knew I loved you until that last morning at Tog's Mill; you had a little streak of soot on your cheek; I knew then."

"Why didn't you tell me!" she cried. "Oh, why didn't you? I thought you didn't care. Why did you go away and leave me?"

Darnay looked at her in suprise. "What could I do?" he asked. "I wasn't free then; besides, I thought that you and Hickie . . . but never mind that now. Nothing matters now except that I love you—desperately. I love you and I can't live without you, but I won't have you unless you'll marry me."

"Oh, dear!" she said in perplexity. "Oh, *dear*, it would be *much* better my way."

He took her in his arms and kissed her tenderly. "There," he said. "How do you feel about it now?"

Sue felt a good deal better about it. She smiled at him with dewy eyes. "Did you know——" she began, and hesitated.

"Did I know what?" Darnay enquired.

"Rembrandt's mother was a baker's daughter," said Sue.

CHAPTER THIRTY-TWO

MR. AND MRS. BULLOCH were sitting by the fire. Mrs. Bulloch was knitting a grey sock, and Mr. Bulloch was reading out tit-bits from the evening paper. The fire burnt merrily in the grate and was reflected in dancing points of light in the lenses of Mrs. Bulloch's spectacles, and on the highly polished surface of her knitting needles. Outside the wind howled, and now and then the windows rattled, but this only served to accentuate the comfort of the cosy room.

"It's a wild night," Mrs. Bulloch said, "and only October too. Winter's starting early this year."

"It is that," Mr. Bulloch agreed comfortably.

"I'm wondering why I got no letter from Sue this week," Mrs. Bulloch said, after a pause.

"Ye've been wondering that all day," declared her husband, smiling. "I could see ye were worrying, and I knew fine what it was. Bella would let us know soon enough if anything was wrong."

"Maybe; but it's not like Sue. She's written me regularly every week, Thomas."

In the silence which followed her remark Mrs. Bulloch heard a car draw up at the street door. She looked at her husband over her spectacles in an enquiring manner.

"Aye, it's a car," he said. "Maybe it's somebody come to the wrong house."

Mrs. Bulloch nodded, "It must be that," she agreed.

She had hardly spoken when the door opened and Sue rushed in like a wirlwind, and flung herself upon her grandparents with cries of affection and delight.

"You lambs!" she exclaimed, hugging them each in turn. "Oh, dear, how lovely it is to see you! And here you are, exactly the same—not a hair altered—and here you've been all these months. I can't believe all the things that have happened—it seems like a dream."

To say that the Bullochs were surprised at her sudden appearance would be ludicrously inadequate—they were dumbfounded, they could not believe their eyes; and, indeed, Sue was so changed that it was only by some sixth sense that they were able to recognise her. They had said good-bye to a quiet, woe-begone, dejected granddaughter, and they were confronted by a radiant young woman with rosy cheeks and starry eyes, a young woman who had thrown her native reserve to the winds and seemed almost beside herself with excitement.

"Sue," exclaimed Mrs. Bulloch, when she had found her voice. "Sue, my dearie, is it really yerself?"

"I don't know, Granny," declared the young woman, shaking her head and laughing. "I really don't know whether it's me or not, but I think it must be me because I'm so pleased to see you."

"Have ye come home to stay?" enquired Mr. Bulloch, patting the gloved hand which lay upon his knee.

"Well—no," said Sue, suddenly grave. "You see, the fact is . . . and I do hope you'll be glad, darlings, because I'm so tremendously happy about it, but I won't be nearly so happy unless you two——"

"Sue, for pity's sake!" cried Mrs. Bulloch, holding her head.

Sue laughed excitedly. "I know I'm daft," she declared; "but I simply can't help it. I'm so happy that I don't know what I'm saying. I'm married, you see."

They stared at her in amazement.

"Yes, it's true," she declared, and to convince them of the fact she drew off her glove and showed them her rings—a plain gold band, very new and shiny, and three big emeralds in a platinum setting.

Mr. Bulloch took her hand and examined the stones carefully—they were beautiful emeralds, and they winked and gleamed in the firelight like cat's eyes. "Sue," he said in a grave tone; "who is it, Sue? Who's the man, and why did ye not tell us and do the thing in order?"

"You know him," she replied. "You know him and like him—it's John Darnay."

There was a moment's silence, and then, as neither of her grandparents spoke, she continued in a low voice. "I know what you're thinking. I thought all that too, but he wanted it—and I love him."

"It's just—we wondered——" Mr. Bulloch began, speaking for his wife in the full confidence that they were at one.

"Oh, please do be nice to him," Sue cried, seizing a hand of her grandparents and squeezing it hard. "He's so fond of you both. He says you're his best friends. Please be nice to him . . ."

"Yes, please be nice to me," echoed Darney's voice from the door.

They looked up and saw him standing there, smiling a trifle shyly.

"I couldn't wait outside any longer," he explained.

I just had to come in and find out what was happening.
ou aren't angry with me, are you?"

"Be nice to him," Sue said again.

They had to be nice to him, of course, for they really
ked him, and, in his new-found happiness, he was
ore irresistible than ever. He smoothed away all their
oubts and allayed their fears. "I tried to live without
ue and found I couldn't," he told them, "so I made
er marry me—that's all."

It was simple enough in all conscience.

"And where are ye going now?" Mr. Bulloch
nquired at last. "Where are ye going to-night, the
air of ye?"

They looked at each other and smiled.

"We're going to Tog's Mill," said Darnay.

"Because we were so happy there," Sue explained.

"But ye'll stay and have supper with us, I'm hoping,"
ut in Mr. Bulloch hospitably.

Mrs. Bulloch frowned and shook her head.

"Is there not enough for them, Susan?" asked her
usband in dismay.

"There's ample," replied the housekeeper; "but it's
heep's head broth. Maybe Mr. Darnay wouldn't care
or that. Maybe ye could go down to the shop, Thomas,
nd——"

"But I like it better than anything else," declared
)arnay, laughing, and glancing at his new wife in a
ignificant manner; "for if it hadn't been for a sheep's
ead——"

"Fancy your remembering *that*!" cried Sue in
mazement.

Bonnywall House was ablaze with light; there was

an air of expectancy in the big, beautifully proportione
rooms; fires had been banked until the flames lea
half-way up the chimneys, and there were flowers i
tall vases—chrysanthemums and red-hot pokers-
lightening the heaviness of the massive furniture.

Admiral Sir Rupert Lang came slowly down the wic
staircase looking about him with satisfaction. He wa
dressed in tails with white tie and waistcoat, and the
was a white carnation in his buttonhole. He was on th
last step when the footman opened the front door, an
Sir James Faulds of Beil appeared.

"Hallo, Rupert!" he exclaimed. "You told me t
come early, so here I am. Jean's coming later with th
rest of the party. You're very smart to-night."

"You're smart yourself, for that matter," replie
his host. "Come into the library and have a drink-
I want to talk to you."

There was a huge silver tray in the library, and on
Sir James counted thirty-two glasses; he looked u
and whistled.

"Yes, it's a biggish dinner-party," nodded Sir Ruper
"I asked everybody in the county and they all accepte
—every man jack."

"Of course. They'll feed out of your hand, Admira
Sir Rupert Lang, V.C., K.C.B."

"Yes," agreed the host complacently, and he pulle
down the points of his white waistcoat with a littl
jerk.

"What's up?" enquired Sir James.

"What's up?"

"Yes, *what's up*?"

"Why do you ask me that? Can't I give a dinne
party without being suspected of evil designs?"

"No," replied his friend promptly. "You can't, Rupert."

"What d'you mean?"

"I come here to-night, and find you all per jink, and as pleased with yourself as a dog with two tails, and all because you're giving an enormous dinner-party—a thing you abhor, a thing you haven't done in the memory of man. It's enough to make anybody wonder what's up."

The Admiral laughed. "Supposing I were to tell you that I realise how remiss I have been in social matters, and have decided to turn over a new leaf?"

"I should merely reply, ' Bunk,' " declared his guest firmly.

"In that case I had better tell you the truth to start with. There's not much time before they arrive, and I want your help."

"My help?"

"Yes. The truth is I'm giving the show to introduce a bride to the county; I want you to be nice to her."

"My dear Rupert, of course I'll be nice to her. Surely there was no need . . . I mean, I'm usually quite nice to young women, especially good-looking ones."

"I know, but——"

"What's she like?" inquired Sir James anxiously. "Has she got a squint, or anything?"

"You know her, Jamie. Can't you guess who it is?"

"No. Who is it?"

"Mrs. Darnay," said the Admiral in a significant tone.

His friend looked at him questioningly. "So Darnay's married, is he? I hadn't heard."

The Admiral nodded. "Yes, he's married. I met him

last week in Bulloch's shop and he told me all about it
He's radiantly happy."

"Most bridegrooms are. Who is the lady—you
haven't told me that yet."

There was a little pause and then the Admiral said
"Darnay has married Sue Pringle."

"Sue Pringle! But, good Lord . . ."

"Why shouldn't he marry her? She's a delightfu
creature."

"He can do what he pleases, of course," retorted Si
James. "I don't care a hang who he marries—it's you
part in the affair that worries me. What are you up
to, Rupert?"

"I told you I wanted to do something for the girl—
well, I'm doing it. That's all."

"I doubt if she will enjoy it," declared Sir James after
a moment's thought.

"Perhaps not," agreed his host; "but she will bear it
for her husband's sake—and bear it gladly."

"You want her to be received by the county, so you're
going to ram her down their throats?"

Admiral Sir Rupert Lang smiled. "You put things
so coarsely, Jamie," he said; "but . . . yes . . . that
was the idea."